Devoted to the Duke

The St. Clairs

Book 1

Alexa Aston

Copyright © 2019 by Alexa Aston
Print Edition

Published by Dragonblade Publishing, an imprint of Kathryn Le Veque Novels, Inc

All rights reserved. No part of this book may be used or reproduced in any manner whatsoever without written permission, except in the case of brief quotations embodied in critical articles or reviews.

Books from Dragonblade Publishing

Dangerous Lords Series by Maggi Andersen
The Baron's Betrothal
Seducing the Earl
The Viscount's Widowed Lady
Governess to the Duke's Heir

Also from Maggi Andersen
The Marquess Meets His Match

The St. Clairs Series by Alexa Aston
Devoted to the Duke
Midnight with the Marquess
Embracing the Earl

Knights of Honor Series by Alexa Aston
Word of Honor
Marked by Honor
Code of Honor
Journey to Honor
Heart of Honor
Bold in Honor
Love and Honor
Gift of Honor
Path to Honor
Return to Honor

The King's Cousins Series by Alexa Aston
The Pawn
The Heir
The Bastard

Beastly Lords Series by Sydney Jane Baily
Lord Despair
Lord Anguish
Lord Vile
Lord Corsair

Dukes of Destiny Series by Whitney Blake
Duke of Havoc
Duke of Sorrow

Legends of Love Series by Avril Borthiry
The Wishing Well
Isolated Hearts
Sentinel

The Lost Lords Series by Chasity Bowlin
The Lost Lord of Castle Black
The Vanishing of Lord Vale
The Missing Marquess of Althorn
The Resurrection of Lady Ramsleigh
The Mystery of Miss Mason
The Awakening of Lord Ambrose

By Elizabeth Ellen Carter
Captive of the Corsairs, *Heart of the Corsairs Series*
Revenge of the Corsairs, *Heart of the Corsairs Series*
Shadow of the Corsairs, *Heart of the Corsairs Series*
Dark Heart
Live and Let Spy, *King's Rogues Series*

Knight Everlasting Series by Cassidy Cayman
Endearing
Enchanted
Evermore

Midnight Meetings Series by Gina Conkle
Meet a Rogue at Midnight, book 4

Second Chance Series by Jessica Jefferson
Second Chance Marquess

Imperial Season Series by Mary Lancaster
Vienna Waltz
Vienna Woods
Vienna Dawn

Blackhaven Brides Series by Mary Lancaster
The Wicked Baron
The Wicked Lady
The Wicked Rebel
The Wicked Husband
The Wicked Marquis
The Wicked Governess
The Wicked Spy
The Wicked Gypsy
The Wicked Wife

Unmarriageable Series by Mary Lancaster
The Deserted Heart
The Sinister Heart
The Vulgar Heart

Highland Loves Series by Melissa Limoges
My Reckless Love
My Steadfast Love
My Passionate Love

Clash of the Tartans Series by Anna Markland
Kilty Secrets
Kilted at the Altar
Kilty Pleasures

Queen of Thieves Series by Andy Peloquin
Child of the Night Guild
Thief of the Night Guild
Queen of the Night Guild

The Book of Love Series by Meara Platt
The Look of Love
The Touch of Love

Dark Gardens Series by Meara Platt
Garden of Shadows
Garden of Light
Garden of Dragons
Garden of Destiny

Rulers of the Sky Series by Paula Quinn
Scorched
Ember
White Hot

Hearts of the Highlands Series by Paula Quinn
Heart of Ashes
Heart of Shadows
Heart of Stone

Highlands Forever Series by Violetta Rand
Unbreakable
Undeniable
Unyielding

Viking's Fury Series by Violetta Rand
Love's Fury
Desire's Fury
Passion's Fury

Also from Violetta Rand
Viking Hearts

The Sins and Scoundrels Series by Scarlett Scott
Duke of Depravity
Prince of Persuasion
Marquess of Mayhem

The Unconventional Ladies Series by Ellie St. Clair
Lady of Mystery
Lady of Fortune

The Sons of Scotland Series by Victoria Vane
Virtue
Valor

Men of Blood Series by Rosamund Winchester
The Blood & The Bloom

Acknowledgements

My thanks to Kathryn Le Veque, who challenged me to try something new. You're always pushing me out of my comfort zone, and I appreciate every time you nudge me from the nest.

My gratitude to my editor, Scott Moreland, whose belief in this book—and me—makes writing a thing of joy.

Chapter One

London—May, 1806

CATHERINE CRAWFORD SAT with her back to the mirror as her maid fussed over her hair, hoping Tilly's efforts would be worth all the time spent sitting still in the chair. Her younger sister, Leah, watched, an enraptured look on her face.

"I can't wait until I'm old enough to go to balls. I love to dance." Leah began twirling around the room, her arms spread wide as she swung them through the air.

"Watch yourself, my lady," Tilly warned. "Wouldn't want another broken arm to deal with, would we?"

Leah stopped at once, her face turning red to her blond roots. "That won't happen again, Tilly," she said quickly, plopping on the bed.

"True. If you stay out of trees, that is," the maid admonished, tugging on one of Catherine's curls a bit too hard.

"Easy, Tilly," Catherine warned.

"On your hair or Lady Leah?" Tilly asked saucily.

She knew she should chastise the maid but Tilly had been in the Crawford household ever since Catherine could remember and sometimes, though the older woman seemed too familiar with the daughters of the house, Catherine knew the servant had a good heart and would fiercely protect both girls if push came to shove.

"Hurry and finish, Tilly," chided Leah. "Or else Catherine will be late to the ball."

The maid fussed a moment longer. "There. I'm done. Close your eyes, my lady."

Catherine did as instructed and Tilly rotated the stool to where it faced the mirror propped on the vanity, eager to see how her auburn locks had been styled tonight.

"You may open your eyes, my lady."

She did as requested and studied her image in the mirror. A slow smile spread across her face.

"You are incredibly talented, Tilly," she praised. "I will be the envy of every girl at the Wethersby ball tonight."

The maid sniffed. "You're already the envy of many, Lady Catherine. I know. I see all the bouquets that arrive. I'm the one who dresses you to meet all those gentlemen who call in the afternoons for tea. I'm the one who accompanies you on your walks with them in Hyde Park. And I see the envious looks cast your way by those young ladies of the *ton* looking for a husband. Mark my words, you'll snap up the best lord when the Marriage Mart is done. Three offers already and the Season's only a month old."

Tilly smoothed Catherine's hair a final time and added, "I'm off to retrieve your mama. She said she wanted to speak to you once I had you ready." The maid looked at Leah. "And it's about time you were in bed."

"Do I have to go, Tilly?" Leah pleaded. "I'm eleven now. I should be allowed to stay up later."

"It's almost nine as it is and it's bad for you. Come on, now. I'll help you undress once I fetch your mama to Lady Catherine." The maid bobbed a curtsey and left the room, Leah still protesting as the door closed.

Catherine sighed. She didn't want to snag a husband.

Not until she fell in love.

She knew it wasn't the done thing. The purpose of the Season was to move up the social ladder. To find a well-bred, wealthy, pleasant fellow that would offer her the protection of his name and rank. She would then wed him sometime after the Season ended and then go about providing him with an heir and, hopefully, a spare. Once she did so, her life would be her own. She could search for a lover, as long as she was discreet about it. That was when love, if it was to be found, might come her way.

In the meantime, her husband would do the same, although men often sought out a mistress soon after they married. At least that's what Catherine had picked up from the gossiping females of the *ton*. Supposedly, a man was free to come and go as he pleased, as long as he did not publicly embarrass his wife. The said wife was to turn a blind eye to all comings and goings and be grateful for having wed a titled gentleman who provided her with financial security, children, and—if she was lucky—affection.

Not at all what Catherine had in mind when she thought of marriage.

Her parents had ruined her expectations. The Earl and Countess of Statham were that rare couple who'd met the first week of her mother's Season and fallen deeply in love. The match had proven suitable to both of their families and they'd spent the last twenty-eight years devoted to one another and their two daughters. She couldn't imagine her father desiring to couple with another woman. He treated his wife as if she were the most precious thing on earth. And to think of her mother in the arms of another man? Laughable.

Because of the beautiful example she'd grown up with, Catherine assumed all married couples loved one another and that when her time came, she would recognize her soul mate in her heart. Instead, she'd been exposed to the ways of society as she'd embarked upon her first Season and didn't like them. At all.

She'd already received three offers of marriage, which was ridiculous. She'd danced with one of the gentlemen once and the other two thrice before they made their offers. Of course, besides dancing with her, they had called on Catherine and she'd poured tea, conversing with them as she tried to get to know them. All three were amiable, handsome men, with beautiful manners and varying amounts of wealth. The problem was, she'd felt nothing for any of them. Though she knew it to be foolish, she wanted her heart to race and a giddiness to overtake her. She thought if she wanted to kiss even one of them, it would be a good sign. So far, none of that had happened. She'd proven popular at events and made it clear that she would entertain no more offers from any gentleman until the Season ended. That would be in less than three months, which caused panic to ripple through her.

What if she didn't find someone to love?

She would be expected to wed. Every woman did. Preparing for the Season had been terribly expensive. Dozens of ball gowns had been made up, with more gowns for parties, the theatre, and the opera. Mama had told Catherine not to worry about the expense but she couldn't help doing so. Mama had said Catherine must look her best in order to attract the right man.

Catherine didn't want to attract a man by wearing a fancy ball gown. She wanted a man who would be attracted to her for *her*—not because of what she wore. She wanted a man who was interesting and kind and could carry on a decent conversation. Already, she'd discovered too many eligible gentlemen of the *ton* had very little to say. It was important for her to fall in love with someone who loved to talk about everything—politics, literature, economics—and not merely the weather. How were you supposed to get to know anyone when all they spoke of was the weather?

Not only did she believe she needed to love a man to marry him, she wanted him to love her in return. How could she be sure if he did?

It was all so very complicated.

A part of her knew her decision would be important not only for her, but for her family. Her father was already in his early fifties, not old but not terribly young. Since Mama hadn't provided the expected heir, much less a spare, the earldom and lands would fall to her uncle. Edward Crawford was nothing but a busybody, always sticking his nose into everyone's business. At least she knew he was gentleman enough to live up to his obligation to take care of her mother and his nieces if her father passed.

She wasn't so sure Cousin Martin would.

Martin Crawford was Uncle Edward's only child, which meant he would eventually inherit Statham Manor and become the Earl of Statham. He was smallminded and had a vicious streak. Martin had pinched her repeatedly as a child when they were young, causing large bruises and making her cry. He'd threatened her not to tell. Being six years older than Catherine, Martin had assured her no one would believe her wild stories about him and so she'd kept quiet. Something told Catherine that if her father and uncle were both gone, Martin would continue the cruelty toward her he'd displayed since childhood.

Because of that, it was imperative that she wed a man who would promise to look after not only her, but her mother and Leah. Just in case the unthinkable became reality.

A knock sounded at the door and her mother entered, closely followed by her father. She couldn't remember the last time he'd come to her bedchamber. Possibly, never. Catherine rose to greet them, uncertainty filling her. She wondered if he would ask her to begin to consider from the many gentlemen of the *ton* which one might become her future husband.

"Oh, you look stunning, my dear!" her mother exclaimed, taking Catherine's hands as her eyes swept up and down her daughter. "Tilly is a genius."

"You look more lovely with each outing this Season," her father declared, kissing her cheek and then bringing a flat, square box from behind his back and pressing her to take it. "For you, child. After all, it is your birthday."

No one had mentioned it all day and Catherine assumed her parents and the rest of the household had forgotten with all the many events they'd been swept up in over the last few weeks.

She pushed the lid up, finding a sapphire necklace inside. Stunned, she raised her eyes and met her father's twinkling ones.

"Do you like it, dearest?"

"Oh, Papa, I adore it!"

Catherine threw her arms around his neck as he chuckled.

"Your mother wanted to give it to you at the start of the Season but I thought we'd wait for your birthday." He gazed lovingly at his wife. "She made sure you would wear blue tonight in order to complement it."

"Give it to me, Catherine," Mama said. "I'll place it around your neck."

She handed the precious necklace over and her mother fastened the clasp. Eager to see what it looked like, Catherine ran to the mirror and fingered the jewels, in awe of receiving such a tremendous present.

Turning to face her parents, she said, "I don't think I'll ever receive a more lovely gift."

"Let's hope you do," her father teased good-naturedly. "That husband of yours, whomever he might be, better shower you with jewelry."

The thought of marrying anyone she'd met so far gave Catherine pause. She looked at her parents, her father's arm around her mother's waist now, and saw how close and loving they were toward one another. Tears misted her eyes.

"Don't cry, dearest," Papa said. "No matter who you wed, you'll always be my little girl."

She hurried to him and hugged him tightly, wishing she never had to grow up and leave his household.

He grasped her elbows and drew her back. "What's wrong, Catherine? I thought the necklace would please you but you seem most upset."

Her lips trembled as she said, "I'm afraid I may never find someone to love, Papa. The way you and Mama love one another."

He kissed her forehead. "Well, if you don't find anyone good enough for you this Season, we'll simply do all of this again next year." He cupped her cheek. "There's a perfect match waiting for you out there, Catherine. I feel it in my bones."

"You mean . . . you don't expect me to wed by summer's end?" she asked.

"Of course not," he said. "Your mama and I want you to be as happy as we've been all these years. If it takes another Season—no, five Seasons—then you'll wait until you find the right man to be your husband. You have no need to rush into a match. The same goes for Leah."

Catherine fell into his arms again, relief pouring through her. She could wait and let love find her, after all, and not be hurried in her decision. Whether he knew or not, her papa had given her a greater gift than the beautiful sapphire necklace.

He'd given her the gift of time.

Chapter Two

Jeremy St. Clair watched the streets of London pass by from the carriage, happy to be in familiar surroundings once more after a year abroad. The sound of English being spoken was sweet music to his ears. He turned to his companion, Matthew Proctor.

"Are you happy to be on English soil again?"

"Safely on English soil," the bespectacled tutor noted. "I hope the English—and Russians—can dispatch Bonaparte soon. If they do, we must go out again and see the cities you should have been exposed to. Especially Paris."

"The Little Corsican has dragged the fight out for years," he said. "I was a boy when he was named First Consul. He's amassed and consolidated his power and gobbled up land during all that time. At least we got to see some of Europe. The few parts not affected by the war."

Matthew shuddered. "Dodging a few shady situations along the way, Jeremy." He paused. "Forgive me. We are in London. I should address you as Lord Sather once more."

Irritation prickled through him. "You will do no such thing, Matthew. After all our adventures together, we are as brothers." Though once the words were out of his mouth, a dark shadow crossed Jeremy's mind. Once, he'd had a brother. Timothy. *He* was the true Marquess of Sather. It should be Timothy who became the next Duke of Everton. Not Jeremy.

"It probably doesn't matter, Lord Sather," his friend continued. "We do not run in the same social circles. I doubt we will meet again after today." The tutor smiled. "Unless one day you wish me to tutor your son, the future Marquess of Sather. I would be happy to do so, knowing he would be as inquisitive and agreeable as his father."

"To have a son would mean I must marry." The thought of having any child startled him.

"And you will. Your father will expect it of you. His Grace will want the St. Clair line to carry on."

"Father has done his best to see that occur," he said lightly, thinking of the three marriages and the three dead wives. "Luke could always take my place," he added, referring to his half-brother, who was eight years his junior.

"The mighty Duke of Everton wants his heir apparent to become the next duke. That's you, my lord. You've a steady head on your shoulders. You will do a fine job when the time comes."

In a way, Jeremy wished Luke could leapfrog over him and take on the responsibility of becoming the next in line. At only fifteen, his half-brother was brash and bold and would carry none of the doubts the more serious-minded Jeremy did. Ever since Timothy had drowned, making the second St. Clair son next in line for the title, Jeremy had questioned why he had survived and why he had to take his brother's place. Once, he had been happy and carefree, without worries—until that day when he'd dragged into Eversleigh, soaked to the skin and half out of his mind.

The day Timothy died.

The carriage pulled up in front the London townhome of the St. Clairs. Turning to Matthew, he offered his hand.

"I suppose this is goodbye." As they shook, Jeremy added, "We've never talked about it before. What will you do now, Matthew?"

"Return to Cambridge. See if they have any positions open for a well-traveled tutor." He laughed. "There are always young men in need of someone to guide and instruct them during their university studies. Even one who can get them out of the occasional scrape."

Jeremy thought a moment. "You will need a reference. I will write a glowing one, of course."

"That would be much appreciated, my lord," Matthew said solemnly.

It pained him to hear his companion of the past year withdraw and speak so formally, as if Matthew and his brilliant mind could ever be subservient to anyone. True, they had known one another for several years, throughout Jeremy's time at Cambridge, but they had spent over a year in one another's company and become the closest of friends. He understood, though, the class system that ruled England. Jeremy had been born into a family of wealth and position. Matthew was the son of a clergyman.

"It's too late in the afternoon to catch a post coach to Cambridge. Would you come in and stay the night? That way, I could write your letter of recommendation and send it with you tomorrow."

Doubt filled Matthew's eyes. "It's a most generous offer, Lord Sather, but I would be more comfortable staying at a nearby inn. I will drop by tomorrow morning, however, to collect the reference. If that's convenient for you, of course."

He knew he wouldn't be able to convince his friend to stay and decided to let the matter go.

"Very well. I'll tell the driver to take you to a local establishment. Would you at least come for breakfast, Matthew?"

"I think not, my lord. Why don't you leave the letter with your butler? I'll collect it from him."

Jeremy touched Matthew's shoulder. "I will see you in the morning," he said emphatically and climbed from the carriage.

He instructed the driver as to which trunk was his and the man retrieved it. A footman had already stepped outside and hoisted it to his shoulder as he greeted Jeremy. Paying off the driver, Jeremy instructed him to an inn less than a mile away, where the man could drop his remaining passenger.

The carriage drove off. He waved at Matthew, who nodded at him. Jeremy realized a door closed on this chapter in his life. He faced the house, three stories in height and located in one of the most suitable squares in London. Steeling himself, he followed the footman inside.

Barton, the butler who had been with the St. Clair family for many years, greeted him.

"Good afternoon, Lord Sather. It is very good to have you home."

"I am happy to be back in England. You're looking well, Barton. Any news?"

"His Grace is in residence, naturally, with Parliament in session. Her Grace arrived from Eversleigh two days ago, in anticipation of your arrival. Lord Luke is finishing his term at Eton and will be home within the next week. And Lady Rachel is—"

"Here!" cried out a joyous voice from the top of the staircase.

Jeremy watched his half-sister race down the stairs. When she still had half a dozen steps to go, she flung herself at him. He caught her and held on as she hugged him tightly, smothering his face in kisses.

"Did you miss me?" she asked, her face flushed with color, her St. Clair eyes gleaming at him.

He pretended to ponder her question and then said, "Only a smidgeon. More importantly, did you miss me?"

A dramatic sigh came from her as he set her on her feet. "You know I did, Jeremy. Did you get my letters?"

"I did, poppet. I answered them, every one. Thank you for keeping me abreast of the happenings in the family. You always have a colorful way with words," he praised.

"It was so boring without you at home," she declared. Then mischief lit her eyes. "Did you bring anything for me?"

He laughed. "Wasn't it enough that I sent you something from every city I stayed in?"

"Oh, I appreciated every gift, Jeremy. You're ever so thoughtful."

She grew quiet and he knew she was thinking of their father. The children of the Duke of Everton received scant attention from their father, no matter their gender or age. He couldn't think of a single gift his father had ever given him and doubted Luke or Rachel had received anything.

Taking her hand, he said, "I'm sure somewhere in my trunk I can rummage through and find something meant for you. It may take hours to unpack, however. I crammed as much into it as possible as I made for home. I don't suppose Manfry is still available?"

Rachel sniffed haughtily. "Manfry hated that you left him behind. He complained that, especially going abroad, you needed a valet. His nose has been out of joint ever since." She smiled. "Don't worry. Cor kept him busy."

Jeremy contained the laughter that threatened to erupt. The true power in the St. Clair family was his formidable grandmamma, the dowager duchess. If Manfry was under Cor's supervision, the valet had been worked to the bone during his master's absence.

From the corner of his eyes, he saw a figure descending the stairs, a woman who looked vaguely familiar. She reached the foot of the stairs and curtseyed to him.

"Lady Rachel, it's time for our reading hour."

"Oh, Miss Bates, Jeremy has only arrived at home. Surely, we can forego reading this one time."

"On the contrary, it's important to keep to a schedule," the governess said. "Besides, Lord Sather will want to wash away the travel stains of the road. Come along, my lady."

Rachel flung him a look of desperation, which he decided to ignore.

"It's important to do as your governess says."

Her bottom lip stuck out in a pretty pout. At eleven, Rachel already had the St. Clair height, as well as the jet black hair and emerald eyes. She would be quite the beauty someday and likely break several hearts before she chose a husband.

"Will you at least take me riding in the morning?" she asked petulantly.

"I'd be delighted to as long as there's a mount available for me. Shall we meet before breakfast?"

Her smile said she'd forgiven him. "I'll meet you in the stables. Don't be late, Jeremy. I don't tolerate tardiness. It's something Miss Bates has ground into me." Under her breath, she added, "Along with countless other things."

With that, Rachel turned and trotted up the stairs, her governess following after her. Jeremy decided that the poor woman must earn every penny of her salary, caring for the headstrong young tomboy.

Barton cleared his throat. "My lord, His Grace has been informed of your arrival and wishes to speak with you in the library."

"Very good, Barton. I suppose Manfry came to town with Cor?"

"He did, my lord. You'll find your chamber prepared. Even now, Manfry will be unpacking your trunk and helping you to settle in."

"Then I will go see Father. Thank you, Barton."

The butler nodded deferentially and Jeremy went straight to the library. He would have preferred washing up first but when the Duke of Everton requested your presence, everything else faded into the woodwork.

Reaching the library, he knocked on the door and heard a voice bidding him to enter. He opened the door and closed it behind him.

His father sat in a chair next to the window, an ever-present glass of brandy in his hand. As Jeremy approached, he saw the past year hadn't been kind to the elder St. Clair. The good looks of his youth had dissipated, thanks to an overindulgence in drink and food, coupled with years of late nights and little exercise. His ruddy complexion seemed more flush than usual and his hair had thinned to the point of baldness. He looked to weigh a good two stones heavier than when Jeremy had last seen him a year ago.

Crossing the room, he bowed. "Hello, Father. How have you been?"

No hand was offered. No gesture of warmth given. Not even a smile escaped the duke's lips.

"Sit," he commanded. "Drink?"

"No, thank you, sir."

Jeremy took a seat across from his father and waited for him to lead the conversation. It was how they'd always communicated. His father barked at him. He answered in as few words as possible.

"Tell me you enjoyed your sojourns."

"Indeed, I did."

"Give me details, Boy."

Jeremy launched into recounting some of the places he'd visited, including the business establishments he'd called upon, as well as estates and farms he'd visited.

"Stop," his father commanded after several minutes, scrutinizing him. After a moment, he said, "What about the fun you had? The parties you attended. The women you met. The drinking and the hunting. What of that?"

"There was some of that," he began. "I thought it important, though, since I am to be the next duke, that I learn about great estates, as well as businesses and which types I should invest in."

"Balderdash! I sent you abroad to open your horizons, Jeremy, not for you to study dull topics as you did at Cambridge for four years. I'm sorely disappointed that you didn't follow my instructions and relish your trip."

"I did have a marvelous time, Father. I attended balls and plays and concerts. Went to museums and viewed the architecture of famous churches. I mingled with society and met fascinating people, including artists and playwrights. It would have been a wasted opportunity, though, not to have taken advantage to extend my knowledge in other areas. Which leads me to say that now I've returned home, I'm eager to become familiar with how our various estates are run."

His father's perplexed look silenced him. Jeremy hesitated a moment and decided to plunge ahead. "I realize you have no interest in the many operations that run on St. Clair lands, but I have a great interest in farming and husbandry. From what I've learned and what I saw in Europe, I believe—"

"No changes," the duke proclaimed firmly. "I have competent managers to deal with those things. What I need is for you to quit being so bloody serious and enjoy being a young man of wealth and position. You're a marquess, my boy. A St. Clair. We're known for our enjoyment of life. It's time you quit being so solemn and appreciate all you have and take advantage of it. Drink! Dance! Find a mistress!"

Jeremy held his tongue. All his life, he'd seen his father engage in irresponsible behavior. He acted as a wastrel, overeating and drinking to excess. Gambling. Fighting. Having countless affairs. The Duke of Everton was an embarrassment to his family. Jeremy had heard the many whispers that disparaged his father behind his back, though never to his face since he was, in fact, the Duke of Everton.

Jeremy planned to be a much different kind of duke. One who would be responsible to his people and careful with his purse. One whose behavior and manners were so impeccable, society would never question them. One who never embarrassed his family. He'd been in plenty of schoolboy fights, defending the St. Clair name and his father's despicable behavior. Once he claimed the title, he would restore honor to his family and act the way a duke should.

In a dismissive voice, his father said, "You can start amusing yourself tonight by attending the Wethersby ball. The Season is in full swing."

"Do you expect me to begin a search for a wife?" Jeremy asked pointedly.

His father guffawed. "That's the last thing I'd expect from you. Sow your wild oats. Find a pretty widow. One of around thirty. Old enough to teach you a few things and young enough to still have her looks and figure. Reconnect with your old friends. Go riding and to your club.

"But whatever you do, you are to stay out of my business affairs," the duke warned.

"I understand, sir."

Jeremy rose and excused himself. His gut told him his father was hiding something. Something that might affect the entire wellbeing of the St. Clair family.

He would find Cor. She would know if anything was amiss.

CHAPTER THREE

JEREMY FOUND HIS grandmother in her sitting room, sipping a cup of tea as she composed a letter at her desk. He observed her for a moment before making his presence known. Her abundant silver hair was swept off her face, showing the delicate bone structure. Dark blue eyes, ever inquisitive, dominated her face. Though she would be seventy next year, only a few wrinkles appeared about her eyes and mouth, the rest of her face unlined. If she didn't laugh so much, she wouldn't possess any wrinkles at all.

His grandmother had been a mother to him since his own passed away in childbirth. The second and third wives his father took tried to mother him briefly but Jeremy hadn't taken to either woman. Luke's mother saw Timothy and Jeremy as a threat to any future sons she would bear the duke and kept her distance after those first few weeks. Rachel's mother was flighty and quite dense—though beautiful to look at—but not much for children. Since both women had also died in childbirth, Jeremy had an odd fear of women giving birth, which made him reluctant to wed. The point of marriage in the upper classes was to procreate so that he would have sons to pass his title and lands to, yet the thought of his wife giving birth made him ill. No law said he had to marry. Once his father was gone and Jeremy inherited the title, he could do as he pleased. If that meant no wife, so be it. Luke—or his son—could become the heir.

He cleared his throat so that Cor would look up. When she didn't, he entered the room and leaned over her shoulder, pressing a kiss to her cheek.

She turned slowly and gave him The Look, one servants and society alike knew.

"Did you think I didn't know you've been staring at me for the last five minutes, Jeremy?" she accused, though he knew she wasn't angry.

He wrapped his arms about her. "You are still the most beautiful woman I've ever seen, Cor. No one holds a candle to you."

Her graying brows rose. "Not any woman you met in your travels?"

"You are still first and foremost in my esteem," he replied smoothly. "Come and sit with me and let me tell you some of what I did during my travels."

"Let me ring for another cup of tea first." She appraised him. "And something to eat. You look famished."

He helped her rise and she rang the bell before he escorted her to a settee and joined her. A servant appeared and received instructions, soon bearing a new tea tray with a delightful assortment of treats. He stacked his plate high as Cor poured tea for them both.

"Your letters were wonderful, you know," she confided. "They were always the highlight of any day in which I received them. You have quite a way with words. Your descriptions were so vivid. Of the people. Streets and shops. The music and food. It reminded me of my wedding trip when your grandpapa took me to Paris."

Jeremy had never known the man but Cor always spoke of her husband fondly. He regaled her for an hour about places he and Matthew had visited, including some of the businesses they stopped at.

"You've always had a head for numbers," she noted, shaking her head. "I'm afraid your brother only has a head for women."

He frowned. "Has Luke gotten some girl into trouble?"

"Trouble seems to find Luke wherever he goes. He was in a good deal of it during his Christmas holidays."

He sighed. "What has he done now?"

"I had to dismiss one of the maids at Eversleigh."

"Was she with child?"

"No, fortunately. She was almost twice his age. I caught them in a compromising position in the conservatory. It seems Luke started paying her three years ago to . . . teach him . . . things."

Shock filled him. "Paying her? What kind of lessons did she offer?"

Cor sniffed. "Kissing lessons, to begin with, starting when he was twelve. They had progressed from chaste kisses to more . . . friendly ones. Luke pressed her—"

"He didn't force her?" Jeremy asked quickly.

"No, nothing of the sort. Luke merely encouraged her to help him expand his horizons as time passed. They'd never engaged in relations, thank the heavens. All but that. She admitted to me that Luke was most likely the best kisser in the county and beyond. He confessed to me that he'd learned how to appreciate a woman. How to worship her body. How to please her in small ways. He said it was all quite useful information that would benefit him in the future."

Jeremy shook his head. "The audacity of that boy. Father should take a firmer hand with him."

Surprise filled Cor's face. "You think your father would chastise him? For all I know, my son encouraged this maid to take Luke under her tutelage. It wouldn't surprise me if he also paid the woman to educate Luke in the ways of the flesh."

"You're right," Jeremy admitted. "I never told you before but Father took me to a bawdy house when I was around fifteen. It was mortifying. He wanted us to share the same tart. He forced me to watch them couple and then wanted me to do the same as he observed and offered advice. I refused and walked out. He never mentioned it after that."

She shuddered. "Now that you're home, my darling, it would be good for you to take Luke under your wing. He needs a good example of what it means to be a true gentleman. I can think of no one finer to guide our Luke than you."

"I will do my duty, of course, Cor. What happened to the maid?"

"Luke begged me not to dismiss her. He claimed everything had originated with him and that she'd gone along in order to keep her position. While I doubted it, I didn't have the heart to turn her out without a reference. She is quite a good maid and they can be hard to come by. In the end, I sent her to a property I inherited from my family. It's isolated, with only a small village nearby. She won't find much to do there but she still has work."

"You are kindhearted, Cor."

She shrugged. "I do my best for this family."

"I'm afraid to ask since the news of Luke has been all bad, but what of Rachel?"

Her face softened. "Rachel is a delight. She reads voraciously. Asks about everything. Her riding skills have improved tremendously."

"Is she still climbing trees?"

Cor chuckled. "Would you expect anything less? I turn a blind eye to some of her activities but, mind you, I know everything she does. As far as Luke goes, he's a good boy, just a bit misguided. His grades at Eton have been excellent. He has tremendous potential. They both do." She paused. "I know they are only half-siblings to you, Jeremy, but you must promise me you'll look after them when your father and I are gone."

He took her hands in his and kissed them. "That won't be for many years, Cor."

She smiled. "You'd be surprised. I've been to my fair share of funerals lately. It seems I have friends dying to the left and right of me. You can do me a favor, however."

"Name it. I am yours to command."

"Escort me to the Wethersby ball tonight. A dear friend of mine will be attending. She lost her husband over a year ago and buried herself in the country. She's only just come to town and I promised I would meet her there. Besides, it would be a good way to let others know you are back in London."

"I can do that but I have a favor to ask in return."

She patted his knee. "You only need to ask, my boy. I doubt I would deny you anything."

"Father seems to be hiding something." He watched as she stilled. "I aim to find out what. I want to tour all of our properties and become familiar with how they're run. He's—"

"I will share with you what I know, Jeremy. Why don't we meet after breakfast tomorrow to discuss matters? Right now, I'm sure you're ready for a bath and a good English meal."

Soaking in a hot bath sounded very appealing but he disliked being put off again. Still, Cor would be true to her word and tell him everything she knew. He supposed he could wait until morning to discover what his father had been up to.

"I'll take your advice, Cor. It will be a bath for me and fresh clothes."

"Evening wear, darling. Don't forget the ball."

"Of course."

He kissed her cheek and made his way to his bedchamber. Manfry was ecstatic to see him and immediately sent for hot water. While Jeremy waited for it to arrive, he dashed off the letter of recommendation for Matthew Proctor and asked Manfry to entrust it to Barton's care. He fully intended to speak with his friend tomorrow but leaving it with Barton would be more convenient.

As Jeremy soaked in the hot tub, he wondered what Cor might reveal about the state of their affairs.

CATHERINE EXITED THE carriage and her father offered her his arm. She took it and he escorted her and her mother inside. They joined the receiving line and were soon greeted by Lord and Lady Wethersby. The viscountess remarked upon Catherine's birthday gift.

"What a sumptuous necklace. It suits you, of course, bringing out the blue in your eyes. Your dance card will be filled in no time, Lady Catherine." With a sly smile, she added, "I'm sure you'll have your pick of the litter by the time the Season ends. Aim for a duke, my girl. With your looks and family name, it's easily within your grasp."

Catherine smiled benignly as she moved away. She couldn't understand the fixation on titles that every woman seemed to possess. Everyone from her own maid to society matrons urged her to do what it took to wed someone above her station, especially a duke. For heaven's sake, there were only so many dukes to go around and even then, most of them were already wed. Once again, she glanced at her parents and wished she could find love.

Or that love might find her.

"I'm off to the card room," her father announced, kissing his wife's cheek and then Catherine's. "Enjoy yourselves."

"Be sure to get your *programme du bal*," her mother urged. "Last time, I believe yours filled up more quickly than any other girl's did. Looking as you do tonight, I believe the same will occur."

She saw her friend, Charlotte, and went to greet her as a footman handed her the dance card. Catherine slipped it into her reticule and joined Charlotte.

"Wherever did you get that brilliant necklace?" her friend asked, her eyes round as Catherine slipped her arm through Charlotte's.

"Today is my birthday. Papa and Mama gave it to me in honor of the occasion."

"Then I suppose I should steer my papa in your papa's direction. Maybe he can learn something from Lord Statham. On my eighteenth birthday, I received a new hat." She sniffed. "Mama is pleased we're friends, you know."

"Why so?" Catherine thought Charlotte's mother a bit pushy, though she realized she had her daughter's best interests at heart.

"You are so popular with the men and your dance card fills so quickly. When a gentleman asks you to dance and I'm standing beside you, they often turn to me and request the same. That pleases Mama greatly. I, on the other hand, simply enjoy your company and believe we'll always be friends," Charlotte declared. "You know, if we both wed at the end of the Season, we might have our first child around the same time. Why, by next Season, you and I could be old married ladies—and mothers."

The thought of her life changing so rapidly frightened Catherine. No man had truly caught her eye, so she asked, "Have you formed any special attachment?"

"Not yet. I have my eye on a few prospects," her friend said mysteriously. "Oh, look. Here comes the horde." Charlotte moistened her lips and smiled prettily.

Catherine looked up and saw a group of eligible suitors headed their way. She raised a gloved hand to hide her mouth, stifling the giggle that threatened to erupt. The men looked like a pack of animals as they approached. A few fanned out in other directions, letting the alpha males of the pack have first dibs.

She watched as her programme began to fill with names. A blond man hovered nearby as she finished speaking with a viscount who had bucked teeth and a lisp. As the viscount moved toward Charlotte, Catherine recognized the waiting gentleman since they'd danced together previously but she couldn't recall his name. That was the problem with the Season. So many social events. Dozens of introductions. Far too many dances with men who then disappeared to dance with another debutante. The evenings, with all the faces and names, became a blur.

"Good evening, Lady Catherine," the man said. "I'm hoping you would do me the great honor of dancing with me again this evening. I so enjoyed your company when we danced together before." His smile revealed white, even teeth as his blue eyes sparkled.

At least this one showed some potential. She needed to at least think about getting to know some of these men beyond casual comments regarding the weather. She offered her programme to him.

"You may claim the supper dance if you wish, my lord."

His eyes lit up, knowing they would not only dance together but spend an extended time in conversation as they dined.

"I'd be most delighted." He wrote his name and returned the card to her.

Glancing down, she said, "I look forward to our dance, Lord Morefield."

After that, Catherine turned down several suitors, apologizing for having no more room on her card, heeding her mother's recent advice before they'd disembarked from the carriage.

As she turned away another disappointed gentleman, Charlotte hissed," How could you have no vacancies left? Most of the men who've asked you to dance have also signed my card. I still have five openings."

"Mama begged me to leave two slots open tonight," Catherine explained. "She instructed me to leave the supper dance and the final dance of the evening free. That way, if I found someone to my liking, I might offer a second opportunity and spend additional time with him. I allowed Lord Morefield to have the supper dance since he somewhat intrigues me. Instead, I left the one after supper and the last of the night vacant."

"Oh, my word! Your mother is a genius, no doubt about it. I shall do the same from now on."

As a few others approached them to ask for a dance and she shook her head, Catherine's gaze scanned the room. She recognized many of the faces as everyone waited for the music to begin. None of them excited her, in particular. If she didn't find anyone else interesting tonight, she would skip the final dance and go find her parents so they could depart before the rush of carriages clogged the road.

Then her eyes fell upon someone she didn't know and her breath caught in her throat. This man hadn't attended any event of the Season. She was certain of that for he would stand out in any crowd.

He was taller and broader of shoulders than the companion he conversed with. His hair was as black as midnight, matching his fitted trousers and coat. His shirt was snow white against his tanned face. She wished she could see what color his eyes were. As he gestured, it was with a fluid grace.

Who was this very handsome stranger—and how could she persuade him to dance with her?

Chapter Four

Jeremy stood conversing with an acquaintance from his Cambridge days. He'd seen Cor settled with her friend and had wandered into the ballroom when he'd run across Neville.

"You simply must try Gentleman Jack's while you're in London, Sather. You were quite the boxer at Cambridge. I placed bets on you on several occasions and won every time."

He'd taken up boxing in his youth because it interested Timothy and anything that Timothy wanted to do, Jeremy wanted to do even more. The brothers had sparred with one another, perfecting their skills over the years. After Timothy was gone, Jeremy thought he might never box again. Then someone had challenged him to a match his second year at Cambridge and he'd accepted. Word of the bout spread across the campus from college to college and a good number of young men turned out.

Jeremy had knocked his opponent out in the third round.

In boxing, he found an outlet for the pent up rage that had swirled through him ever since he'd lost his brother. Never one to back down from a challenge, he'd gone on to fight several times over the next couple of years, losing only once. He'd eaten something that violently disagreed with him the evening before and had spent most of the night bent over his chamber pot, puking his guts out. In a weakened state the next day, he should never have fought. Still, the fight went a good six rounds before he succumbed to his fatigue.

"I may investigate that, Neville, though I haven't boxed in over a year."

"I'd be happy to introduce you to the man himself," his companion said. "Oh, is that Morefield? You two were friends, weren't you? From your Eton days, I believe."

He looked across the room and spotted his fair-haired friend—and the luminous beauty Morefield stood in front of. She wore a dress of deep blue and a sapphire necklace around her neck. Her auburn hair was artfully arranged and a contrast to her pale, smooth skin. In all his travels, he'd never seen a more beautiful woman.

"Who is that with Morefield?" Jeremy asked, unable to take his eyes from her.

Neville laughed. "That divine creature is Lady Catherine Crawford, older daughter of the Earl of Statham. She's proven quite popular during her come-out. I hear she's already been made three offers. Or it might be four."

He tore his eyes from the beauty and stared at Neville. "Has she accepted any of them?"

"Not from what I've heard. *Ton* gossip says the lady refuses to entertain any more offers of matrimony until after the Season ends."

An urgency to speak to her filled him. "Do you know her, Neville? I'd like to be introduced. Now."

"Afraid not, Sather. She's a bit out of my league, so why bother? Why don't you ask Morefield to do the honors?"

He would. The viscount owed him.

"Good talking with you, Neville," he said abruptly and made his way toward his old friend, who now headed in his direction.

As they crossed paths, Morefield caught sight of him and smiled. Pumping Jeremy's hand enthusiastically, he said, "You've returned home. It's very good to see you, Sather."

"The same, Morefield. I only arrived in London a few hours ago. What have you been up to?"

The viscount had only recently finished his studies and spoke of that before he launched into a discussion regarding a pair of horses he was considering purchasing at Tattersall's.

"Why don't you come with me, Sather? You've always had a keen eye for horseflesh. Or are you going to bury yourself in the country or some other such nonsense?"

Jeremy's closest friend had been his brother. After Timothy's death, he found it hard to be around other friends and, gradually, most of them had fallen away. He was no longer a lighthearted boy but a man filled with guilt for having survived. He'd become something of a loner during his time at Cambridge, concentrating on his studies. Morefield was one of the few he'd spent time with, though not often, and he regretted letting their friendship lapse.

"I'd like to call in a favor," he began.

Morefield stilled, his face growing serious. "You have every right to. I told you, years ago, I would do anything for you. You saved me, Jeremy. I wouldn't be here today but for you."

The viscount referred to when they were schoolboys. Morefield was a year younger and quite small for his age. When he'd arrived at school as one of the new boys, the older ones had bullied him unmercifully, reducing the newcomer to tears while their blows kept him covered in fresh bruises. Jeremy had little tolerance for bullies but hadn't known Morefield and stayed out of the fray.

Until the night he couldn't sleep.

Though against school rules, he left his bed in the wee hours of the morning. He found walking quieted his mind when it was racing. If he moved about, it calmed him and once he returned to his bed, he would be able to fall asleep easily. It happened at least once a month and he'd come to learn all the nooks and crannies of the school during these late night treks.

On one occasion, he'd moved through the halls, silent as a ghost, and longed to have some fresh air. Knowing he couldn't leave the building, for a reason he would never know, he ventured up to the bell tower, a place he'd never been. As he ascended the stairs, he heard weeping as he never had. As if someone's heart was being torn from his chest. When he reached the top and found the trap door to the belfry open, he climbed through it—and found Eric Saunders with a sheet knotted around his neck, his face ravaged with pain.

The younger boy's eyes grew wide when he saw Jeremy.

"What are you doing here?" he said, choking on his words.

Jeremy saw Eric had stopped tying the other end of the sheet and realized the boy had been about to kill himself. He would have stepped through the trap door, his neck snapping in an instant.

"Is it because of the abuse from the older boys?" he asked softly.

Eric nodded, his eyes lowered in shame.

"They're all bigger than me. Stronger. They've threatened and tormented me until I can't take it anymore." Fat tears rolled down his pale cheeks. "I don't want to live anymore." He raised his eyes to meet Jeremy's, his face defiant. "You can't stop me."

Though only a year older, Jeremy could easily keep the boy from harming himself but he ventured, "No, I can't. Only you can stop yourself. That's what I'd do if I were you."

Eric sniffled. "You would? Oh, of course you would. You're a St. Clair. You're a favorite of all the teachers and the other boys alike. You'd never want to do away with yourself. You St. Clairs lead a charmed life. Everything comes so easily to you."

Knowing the boy was within a hair's breadth of ending his life, he said, "Everyone has pain, Eric. They don't always show it. Or they bully others to keep their own sadness at bay. My mama died giving birth to me. My stepmamma just gave birth to my half-brother. She died, too. I know Mama looks down upon me from heaven but that doesn't mean I don't miss her. I never got to know her. I would give anything for a single day with her. Life is unfair like that sometimes."

He took a step closer. "Life is cruel to you right now but you shouldn't give in. You're very smart. You come from a good family. In time, you'll grow tall and strong. Don't let them win, Eric. Don't give in. Don't hurt your family like this."

The boy sank to his knees, his sobs coming in heaves. Jeremy went and touched his shoulder in comfort.

"I would like to be your friend. I'll ask my brother to do the same. If you have two St. Clairs on your side, no one will ever threaten you again. Would you care to make friends with me, Eric?"

Slowly, the boy nodded. Jeremy insisted Eric loosen the knot from his neck, somehow knowing it was important for the younger boy to take control of his situation and not have Jeremy do it for him. The two boys had returned to their dormitory without further conversation.

He pulled Timothy aside the next morning before breakfast and told him what had happened and how frightened he'd been that Eric might kill himself. Both boys were ready that night when the bullies came to harass Eric Saunders. Together, they pushed through the circle surrounding Eric. Timothy shoved aside two of the worst as Jeremy helped Eric to his feet. Jeremy had calmly told the ruffians that Eric was a friend to both St. Clairs and if anyone had a problem with that, he and Timothy would clarify the situation—with their fists.

The group around Eric had dissolved. No one ever tormented him again.

As Jeremy now looked at the fully grown man who'd been that sad little boy, he was thankful he'd been there that night and kept Eric from harming himself.

"What would you have me do, Sather? Name it."

"I would like an introduction to Lady Catherine Crawford," he replied.

Morefield looked astounded. "That's it? You saved my life and that's all you'll claim?"

Jeremy felt adrift, especially after his travels. Timothy had been gone almost a decade. His father's debauchery meant he might pass in the near future, making Jeremy the new duke with a multitude of responsibilities. By tomorrow, Matthew would be on the road to Cambridge and gone from his life. Jeremy had parted ways with so many of his friends until he felt alone, except for Cor. He felt every bit as lost as young Eric Saunders had all those years ago.

Who knew? Lady Catherine might be the one to save him.

When he failed to reply, Morefield frowned. Still, he rallied and said, "I'd be happy to make the introduction. By now, though, I doubt she has any openings on her dance card."

Jeremy grinned. "Perhaps you'd consider allowing me to take your slot."

"Ah. So, the favor grows? And here, with all the time that had passed, I didn't know if you would ever call it in." He put an arm around Jeremy's shoulder. "You may claim the supper dance, old friend. Come, let us speak to her."

Morefield led him to where Lady Catherine and her companion stood. Bowing, he said, "Lady Catherine, Lady Charlotte, allow me to introduce to you my dearest friend, the Marquess of Sather. He has recently returned from abroad and is eager to participate in the events of the Season. He would be delighted to make your acquaintance."

They exchanged curtseys and bows and then Morefield said, "I'm afraid I must beg off of our dance, Lady Catherine. Urgent business has arisen and I must leave at once to attend to it."

Her brow wrinkled in concern. "I'm most distressed to her that, my lord. I hope everything will work out to your satisfaction."

"Will you be at the Rutherfords' ball tomorrow night?" he asked. "If so, would you consider saving a dance for me?"

"I'd like nothing better than to do so," she replied.

"Then I will bid you good evening." He bowed and left them.

Another gentleman stepped forward and engaged Lady Charlotte in conversation. As she turned toward him, Jeremy said, "Might I request a dance with you, Lady Catherine?" noting her eyes were as deep a blue as the sapphires she wore.

He took her card before she could offer it to him and boldly struck through Morefield's name. Her lips twitched in amusement.

"I see you were to have the supper dance together." He scrawled his name beside it and added, "I see you have two other numbers open. Might I be presumptuous and ask for the final dance of the evening, as well? The better to make your acquaintance."

Her slow smile turned into a radiant one. "I'd like that very much, Lord Sather. But please, don't ask for the remaining slot on my card. It's bad fashion, you know, to dance with a partner more than twice."

He returned her card, catching a whiff of vanilla. "Who makes such silly restricting rules? If I found an interesting partner, I would claim every dance from her," he teased.

She cocked one eyebrow at him. "You would tempt the gossips of the *ton*?"

"I would, my lady. And give them something to gossip about," he added suggestively.

Lady Catherine burst out laughing. Her rich laughter was contagious, causing him to do the same, drawing the eyes of those standing nearby. He swallowed, trying to contain his laughter and failing miserably. Inhaling deeply, he calmed himself, though his spirits soared.

Taking her gloved hand, he kissed her fingers. "Until the supper dance."

With that, Jeremy left, his heart pumping wildly.

Chapter Five

"I AM SO sorry, my lord," Catherine murmured to her partner, her tone apologetic.

It was the third time she stepped on someone's toes as she'd danced this evening. Normally, she was light on her feet and considered quite an accomplished dancer. Tonight, though, thoughts of the Marquess of Sather filled her head to distraction.

She'd caught a glimpse of him twice since he'd signed her *programme du bal*. Once, he was dancing with a beautiful blond, the daughter of a duke. The pair talked animatedly, causing Catherine to grip her dance partner's shoulder so tightly that he visibly winced. The second time, Sather was sipping punch, standing with a group of titled gentlemen that were said to be among some of the best catches of the Season. She wondered if he were friends with any of the men. The earl standing next to Sather had been one of those who'd already offered for her. Catherine couldn't help speculate if her name had come up during their conversation and what the earl might have said to the handsome marquess.

Oh, he was so very handsome. Though his countenance seemed serious, he had piqued her interest with his teasing remark about creating a little gossip within the *ton*. Despite knowing better, Catherine hadn't been able to politely contain her laughter. Instead, it had erupted without warning—and the Marquess of Sather had surprisingly joined in. His sonorous laugh came from deep within his belly. It wasn't the refined, indulgent chuckle she was used to hearing from others at *ton* events. No, his laugh was genuine and honest and made her wish she could strike every name from her dance card and spend the rest of the evening with him.

At least they would be able to sup together after their dance. She looked forward to learning more about him. Since he hadn't been in London until only recently, she'd never heard his name mentioned. She knew nothing about him except for his title and that he was a good friend of Morefield's. That spoke well of Sather, to know he had Morefield's friendship. He had seemed very kind, which was why she had considered spending extra time with him tonight. Now, though, all thoughts of Morefield fled as her mind filled with Sather's image.

Only one more dance to go.

The music ended and her dance partner returned her to where he'd claimed her for their set. Charlotte had already arrived and stood next to a girl that Catherine immediately recognized as the one who'd danced with Sather. Catherine thanked the earl for partnering with her, knowing he'd never ask her to do so again, thanks to her utter distraction and his probable bruised toes.

"I don't believe we've met," she began, nudging Charlotte.

"Oh, this is Lady Amanda Rutherford. Please meet my closest friend, Lady Catherine Crawford," Charlotte said. "Lady Amanda's parents are hosting tomorrow night's ball."

"It's a pleasure to make your acquaintance," Catherine said. "What does your dress for tomorrow evening look like?"

Lady Amanda went into excruciating detail about her gown, almost boring Catherine to tears, but she wanted to have some conversation between them before she mentioned Sather. Finally, the young woman took a breath.

"It sounds delightful. I look forward to seeing you in it." She paused. "Did I see you dancing with the Marquess of Sather earlier?"

"Yes. Jeremy returned from abroad only late this afternoon."

So his given name was Jeremy.

"You must know him quite well to address him by his Christian name rather than his title."

Lady Amanda smiled. "Jeremy's brother and mine were friends at Eton. Both Jeremy and Timothy came to visit us on several occasions and Marcus went to Eversleigh, as well. Marcus was thick as thieves with both St. Clairs for several years." A shadow crossed her face. "I fear Timothy was the link between them, though. Once he passed, Marcus and Jeremy's friendship fell by the wayside." She brightened. "Still, it was good seeing Jeremy again. I hope he will come to more events now that he's home again."

Catherine felt obligated to ask, "Do you have a particular interest in him?"

"Jeremy? Not at all. Even after such a long time of not seeing him, we fell into our usual pattern of picking at one another, much like a brother and sister." Lady Amanda paused. "Why? Are you interested in him?"

Not wanting to reveal how taken she was with the marquess, Catherine said, "He and his friend, Viscount Morefield, both asked me for a dance this evening. I know something of Morefield but was curious about his friend since I've never seen him this Season."

Lady Amanda's eyes lit up. "I danced earlier with Morefield." Lowering her voice, she tilted her head closer and confided, "Now, he's one I find most interesting. Handsome. Well spoken."

She nodded. "He has made a good impression on me, as well." Seeing how Lady Amanda felt, Catherine said, "You would make a striking couple. You are both blond and would have adorable children."

A hopeful look blossomed on the young woman's face. "I think so, too. I only need Morefield to think the same. He's a bit shy."

"The next time I speak with him, I will be sure to sing your praises," Catherine promised.

Her next partner was a lisping viscount. After the usual talk of the weather, he ended their conversation. She concentrated on her dance steps in order to save his toes and was happy when the dance ended and he parted from her. Her insides already fluttered in anticipation and it grew tenfold as she watched the Marquess of Sather stride confidently toward her. She reminded herself not to become tongue-tied. He was only one man, albeit an incredibly handsome one. Looks faded over time. Conversation and common interests would be what remained. She needed to see if this man showed potential in either area. Now that her father had granted her the option of ending her first Season without being forced to choose a husband, Catherine had the luxury of truly getting to know different suitors without rushing to the altar.

She very much wanted to learn all about Jeremy St. Clair.

He bowed as he reached her, his smile reaching his eyes, unlike so many men of the *ton*.

"I believe the supper dance is ours, Lady Catherine."

He offered her his arm and escorted her onto the ballroom floor as the strains of the waltz began. Catherine shivered in anticipation.

"Are you cold?" he asked.

"Not a bit," she replied. "It's the first waltz of the evening. I enjoy dancing to it."

As he clasped her right hand and slid his arm about her, he said, "Tonight, so do I." Amusement twinkling in his emerald eyes as he swept her away.

Right away, she noted his skill as a dancer. His grasp on her was light and yet firm at the same time. Effortlessly, he steered her along the polished floor, twirling her about so that her skirts billowed. For a moment, Catherine could have sworn she was floating, not dancing. As they continued, she felt the warmth of his hand against the small of her back as well as in their joined hands. He held her slightly closer than he should have, causing her breasts to brush against his muscled, broad chest. Her nipples puckered and she ached to rub them against him. The thought shocked her and, yet, it seemed exactly what she needed to do. His clean, masculine scent filled her with every breath she took.

"You are a delight to dance with, Lady Catherine." Those green eyes gleamed at her with interest.

"I already knew you were a skilled dancer. I observed you earlier dancing with Lady Amanda."

"I haven't seen Amanda in a good ten years. She's grown into quite a beauty." His mouth moved to her ear. "But she cannot hold a candle to you." His lips grazed her earlobe and then moved away.

Something unknown rippled through Catherine. Something she had no name for. Unless it was . . . *desire*. She clutched his fingers more tightly and his low chuckle confirmed she was right in her thinking. Butterflies exploded in her belly.

"Lady Amanda is quite taken with your friend, Morefield," she said breathlessly.

He nodded sagely. "Morefield can be a bit reserved. I will let him know. It will boost his confidence. He's a fine man. Amanda could not do better than Eric. He would make an excellent husband and father, as she would wife and mother. I can tell he's ready to settle into matrimony."

"And what of you, Lord Sather? Are you at the Marriage Mart to browse for a wife?" she asked boldly.

His arm tightened about her." I hadn't thought so," he said carefully. "I'm only twenty-three. That's why I wanted to see a bit of the world after I graduated from Cambridge last year." He gave her a long look as the music died. "My father and grandmamma encouraged me to come tonight. I'm a bit of a loner and they wish for me to mix more into society."

Catherine was aware of others passing by them yet Jeremy St. Clair made no move to release her.

"To answer your question, my lady? My position may have changed, thanks to the company I'm keeping."

With that, he slowly released her and tucked her hand into the crook of his arm. "I believe supper awaits us."

As if walking on air, Catherine glided along beside him toward the room where the buffet had been laid out.

JEREMY HEARD THE clock chime midnight as he escorted Catherine Crawford to a table away from the large ones in the center of the room. The one he chose was in a corner and seated only two. She placed her reticule on it.

"Do you have anything particular you enjoy?" he asked, wanting to please her with choices from the buffet.

Those magnificent blue eyes lit up. "I know I'm not supposed to reveal this to a gentleman but I adore eating, especially if sweets are involved." She hesitated a moment and then asked, "Might I accompany you?"

"An excellent idea," he proclaimed, glad to remain in her company even going through the buffet line.

They joined a queue at the nearest table, where a group of servants doled out whatever was requested. His companion passed on the white soup and chicken but asked for both sliced ham and poached salmon. She only wanted a few glazed carrots and then the rest of her plate became heavy with cheeses and desserts.

"A large helping of the trifle, please," she instructed a maid. "And plenty of the dry cake, too." She leaned toward him, placing a hand on his forearm. "I drown it in strawberries and whipped cream." She had the maid scoop sliced strawberries atop the pound cake and then asked for three large spoonfuls of cream to rest atop it.

"And one piece of the pie. I'd like more but I might burst."

"I'll ask for two different kinds and you may share a few bites from my plate," he suggested.

Armed with their supper, he led her back to the corner. Placing their plates down, he seated her.

"I'll return with something for us to drink. Madeira? Ratifia? Lemonade?"

"Lemonade would be nice. It's rather warm in here."

"If you'd like, we can stroll outside in the evening air once we dine."

Jeremy left, unsure why he'd mentioned a stroll. He had no business taking up Lady Catherine's time. She was a beautiful woman in search of a husband. He wasn't husband material. He didn't want a wife, much less need one. He had no plans of having any children and that was the only reason to take a wife.

Yet something called out to his very soul every time he gazed at her, causing his heart to soar and making him flirt with her.

He dismissed the imaginary call. He would enjoy supping with her but somehow rescind his earlier remark. Giving her the impression that he was considering a bride was utterly wrong. She seemed too sweet and kind for him to give her false hope.

He collected a claret for himself and the lemonade she'd requested and returned to their isolated table. By choosing a table for two, he'd already caused the gossiping tongues to wag and could have kicked himself for linking their names together on his first evening in London.

She gave him a warm smile as he handed over her drink and sat.

"Who is the real Jeremy St. Clair?" she asked.

"I'm surprised you already know my name."

"Lady Amanda called you Jeremy and mentioned that you and your brother used to visit her family."

A dark cloud suddenly settled over him at the mention of Timothy. Perceptively, she leaned toward him and said, "I'm sorry if I brought up unpleasant memories, Lord Sather. Lady Amanda mentioned your brother had passed. It was cruel of me to mention something that still affects you so deeply."

Tears welled in her eyes and, without thinking, he reached and took her hand.

"Timothy's memory is never unpleasant to me, Lady Catherine. He was my best friend. I've missed him every day since he's been gone. He should have been the marquess. As a second son, I was destined for the army. I should be there now, with other friends, fighting against Bonaparte. Instead, I'm to be the eventual duke and must remain in England."

She placed her free hand atop his. "Your brother must have been a good man since he was not only your brother but your best friend. Tell me about him. I'd love to hear what he was like and what you did together as boys."

She removed her hand and he did the same, freeing hers up so she could eat. Again, he'd done something that might draw the eyes of others. Hopefully, with their table in the darkened corner, no one had seen them touching.

As they ate, he began speaking of Timothy, which he hadn't done in years. In fact, never. Once Timothy drowned, no one in the St. Clair house spoke his name, thanks to his father's edict. Jeremy's friends, after giving him their condolences, never mentioned him. It was as if Timothy had never existed. A part of Jeremy died with his brother and what was left became lost by not being able to speak of his closest friend and the biggest influence in his life.

The floodgates opened and story after story poured from Jeremy. At first, it hurt to talk about things he'd done with Timothy. Gradually, the hurt lessened and only the good times remained as he told Lady Catherine of growing up at Eversleigh. The things Timothy had taught him, from hunting and fishing to riding and boxing. He laughed until tears nearly fell as he told her of several scrapes they'd gotten into at school and how the St. Clair charm helped the pair escape punishment on more than one occasion.

She dabbed her lips with her napkin. "How I would have enjoyed knowing Timothy. He lived life to its fullest in the short time he was here."

Jeremy realized that not only had they both cleaned their plates as they conversed but that most of the buffet room had emptied of ball guests. This lovely woman had done what no one else had before. She was almost a stranger to him yet he felt closer to her than anyone, other than Cor.

"I'm sorry to have dominated our dinner conversation, Lady Catherine. We've talked about nothing but me. I should like to learn more about you."

"Oh, but I've enjoyed hearing about your antics," she said, her lips curving in a smile. "You and your brother were quite the scamps. I'm afraid I am boring in comparison."

"Thank you for allowing me to speak of my brother to you. I haven't since his death."

Her brows knit in puzzlement. "Why not? I adore my younger sister, Leah. If anything ever happened to her, I would most certainly remember her with both family and friends."

"My father wouldn't allow it," he revealed. "He forbade Timothy's name from being spoken by family and servants alike. At school, our friends probably thought it awkward for me to hear talk about Timothy so they, too, never mentioned him. It was a relief tonight to talk about him openly, with joy, and recall such fun, sweet memories." He paused. "You've given me a gift tonight, Catherine. You've given me my brother back. For that, I will forever be in your debt."

Chapter Six

HIS WORDS—AND THE emotion behind them—moved Catherine. To think this man hadn't spoken of his beloved brother in years and yet he'd opened up and shared special memories with her. It touched her to her core.

She looked at Jeremy St. Clair with new eyes. She'd been taken by his dashing looks and charm. His smooth moves on the dance floor. But the depth of character he'd revealed made her appreciate him even more.

She realized she'd never learned so much about a person in such a short time. Though Catherine had only spent an hour in this man's company, she believed she knew him better than anyone of her acquaintance. Even her conversations with her parents and Leah, as well as her friends, had always been ones that skimmed the surface. In her eighteen years, no man had revealed so much of himself to her, let alone any of her girlfriends. The marquess had spoken of so many events from his past and she'd eagerly asked questions, forming a solid picture of the boy he'd been and seeing how his experiences had shaped him into the man he was.

The time spent in his company had passed swiftly. Looking around, she saw they were the only remaining couple in the buffet room. Already, servants scurried about collecting dirty dishes and silverware.

"You owe me nothing, Lord Sather," she assured him. "Your conversation was open and refreshing. I haven't enjoyed anyone's company this much for the entire length of the Season."

He rose and assisted her from her chair. "I should return you to the ballroom before your next partner comes looking for you."

Noting the rueful look on his face, Catherine silently thanked her mother and said, "I have no commitment for now. You might recall no one had claimed the post-supper dance." She paused. "It would be nice to take a turn outside. You did mention a stroll. I would appreciate some fresh air."

His smile caused her heart to skip a beat. "I can think of nothing more that I would like to do."

He offered her his arm and led her from the room toward the ballroom. Locating a set of open French doors, they stepped out into the May evening. Immediately, a cool breeze caressed her heated skin. Catherine saw two other couples walking slowly. One woman's head rested against her companion's shoulder.

"Enough of me and my past," he said as he slowly led her around the terrace. "Tell me about yourself, Lady Catherine."

She noticed he'd addressed her formally again, unlike when he had called her by her first name moments ago while they were still at the table.

"I'm not sure there's much to tell. I haven't led as exciting a life as you have, what with your adventures with Timothy and going away to school." She thought a moment. "I will say that I come from a very loving family. Mama and Papa are devoted to one another and open with their affection toward each other. They have always made Leah and me feel we are treasured."

"They indulge you?" he asked.

"Not in the way you think. Material things mean little to either of my parents. Leah and I have been raised to feel the same. We rarely exchange gifts. Time spent with one another is more valued than a new hat or pair of gloves."

"What of the magnificent necklace you wear?" he prodded.

She fingered it lightly. "It's more an exception to the rule. I received it tonight, for my birthday. I've never been given anything so grand. It is something I will wear with fondness the remainder of my life, knowing it is from my parents and recognizes the fact that I am now a grown woman."

"Tonight was your birthday?"

Catherine laughed. "I suppose last night was for it's well past midnight, my lord."

"I wish you belated birthday wishes, all the same. What do you enjoy doing?"

"I adore reading. Sometimes, I make up stories for my sister. She's forever telling me to write them down. She thinks I could publish them and entertain other children with my tales."

His gaze caused her cheeks to warm. "I think you could do whatever you put your mind to." He paused. "What else?"

"I enjoy riding. Dancing. Arranging flowers. We only come to town each spring to be with Papa while Parliament is in session. This year, I haven't spent much time with Leah, thanks to all of the events I must attend and all the obligation calls I must return. To be frank, I'll be happy to be back in the country so I can enjoy life at a slower pace."

"How old is Leah?"

Catherine chuckled. "She is eleven but sometimes I feel she's older than I am. She's very inquisitive and friendly."

"My half-sister, Rachel, is also eleven. She is intelligent and curious, as well. Perhaps we should have the two of them meet."

"Oh, that would be lovely. Leah has been somewhat lonely with me gone so often this spring. She has no friends her age in town."

"That settles it. With your permission, the two of us will call on you tomorrow afternoon so the girls can meet and see if they enjoy one another's company."

Catherine looked at him thoughtfully and asked, "Are you doing this for their sakes or would you ask to call if neither of us had a sister?"

He stopped and faced her, his hands rising to cup her cheeks. A frisson of pleasure rippled through her. Then her heart began beating erratically as she saw the heat in his eyes.

"I, too, would like to visit tomorrow because I enjoy your company."

His head bent toward hers and Catherine knew she was about to be kissed. She'd practiced doing so for hours, pressing her feather pillow to her mouth, in case this very thing occurred.

When his lips touched hers, though, it was nothing like she had imagined. He brushed his softly against hers, causing the blood to pound in her ears. When he began to pull away, she clutched his coat and moved toward him. His hands skimmed her neck and settled on her shoulders, holding her in place.

Afraid he wouldn't kiss her again, Catherine started to tell him why he should just as his mouth touched hers once more. Somehow, she must have given him an unspoken invitation because his tongue swept inside her mouth and, suddenly, she was falling. Her fingers tightened as a moan escaped from her. He tasted like the claret he'd drunk, as well as the strawberries they'd shared. The sandalwood soap he'd used rose from him, making her dizzy.

He broke the kiss and looked over his shoulder as he released her. Catherine swayed slightly and he took her hand and placed it on his forearm, leading her back toward the French doors and the ballroom. When they reached them, he halted.

"Forgive me, Lady Catherine. I did not mean to take advantage of you. Fortunately, no other couples were in sight."

"You're . . . apologizing?" All the blissful feelings fled, replaced by ones of insecurity.

"As I should. A gentleman should never—"

"I don't care. I wanted you to kiss me," she confessed.

His eyes widened. One brow shot up, giving him a rakish look.

"I've never been kissed before. I've practiced on my pillow at night, hoping someone would want to kiss me." She bit her lip. "From what you say, you did so and didn't want to. Or didn't think you should." Her eyes searched his. "How do you think that makes me feel?"

He let out a long sigh. "I did want to kiss you," he said softly. "Very much. And I'm selfish enough to be pleased that I'm the first man you've ever kissed."

His words did more than mollify her. He'd *wanted* to kiss her. Joy swept through her. The Marquess of Sather had kissed her because he wanted to. Yet the stern look on his face told her he probably wouldn't in the future. That he thought it had been a mistake.

"Lady Catherine, you must understand . . ."

"No. Don't say it," she ordered. "If you tell me you regret it, I'll die of embarrassment. You'll probably think me brazen but I enjoyed my first kiss. I can't imagine any man I would rather kiss than you. And if you choose never to speak to me again because I've been so blunt, I will understand. I won't be happy about it but I will soldier on. Please do not feel obligated to call on me tomorrow, my lord."

She released her hold on him, ready to flee before she made a bigger mess of things than she already had. He caught her wrist and she turned, looking him in the eye.

"I look forward to calling on you. And introducing our sisters."

Catherine swallowed. "Very well," she said stiffly.

He took a step closer and said, "I will see you tomorrow. And again tonight. For our dance."

JEREMY RELUCTANTLY RELEASED Catherine and watched her cross the ballroom, the sapphire ball gown clinging to her in all the right places.

He turned away, afraid he might chase after her, and returned to the night air to clear his head. He raised a gloved hand and could still smell her perfume.

Though he'd been to his fair share of *ton* events, no woman had been the breath of fresh air that Catherine Crawford was. Not only was she a rare beauty, but kindness radiated from her. As he paced, he couldn't believe all of what they'd spoken of. It was as if Jeremy had been slumbering for a decade and suddenly awakened, all his senses coming alive. Being able to talk about Timothy once again had been more than a relief. It had renewed Jeremy's spirit. No longer would he keep the memories of his brother shoved into a far corner of his mind, locked away. Catherine had opened that locked box and allowed Timothy St. Clair to live once more, if only through cherished memories. Jeremy saw how wrong his father had been to order everyone to keep Timothy's name from their lips. He would never keep quiet about his brother again and encourage others who'd known Timothy to do the same.

Exhilarated, Jeremy returned to the ballroom, where he danced with two young women who looked at him worshipfully. He politely spoke of the weather and the string quartet's performance and how much he'd enjoyed the evening's buffet selection before excusing himself and moving to the card room. He wanted to meet Catherine's father and see for himself the kind of man who shrugged off material possessions and raised such a remarkable daughter.

He saw Morefield standing with Neville, drinks in hand, and made his way toward them.

"Hiding in the card room?" he asked, knowing his friend had told Catherine he must leave the ball to attend to urgent business.

Morefield shrugged. "I didn't know where else to go. As it is, I've already lost all I can afford to this evening. Might as well make my way home. Say, would you care to go riding tomorrow morning?"

"I can't. I already promised Rachel I would take her. How about the day after?"

"Why don't you meet me at the club instead? We can have luncheon," Morefield suggested. "You're welcome to come, Neville."

"Splendid idea," agreed Neville. "I think I'll get back to the cards. My losing streak has to end sometime. I'm surprised to see you here, Sather. You rarely play."

Jeremy enjoyed cards and was an astute player but he associated gameplay with his father. The duke's well-known forays into gambling were legendary among the *ton*. Because of that, he played infrequently, though he usually won when he did.

"Before you leave, Morefield, point out Lady Catherine's father."

His friend gazed across the room. "There. At the last table on the left. In the gold waistcoat. That's the Earl of Statham." Morefield gave him a questioning look but Jeremy ignored it.

"I see two vacant spots, Neville. Join me?"

The two men crossed the length of the room and stood behind the empty chairs.

Jeremy indicated the seats. "Are these taken?"

The Earl of Statham said, "Not at all. Play just broke up. We were waiting for a few more players to round out the table. Please, have a seat." He turned to the dealer across the table. "Call for a new deck."

Jeremy and Neville sat and introduced themselves. He already knew two men present, one from his Cambridge days and one who was an acquaintance of his father.

While they waited for a new deck of cards to arrive, he turned to his left and said to the earl, "I danced with your daughter tonight."

Statham's face softened. "Ah, my Catherine is a lovely jewel, the same as her sister and my wife. You said you were Sather? Are you related to Hemmings?"

"No." With dread, he added, "I am the heir to the Duke of Everton."

A look of displeasure flickered across Statham's face. He hid it quickly but Jeremy knew he must address the issue.

"My lord, I beg you not to judge me on my father's reputation," he said earnestly. "My mother died in childbirth and I was raised by my grandmamma. I believe I take after her in character far more than I do my father, whom I rarely see."

Statham nodded, understanding lighting his brown eyes. "The dowager duchess is a formidable woman with an impeccable reputation. If you have claimed her good sense and morals, then you are a man to be admired, Lord Sather."

"I hope to prove to you that very thing. I am coming to call on your daughter tomorrow afternoon."

"I see."

"I plan to bring my half-sister, Rachel, who is the very age of Lady Leah. I'm hoping they will enjoy one another's company."

"Well played, Lord Sather."

"I beg your pardon?"

The earl looked at him with new eyes. "Above everything, my daughter values family. What better way to impress her, beyond flattery and ubiquitous bouquets, than to show her you feel the same." He paused. "You *do* esteem family, my lord?"

Jeremy thought a moment and then spoke from his heart. "While my father has not been a strong influence in my life, Cor certainly has. She's instilled in me the importance of family. My father is careless and not involved in the lives of my half-brother or half-sister. It is up to me to guide them. Cor convinced me Luke and Rachel are my responsibility and I don't take that lightly. Nor do I take lightly the duties and obligations that will befall me upon being the Duke of Everton. I assure you, Lord Statham, that I will be a far different duke than my father when the time comes."

The earl smiled benignly. "Then I look forward to learning more of you, Sather. I suppose I will have to make sure you stay for tea tomorrow. Bring your grandmamma, as well as Lady Rachel. I would enjoy visiting with the dowager duchess, as would Lady Statham."

"I will see if Cor is free and if so, I'm sure she'll accompany us. I'm only sorry I cannot fetch Luke from Eton so that all the St. Clairs could be represented tomorrow."

Statham laughed heartily and Jeremy could see where Catherine had gotten her deep, rich laugh.

He noticed cards being dealt and picked up the two in front of him. After winning two hands and losing another, he excused himself and returned to the ballroom. He found three dances remained before the final one of the evening. Searching the room, he spied Catherine's sapphire gown. She danced with a man old enough to be her father, a marquess who had never wed and had a string of mistresses. The gentleman spent more time looking at Catherine's bosom than appropriate. Jeremy forced himself to remain in place instead of storming across the ballroom and slamming his fist into the man's face.

Fortunately, the dance ended and her next partner behaved more admirably.

Jeremy watched how graceful she was, caught up in the music, her face flushed. Again, he doubted he should become further involved with her but found himself helpless to fight the strong attraction he felt toward her. He hadn't come to the Wethersby ball looking for a wife. It was the last thing on his mind. Something he'd never planned on doing. And now, it was the only thing that he could think of.

Making this woman his.

Chapter Seven

Catherine's head spun from all the dancing she'd done. She'd had a partner for every dance since she'd returned to the ballroom. Fortunately, one suitor never showed up, allowing her to catch her breath. She and Charlotte drank a cup of punch to quench their thirsts.

"I'll forever be in your mother's debt," her friend said. "Saving the two most important dances on my card was well worth my while. Cheltham took the supper spot. I took to him so we will partner again for the last dance of the night. What about you?"

"I will end the evening with Lord Sather," Catherine said, trying to calm the butterflies in her stomach as she thought of being in the marquess' arms again.

Charlotte gave her a knowing look. "Everyone noticed how he led you to a table for two. You were the talk of supper. You both laughed quite a bit."

She felt her cheeks pinkening. "Sather is very entertaining." She paused. "He's coming to call tomorrow."

Charlotte's eyes lit up. "I knew I sensed something between the two of you. I wonder what flowers he will send."

Catherine didn't care about flowers. She'd received so many bouquets since the Season began that they'd lost meaning for her. "He's bringing his sister. She's Leah's age and he hopes they'll get on."

"Hmm. A doting older brother. As much as you prize family, he's certainly found a way into your heart."

If only Charlotte knew how much Jeremy St. Clair had already wriggled into Catherine's heart—and soul.

"Would you like to shop in the morning with me?" her friend asked. "I need a new pair of gloves."

"I can't. I promised Leah that we would go to the bookstore. She's desperate for an outing that just the two of us can take."

"Very well. Let's go the day after. By then, Sather will have called and most certainly you will have danced with him again at the Rutherford ball tomorrow night. Since he is childhood friends with Lady Amanda, he's certain to be there." Charlotte smiled. "I'm sure we'll have much to talk about."

Catherine agreed and finished her punch. She danced twice more and then saw Sather approaching her. Her heart fluttered wildly in her chest as she smiled at him.

"Lady Catherine." He bowed to her and took her hand in his. "I believe this dance is meant for us."

They moved to the center of the ballroom. About a quarter of the couples who'd been present at the height of the ball had now left, leaving more room on the dance floor. As the string quartet launched into another waltz, the marquess drew her near, one arm about her and his hand taking hers.

This time, they did not speak. Instead, the music spoke for them as Sather twirled her about the ballroom in grand fashion. She felt light on her feet and giddy on the inside as she smiled up at him, his gaze never leaving her during the entire dance. When the last note sounded, he brought them to a stop.

"May I return you to your parents?"

"Please." Catherine looked about. "There. Mama is in green, speaking to that striking older woman. Oh, she has beautiful posture. She must have been a true beauty in her day."

He grinned. "That woman is my grandmamma. Come, I want you

to meet her." He tucked her hand into the crook of his arm and they wove their way through the parting couples.

Her mother beamed as they arrived. "Catherine, darling, you must meet the Dowager Duchess of Everton. I only learned tonight that she and my mother were the best of friends as young girls."

The duchess assessed Catherine, her head high but her eyes twinkling. "Lady Catherine, it's a pleasure to meet you." Her eyes flicked to Sather. "I see you have met my grandson. I believe you danced twice tonight."

"Yes, Your Grace, we did. Lord Sather is a most excellent dancer."

The old woman nodded sagely. "Jeremy is excellent at many things. I'm only glad he's come home to England. I have missed his company this past year, though he did write beautiful letters to me regarding his travels." She paused. "Have you met the Countess of Statham?" she asked her grandson.

"No, though I've had the pleasure of meeting the earl during card play tonight." He bowed to her mother. From the look on her mother's face, it was obvious she was taken with Sather's charm.

"Speaking of the earl, Cor, I told him that Rachel and I were calling on Lady Catherine and her sister tomorrow afternoon. He asked if you might wish to accompany us and stay for tea."

Catherine wondered why he addressed his grandmamma as Cor and thought she would ask him about it tomorrow. She had a thousand things she wished to learn about him. In a dozen hours, he would be at her house, seated next to her. She shivered with anticipation.

"I would be happy to visit with Statham." The dowager duchess faced Catherine. "And you, too, Lady Catherine. You've made quite an impression on the *ton* during your come-out."

"Thank you, Your Grace. I look forward to spending more time with you. Do you have any sweet that you prefer? Our cook is most talented and would be happy to make something special for you."

The dowager duchess laughed. "My grandson is the one with the sweet tooth. Rachel, too." She looked at Sather. "It's unusual to bring one's sister when you call upon a lady."

"Lady Leah is the same age as Rachel. I thought they might have something in common," he replied.

The Earl of Statham arrived and greeted everyone. "Has Sather asked you to tea?" he inquired of the dowager duchess.

"He has and I'm delighted to accept your invitation."

"Then we will see you tomorrow." The earl turned to his wife. "Ready, my love?"

"We are."

They said their goodbyes and then Catherine's father led them outside. As usual, carriages were everywhere. They found their coachman, who bounded down from the driver's seat and assisted her mother and then Catherine into the carriage. She thought she caught a whiff of whiskey on his breath and wondered if he'd abandoned the coach to spend time in a tavern.

Her mother regaled them with a few stories the dowager duchess had shared as they sat some minutes before the coach took off.

As they traveled through the streets of London, her father asked, "What is your opinion of Sather, Catherine?"

"I have a high regard for him," she replied. "We danced twice and took supper together. He is most interesting. More than any man I've met during the Season."

Her mother smiled. "He's from a very good family. The St. Clairs have held the dukedom for many years and have numerous properties scattered throughout England. The dowager duchess herself possesses an estate that came to her through her own family, before she wed."

"Though I liked Sather, I would beg to differ, my dear," her father said. "The current Duke of Everton is an embarrassment to his title and family. I can't remember the last time I saw the man sober. And he has yet to show up at Parliament this session."

Catherine spoke up. "Sather told me he is not close to his father. He conveyed disapproval of the duke without being disrespectful. He's very close with his grandmamma, though. She seems to have been a strong influence on him and has been the one to raise him."

"Hmm. He seems like a capable young man with a good head on his shoulders," the earl said. "What do you think his intentions are, regarding you?"

Catherine sensed her cheeks heating and was glad the carriage was dark.

"I think we have a real chance at becoming friends. And maybe more."

"Friends? A man and a woman don't become friends," her mother chided. "No, the marquess is definitely interested in you, Catherine. You must know you would have our approval if he wished for a match between our families."

"Don't get ahead of yourself, Mama," she warned. "Though I learned much of him tonight, I would need to know other things." She paused. "And I would need to fall in love with him. Like you and Papa. I couldn't possibly settle for anything less."

"Love is grand," her father said, "but if you are compatible, that's a good start. Love can grow from friendship, Catherine. Remember, you may take your time. There's no rush to wed. If you're drawn to Sather and he offers for you at Season's end, though, I'd consider it. You're both attractive, intelligent people. I think it would be a good match."

"Even if we are not in love?" she asked softly.

"Even then," her father confirmed. "What you see between your mama and me is the result of many years together. Yes, we are deeply in love, but it started as a physical attraction—with a bit of friendship mixed in. By our wedding day, I knew I loved her but that love from long ago is nothing to compare to the depths to which it has grown over our years together. For a decade, it was only the two of us, before you arrived. It gave us ample time to know one another and grow together, both in friendship and love."

Catherine knew that was the only disappointment in her parents' marriage. It had taken her mother ten years before she gave birth to a child. Another seven years passed before Leah arrived. No babies had come since then. With no son, the earldom would pass to her uncle, Edward, and if he were gone, the title and lands would go to his son, Martin. Though her father never spoke of it, she couldn't help but think he was slightly displeased that the woman he worshipped had been unable to provide him with an heir.

Suddenly, the coach, which seemed to be traveling too fast, bucked as a wild horse. Catherine was tossed to the floor. She pushed herself up and sat back on the seat across from her parents.

"I think Robert has been drinking," she announced. "I thought I smelled whiskey on his breath when we left the Wethersbys'."

The coach lurched again and her fingers tightened on the velvet seat. Her father lifted his cane and rapped on the roof of the carriage.

"Slow down, Robert. At once!"

Instead, the horses seemed to run even faster as the vehicle begin swaying from side to side. Fear filled her. The team must be out of control to be moving at such a great speed.

Then they crashed into something and the carriage flipped on its side, tossing its occupants about. It rolled again, flinging them once more. Catherine screamed as her head collided with something hard and her leg snapped at the same time.

For a moment, all was still within the coach. She could hear the wheels outside spinning and then the agonizing cries of injured horses. Something warm trickled down the bridge of her nose and she wiped it away. Her leg ached something awful. She knew it must be broken. Her head began pounding fiercely.

Shouts came from outside. Someone tried to open the door. Confusion filled her. She wondered where her parents were as something dripped into her eyes. Catherine heard her mama gasp and moan. No sound came from her papa. Then darkness swallowed her whole.

Jeremy allowed Cor to speak to a few more people before he steered her toward their coach. He waved off the driver and helped his grandmamma in and then followed, sitting across from her.

"Did you enjoy your time at the Wethersbys' ball?" he asked. "I know it was your first event to attend since your arrival in London."

"I had a wonderful time catching up with everyone, especially my friend." She eyed him with interest. "It seems to me that you, too, enjoyed your first *ton* outing."

"It was good to see some of my friends," he said guardedly.

In truth, his spirits soared higher than a kite on a blustery day. All because of Catherine Crawford.

It was madness to think he might have found the one woman that completed him, especially when he had no intentions of making a lifetime commitment to any female. Yet he'd been the happiest he'd ever been in her company, a thrill of what was to come building inside of him. Already, he counted the hours before he would see her again. The ease with which they'd spoken, as if they'd been acquainted for years, was part of his euphoria. He thought about how much she put family on a pedestal and how she believed in love.

For Jeremy, he'd never seen that love existed, at least between a man and woman. The three women his father had wed had come with large dowries, if Jeremy believed their gossiping servants. He saw little affection between them. His grandfather had passed before Jeremy was born. He wondered if Cor had loved him. Though most of his friends had fallen away over the years, he couldn't think of one of them who had married yet, much less been in love. At *ton* events, wedded couples rarely interacted. Society's unwritten rule asked that a woman provide an heir and a spare and then she could do as she pleased, while a man could take a mistress at any given time, before or during marriage.

He'd never remotely felt any kind of attachment or affection for any woman of his acquaintance. Jeremy was no angel, having sowed enough wild oats at Cambridge and while on his travels through Europe. None of those women appealed to him in any way, shape, or form.

Except Catherine.

She possessed not only beauty but the good name and fortune that society required—yet so did dozens of other women who were present at tonight's ball. He found it hard to explain to himself why he was so drawn to her. Some intangible that refused to be named.

Love?

He wouldn't have thought so before tonight.

Cor pulled him from his thoughts. "Jeremy St. Clair, I am asking you about Lady Catherine."

"What about her?"

"It was obvious you connected with her in some way. I noted you danced twice with her and only once with others. You both seemed quite engaged in your supper conversation. My goodness, I've never seen two people laugh so much."

He shrugged. "She puts me at ease. We spoke of . . . many different things. Even Timothy."

Cor's brows rose. "I see. Tell me, Grandson—how do you feel about her? When you're dancing together. Strolling. Talking."

Letting down his guard, he said, "As if I'm myself. The real me who's been hidden away for so many years. The Jeremy St. Clair who enjoyed life to the fullest." He sighed. "She makes me feel alive, Cor. As if every bone within me wants to move with joy. When she was in my arms, it felt right. That someone was by my side and would stand with me against the world."

He raked his hands through his hair. "I can't get her out of my head. I can still smell her subtle perfume. Hear her laugh. I don't know if I'll be able to sleep tonight because I'm excited to see her again."

Cor patted his knee. "I'm sure Lady Catherine is as taken with you as you are with her."

"I hope so. Or I don't. Cor, I never wished to wed," he admitted. "Father tried thrice and made a disaster of each marriage. He was a terrible husband and an even worse father. I know he's your son but—"

"No apologies needed, my boy. The important thing is you are *not* him. You are a very good man, Jeremy. As you mature, you'll become an even better one. You will make a good husband and wonderful father, for you know to act the opposite of your own father. You will lavish attention upon your children—and your wife. It remains to be seen whether Lady Catherine will be that wife or not."

She took his hand. "Tomorrow will take care of itself. Either your eagerness to see the girl will die out—or it will magnify. If it hits the point where you don't think you can live without her, then she is the one for you."

"Is that what love is, Cor? When you so desperately need to be with another?"

She smiled mysteriously. "It's a part of it."

The coach slowed and Jeremy said, "It looks as if we're home."

He opened the door when the carriage came to a halt and jumped out, handing Cor down. They started toward the house when the front door flew open. Barton appeared, looking disheveled. Jeremy's heart sank, knowing the news would not be pleasant.

"My lord, Your Grace, thank goodness you're home."

"Is it His Grace?" Cor asked, her voice steady as always.

Barton nodded. "His Grace came home from his club an hour ago, his speech slurring and his gait irregular. It wasn't his... usual manner. Simmons got him to his chamber and then His Grace collapsed. I sent for Doctor Walmsley at once. He is with His Grace now."

Dread filled Jeremy. He looked to Cor. "We should go to him."

Taking her arm, he led her into the house and up the stairs, Barton following closely behind them. They reached his father's bedchamber as Walmsley ventured from the room.

Seeing them, the physician shut the door, his face grave. "It's apoplexy. I doubt His Grace will survive the night."

Chapter Eight

Jeremy closed his eyes for a moment, letting Walmsley's words sink in. He steeled himself and opened them.

"Can we see him?" he asked.

The doctor nodded. "He's fading fast. His speech has been affected. I'll warn you that he may be confused. He may also have difficulty understanding what you say to him. Speak in soothing tones. Don't mention what's happened. We don't want him to panic."

"Barton, see that Doctor Walmsley has a room nearby," Cor said, calmly taking charge. She looked to the physician. "Get some rest. I'm sure you were dragged here from your bed. Jeremy and I will stay with my son. We'll call you if you're needed."

"Thank you, Your Grace."

"If you'll follow me?" Barton led Walmsley to the room adjacent to the duke's as Jeremy and Cor entered the bedchamber.

His father lay propped against a few pillows, his normally ruddy face pale as a bedsheet. His sparse hair was plastered to his head. The right side of his face seemed misshapen and his mouth drooped downward on that side. One eye seemed almost swollen shut.

"Uuhhgghh."

He had no idea what his father tried to say. He uttered the noise again, his desperation obvious. Cor took a seat next to the bed and Jeremy stood behind her. She took her son's hand in hers and patted the back of it with her other.

"There, there, Stephen," she said soothingly. "I'm here now. So is Jeremy. We won't leave. We will stay with you."

The Duke of Everton groaned. The noise sounded like a wounded animal, one caught in a trap that knew escape was impossible.

"It's just a setback, Father," Jeremy said with a confidence he didn't feel. Instead, trepidation filled him as he stared at the shell of the man he'd known.

"Do you have anything you need to say?" Cor urged.

"Oh-ry. Oh-ry."

"You're sorry?" she repeated.

"Uhm."

"That's good, Stephen. You have many things to be sorry for. You've treated me abominably over the years and all but ignored your three children. It's good to make amends at the end."

Jeremy placed his hand on her shoulder and squeezed it in warning.

Cor looked up at him. "I know what I'm doing. He should be accountable for what he's done. Maybe he can go to his Maker with a clear conscience."

Tears streamed down Stephen St. Clair's face. He shuddered and mumbled something unintelligible again.

"Despite your lack of effort, your children have all turned out well," Cor continued. "Jeremy will make a fine Duke of Everton. I know you have provided for Luke, as well." She glanced up. "Luke is to inherit Fairhaven and become Earl of Mayfield. It's all spelled out in Stephen's will. He's also provided an ample dowry for Rachel. I made sure both children would be looked after."

"Ade ess," his father said. "A uge ess."

"You certainly have made a mess," she chided. "It will be Jeremy who must deal with the repercussions. Thank goodness he has my strength of will and character, as well as the St. Clair charm and intelligence. Your father indulged you too much, Stephen. He never made you answerable for your actions. You behaved your entire life as if you were better than others. True, most dukes do, but you hurt too many others along the way. I hope you see the error of your ways."

He nodded, his eyes watery. "Orry."

"I know you are," Cor said. She lifted her son's hand and pressed a kiss against it. "Despite your ornery disposition, I have always loved you, my boy. I did then and I do now but I am unhappy that the way you lived your life will affect your heir and our family."

Drool slid down the duke's chin. Jeremy whipped out a handkerchief and wiped it away.

His father looked him in the eye. "Ank oo."

"You're welcome," he managed to get out, his throat thick with emotion.

"Rest, Stephen," Cor said. "We won't leave you. We will be here by your side when you awaken." She smoothed her hand over his brow and he closed his eyes.

Silence filled the room. Jeremy released his grip on Cor and brought another chair over. Placing it next to her, they kept a vigil as Stephen St. Clair's breathing grew more labored. With each raspy breath, Jeremy wished he could do so much of his life over with this man. He'd wanted a father who readily spent time with him. Took him shooting and riding. Ate meals with his family and shared stories with them.

It was too late now. His father shuddered several times, letting out a wheeze that sounded painful. Then he stilled.

"Fetch Walmsley," Cor ordered.

Jeremy rose and wrapped his arms about her. He kissed the paper-thin cheek. "I'm sorry, Cor."

"I am, too. Stephen wasted all his potential. His life had no meaning. He did no good for others. It saddens me."

He kissed her again and then went to awaken the physician. Walmsley returned with him and gave a cursory exam.

"His Grace is gone."

"Thank you for coming, Doctor Walmsley," Jeremy said. "I know you did all you could."

He escorted the doctor downstairs.

"Send for me if you or Her Grace need anything. A sleeping powder. Whatever."

"We will."

After letting the doctor out, Jeremy trudged back up the stairs. By now, Barton and Simmons stood in the hallway, ready for instructions.

Cor opened the door. "He's passed. You know what to do."

Barton stepped forward. "We will handle everything, Your Grace. You need to get some rest."

"Thank you, Barton." Cor walked slowly down the hall and Jeremy knew how grief blanketed her.

As for himself, he felt nothing. No emotion. Only an emptiness inside.

"Your Grace, Manfry is waiting for you in your chamber," Barton informed him.

"Thank you," he said and wearily started down the hall.

Only as he reached to turn the doorknob did it occur to him that Barton had addressed him as the new Duke of Everton.

WORRY CONSUMED JEREMY as he dozed and woke over the next few hours. He knew how woefully unprepared he was to be the next Duke of Everton. He'd never looked at any estate records and had no idea how much income the St. Clair estates generated. Hundreds of servants and tenants resided on St. Clair lands but he hadn't a clue as to how many. He didn't know what crops they grew or what livestock was bred. He'd met his father's barrister in passing but doubted he could pick the man out in a crowd.

It was why he'd stopped at various businesses during his travels and met with their managers. He'd become acquainted with different members of the nobility in cities along the way and had asked questions of them—and their stewards. He had a burning desire for knowledge, coupled with wanting to restore splendor to the tarnished St. Clair name when his time came to become elevated in position.

If only he'd had more time to prepare.

It was why he'd cornered his father yesterday when he'd arrived. As usual, Stephen St. Clair put his son off, encouraging him to indulge in pleasure. Cor had promised to talk with him in more detail. Despite being a woman, he knew she had her fingers on the pulse of everything that happened within the family.

When he next opened his eyes, he saw a silhouette in the window seat. Rachel, dressed in her riding clothes, sat with her feet in front of her, her chin resting atop her knees. She stared out the window listlessly.

Jeremy slipped from the bed and hastily put on his dressing gown before joining her.

Sitting next to her, he put an arm around her.

"Papa's dead, isn't he?" she asked.

"He is," Jeremy confirmed.

They sat in silence until she said, "I went to the stables to meet you. When you didn't come, I came back to the house. None of the servants would look at me." She paused. "Then I noticed the black armbands they wore."

He kissed the top of her head.

"At first, I thought it was Cor because she's old. I ran upstairs and into her room. She was sleeping, though. I could tell. Her chest went up and down. So I came here."

Rachel choked on her last words and tremendous sobs erupted. Jeremy enveloped her in his arms, rubbing her back, hoping to comfort her.

She raised a tearstained face to him and said, "I'm not crying because I'm sad and will miss him. I'm crying because I feel guilty. Because I'm not sad. I won't miss him at all. I must be a terrible person."

He pressed a kiss to her brow. "You aren't terrible. If you are, then you must accuse me of the same. I was with him when he died. And I felt nothing." He leaned against the wall and pulled her head to his chest.

"Do all fathers ignore their children as he did?"

Jeremy thought of Lord Statham and his great love for his wife and two daughters.

"No. Some men value their children and make time for them. We weren't fortunate enough to have one of those."

"It's unfair that none of us had mothers. Not me. Not you. Not Luke."

He sighed. "Life is not always fair, Rachel."

She gazed up at him. "Will you be my guardian now?"

"Of course. Who else?"

She frowned. "I thought maybe Cor might be but she could die before I'm grown."

"As the new Duke of Everton, you are my responsibility. Luke, as well."

Rachel thought a moment. Hesitantly, she said, "I know as the duke you will have all sorts of obligations. Will you . . . will you still make a little time for me, Jeremy? You've only come home and I've missed you so much. I was lonely the whole year you were gone."

He laughed heartily. "I will always make time for you, pet. Why, I'll be so doting that you will complain to your friends how I smother you."

Saying that, his thoughts turned to Catherine for the first time and how he and Rachel were supposed to visit her and Leah this afternoon. He would need to send a note explaining the circumstances of why the visit had to be postponed.

Rachel's stomach gurgled noisily and she giggled.

"It sounds as if someone is hungry. Run downstairs. I'll join you in the breakfast room in a few minutes." He kissed her cheek and stood.

"Don't be long."

"I won't."

Quickly, he dressed, not bothering to ring for Manfry. He sat at his escritoire and composed a brief note to Catherine, apologizing for missing their visit and telling her he would call once he returned from the funeral at Eversleigh. He would ask Barton to be sure to send flowers to her, as well. Jeremy folded it. He supposed he should have gone downstairs to his father's study and used the ducal Everton seal but he didn't want to bother. He'd signed the note as Sather, so she would know it was from him.

Jeremy left his chamber and hurried downstairs and was surprised to see Matthew Proctor pacing in the foyer. He placed the letter on a nearby table.

"Good morning, Matthew."

His friend turned. "Your Grace." He hesitated a moment and then offered his hand. "My condolences on your loss."

"Thank you. Are you here for your letter of recommendation?"

Matthew nodded. "I almost didn't ring the bell when I saw the black wreath but after being gone from England a year, I need your recommendation in order to find a post."

Barton appeared with a letter in hand that Jeremy had given the butler for safekeeping. He said, "I'll take that."

The butler handed it over and left.

Jeremy slid the letter into his coat pocket. "You won't be needing that. Come, join me and my sister for breakfast."

"Your Grace, I don't think—"

He waved away the protest. "We'll eat first—then I have a proposition for you."

Leading Matthew into the breakfast room, Jeremy saw Rachel had already started. He introduced her to Matthew and then both men filled their plates from the sideboard. As they ate their fill, he encouraged Matthew to talk about their recent travels as a way to take Rachel's mind off the death of their father.

Once they finished the meal, he invited his former tutor into the downstairs study. He noticed a servant had cleared the desktop. All traces of his father had vanished.

"Have a seat."

Matthew sat, obviously puzzled why Jeremy had claimed the reference letter.

Taking a seat behind the desk, he said, "I'm ready to offer you a job."

"What?" Astonishment filled his friend's face.

"You can claim the letter and travel to Cambridge if you wish but I have great need of you here. With my father's death, my duties will be legion. I have much to learn about our various estates and holdings. I will need a secretary to keep everything in order for me. Someone I can trust to accompany me to meetings and share advice when I ask for it."

"I am to be this secretary?" Matthew asked, doubt in his eyes.

"I know of no man more intelligent than you. You accompanied me to factories and mills and large estates on our travels. You know what interests me. You have a good head for business. And I trust you. I fear sycophants galore will come out of the woodwork, all flattering me while wanting something from me. I need someone I can count on and confide in. Someone I know and can trust."

He offered a starting salary and saw Matthew's eyes widen.

"That is far too generous, Your Grace."

Jeremy grinned. "Not for all the work I plan to pile upon you. Take the position, Matthew. If it doesn't suit you after six months, then I will release you from your obligation and return the reference letter to you."

He stood and offered his hand. Matthew took it, beaming from ear to ear.

"Thank you, Your Grace."

"It's Jeremy. At least when we have privacy."

Matthew hesitated and then said, "If you insist."

"I already have your first task. Retrieve my brother from Eton. The term is near the end. It won't matter if he misses the last few days for his father's funeral. I'm sure the school will be understanding."

"You've always referred to him as your half-brother," Matthew pointed out.

"I know. It was wrong of me to make that distinction. Luke and Rachel are my family. I will be their guardian now. I'm dispensing with the half and going with the whole." He sat again. "Let me dash off a note to the headmaster for you to present on my behalf."

Once he'd finished it, using the Everton seal, he gave it to Matthew and said, "I'll let Barton know to have the coach prepared. Be sure Luke packs everything in his trunk since he won't return until next term."

"Thank you again, Jeremy," his friend said. "I won't let you down. This is a rare opportunity. I promise I won't waste it."

"I know you won't. Meet the coachman outside."

He rang for Barton and explained what he needed. The butler assured him it would be taken care of.

"What else needs to be done?" he asked the longtime retainer.

"Her Grace is managing all the necessary details," Barton informed him. "She asked for you to come to her sitting room when it is convenient for you."

"I'll see her now."

Jeremy headed upstairs and found Cor dressed, though she still sipped on her morning hot chocolate.

"I've arranged to have Luke brought from Eton to London," he told her. "I know there are a thousand more particulars to see to in order to bring Father's body back to Eversleigh."

"I've ordered the pine coffin. Stephen is laid out in the dining room for those who wish to come and pay their respects before we leave for Eversleigh. Simmons prepared him. I've ordered lilies, of course."

He knew both the fresh-cut pine and the flowers would cover the smell of the body's deterioration.

"When should we leave for Eversleigh?" he asked.

"The day after tomorrow. That will give anyone in town who wishes a chance to view him to do so either today or tomorrow."

"We'll need to meet with his solicitor when we return to town," he noted. "I've hired Matthew Proctor as my secretary to help me wade through everything."

Cor nodded. "A wise choice." She took his hand, sadness blanketing her. "We must talk, even before you see the St. Clair solicitor or speak to any of the estate managers."

"What is it, Cor?" When she didn't speak, he prodded her. "Go ahead. As the new Duke of Everton, I need to be prepared. I've long thought Father hid something from me. I need to know what he concealed if I'm to be effective and begin to make the necessary changes to restore our family's name."

She nodded. "You're right. There's no way to gloss over this."

She paused, and he sensed her reluctance to reveal what she knew. He braced himself for whatever she would say.

"Your father's gambling has almost bankrupted the St. Clairs, Jeremy. You have next to nothing to inherit, I'm afraid."

Chapter Nine

CATHERINE AWOKE TO excruciating pain in her leg and gasped. Her sharp intake of breath sent spikes of pain through her head and she raised her hands to cradle it.

"Lie still," a voice warned. "Rowney, you know what must be done."

She looked up and saw two men hovering over her. Before she could ask what was happening, one of them yanked sharply on her injured leg as the other pushed and pulled it. Her scream resounded through the room.

"It would be better if she fainted again, sir," the man who'd jerked her leg said. He still gripped her foot and ankle tightly, keeping her from moving it as the other man kneaded and pulled more.

"What are you doing?" she cried.

The older gentleman paused and released the pressure on her leg. "I'm Mr. Jones, your surgeon. I'm trying to set your leg, my lady. Legs are more difficult to remedy than a fractured arm, thanks to the size and strength of the muscles they contain. I need to get this right—else your right leg will be shorter than the left. Be patient."

He returned to manipulating her leg again and the pain caused her to see red and then black. When she came to, the surgeon fussed with her forehead.

Seeing she was conscious again, he told her, "Your leg has been stretched in order to put the bones in their natural position. I've encased it in plaster so it will mend. I'm attending to your head now."

Reaching behind him, he handed her a cup. "Drink this."

Catherine looked at it with suspicion. "What is it?"

"Laudanum. It will help you with the pain of your leg and the stitches I'm about to sew."

Her leg ached so badly that she downed the liquid in the cup in one swallow. The surgeon dipped a cloth in a basin and blotted it against her forehead. She sucked in her breath.

"That stings," she accused him.

His grim look told her it would do worse than sting.

She glanced down at her leg while he readied his equipment. "How did this happen?"

"You don't remember?" he asked.

"No," she said slowly, although a feeling of dread suddenly filled her. She tensed as she heard a scream echoing in her mind. A flash of motion sent a dizzying rush through her.

He blotted a cloth against her brow. "Rowney, come hold her down."

Panic swept through Catherine as the assistant came toward her. "No," she begged softly as her eyelids fluttered. Weariness filled her.

The young man gripped her elbows, pinning them to the bed. Her heart beat wildly but struggling was beyond her.

The surgeon said, "Go to sleep, my lady. This will all be over when you awaken."

She fought the urge even as her eyes closed and then succumbed, too tired to fight anymore.

When she awoke again, Tilly sat in a chair next to the bed. Her maid's eyes were rimmed with red and swollen from crying.

"Oh, my lady. You're awake."

Catherine swallowed. Her mouth was so dry. Her tongue darted out to lick her lips and found them dried and cracked.

"Tilly?"

"Hush, now. You're going to be fine. I need to get a little broth in you. Does that sound good?"

She nodded but a sharp pain filled her head. The leg ached dully.

Tilly helped her sit up some, propping a few pillows behind her, and then held a bowl to her lips. The broth was tepid but tasted so good. She drank it all. Her maid eased her back onto the pillows.

"Go to sleep, Lady Catherine."

"Where is Mama? Papa?"

"Don't you worry about them, my lady. Get some rest."

The next time Catherine woke, her head throbbed dully but the pain had receded. Once again, Tilly greeted her, rising from the chair next to the bed.

"How . . . long . . . have I slept?"

"A good long while, my lady. You needed it. After what happened."

She thought a moment. "What did happen, Tilly?"

The maid clucked her tongue. "Poor child. The surgeon said you might have trouble remembering. You banged your head hard. He put in four stitches."

Her fingers went to her forehead and felt the straight line of stitches an inch below her hairline.

Tilly brought the back of her hand to Catherine's cheek. "You don't seem to have a fever. That's a good sign. Very good. Are you hungry? Mr. Jones said you should start with bread and broth."

"I am."

"I'll go fetch some for you. Be back in a jiffy."

Catherine watched Tilly go and closed her eyes. Her entire body ached as if she'd been bruised and battered. It reminded her of when she'd fallen off a horse at age nine. She'd lost control of it when a storm approached. Thunder frightened the beast and it had taken off running, throwing her in the process. Every muscle in her body hurt for a week.

She opened her eyes and searched the room. She was in her own chamber but had no recollection of returning here. What was the last thing she could remember?

Jeremy St. Clair...

The image of the handsome marquess filled her mind. He was coming to call on her today. She glanced down at her leg. She wouldn't be able to see him like this.

Wait.

She recalled meeting his grandmamma. Leaving the ball. And then...

"No!" she cried weakly.

She remembered. Everything came rushing back faster than flood waters sweeping objects along a road. The carriage out of control. Tumbling. The darkness. Mama's groans. Papa silent. Fat tears fell down her cheeks.

What had happened to them?

Tilly entered the room with a tray. She stopped in her tracks. Catherine knew her dismay must be obvious.

"I remember an accident. What happened, Tilly? Where are Mama and Papa?"

The servant set the tray down. She perched on the bed and took Catherine's hands.

"Robert must have been drinking. From what we know, he lost control of the team. A witness said he stood, yanking hard on the reins, trying to slow the horses down. He was thrown from the coach." Tilly paused, her eyes downcast. "He didn't make it."

Catherine absorbed this information, fearful of what she would learn next. "Go on."

"The team ran through the streets with no driver. It crashed and the carriage turned upside down. It's how you were injured, my lady."

"And my parents?" she insisted, tears filling her eyes.

Reluctantly, Tilly met her gaze. "Lord Statham was badly injured.

They are still tending to him. The countess... she... she... she didn't make it."

Misery swept through Catherine. She would never see Mama again. Never speak with her. When she married, Mama wouldn't be there. Her babies would never know their grandmamma.

Sobs broke from her, causing her head to ache, but she couldn't stop them. Mama was gone and she had to face the possibility that Papa might die, as well.

"Leah," she whispered. "Where is Leah?"

"Her governess is with her," Tilly assured Catherine.

"Bring her to me. Now," she ordered.

"Why don't you eat your—"

"I said now, Tilly."

"Yes, my lady." The maid scurried from the room.

Minutes later, Leah ran through the door. She froze in her tracks only feet from Catherine's bed.

"I know I must look a fright," she apologized.

"No, you don't," Leah said, wringing her hands, something she did when she was uncertain or nervous.

"Come up on the bed with me," Catherine urged. "I need you, Leah."

Her sister gently climbed onto the bed and lay next to her. She took Catherine's hand.

"Mama is gone," she whispered.

"I know."

"Papa is... he's... not good. What if he dies, Catherine? What will we do?"

She squeezed Leah's hand. "Whatever happens, we will always have each other."

Cor's words stunned Jeremy. He'd long known of his father's gambling. The entire *ton* did. He'd also heard whispers that his grandfather had done the same.

"How can we be penniless?" he demanded. "We have dozens of estates filled with tenants and servants. Investments in companies. The St. Clairs are worth a fortune in land alone."

"That was in the past," she said gently. "Your grandfather also gambled and started this downward slide. The cost of Stephen's gambling, coupled with bad investments, spiraled out of control. Of course, keeping up several households while paying for servants' salaries, horses and carriages, fine food, and respectable wardrobes, tipped the scales. His lines of credit have been run up to excess all over town and beyond. Your father has slowly been selling off land and properties. There's still a good half-dozen left but in order to pay his debts, you'll need to sell most of what's left—or end up in debtors' prison."

Jeremy reeled from hearing all of this. "I never would have taken off for a year of travel had I known. Why didn't he tell me? Why didn't you?" he accused.

"It wasn't my place," Cor said. "I chastised Stephen and told him you must be made aware of the dire situation. Instead, he encouraged you to leave England, knowing after your time at Cambridge that you would want to become more involved in the family's finances." She sniffed. "He thought he could win back all he'd lost at the tables. Instead, all he did was sink further into debt."

Bitterness filled him. "Even yesterday, after I returned, I begged him to let me become more involved in estate business. No wonder he pushed me to attend *ton* events and make merry. He knew, soon enough, my life would be one of misery as I spent the remainder of it cleaning up his mistakes."

He stood and began pacing about the room. His bitterness turned to rage against a man he'd barely known and had never respected. One who'd selfishly pursued his own delights to the detriment of his family. It would be the surviving St. Clairs—and chiefly, Jeremy—who would suffer.

Cor urged him to sit again and he did, exhaustion filling him.

"What am I to do?" he asked dejectedly.

"First, we must bury your father at Eversleigh. It's our duty. Once word of his death reaches others, his creditors will present you with their bills. That will give you a good idea of what is owed. It's also possible that other gentlemen he gambled with might present papers of debts he owed from various card games. I've learned what estates Stephen already parted with. Meeting with his solicitor and banker will clarify what's left."

Jeremy nodded. "Once I know those figures and the status of what we still owe, I will know which estates and land must be sold off. It worries me that even then, what we receive from those sales won't be enough."

She lay a hand atop his. "Something that would help immensely would be for you to marry well. Immediately. You need a bride with an extremely large dowry. It won't totally save the family fortune but it would give you fresh capital to invest. I know how you have a head for business and have been eager to apply your knowledge." She smiled. "A plethora of anxious mamas will eagerly push their daughters your direction, all for the opportunity to marry a duke. Surely among them, you can find one that will bring a prodigious dowry."

Jeremy wondered if Catherine Crawford's dowry would suffice. Knowing he must marry to keep the St. Clairs from ruin, he couldn't see himself with anyone but Catherine.

He rose, determination filling him. "Cor, if you will excuse me?"

"Are you off to see Lady Catherine?" she asked sharply.

For a moment, he was taken aback and then said, "You are perceptive, as always."

"I saw the way you looked at her. What will you say to her?"

"I will ask to speak to her father and make known my intentions before I delicately bring up the matter of the marriage contracts and the amount of her dowry."

"You realize we don't know how much you are in debt at this point."

"I understand—but I can't see myself spending my life with any other woman."

Her eyes narrowed. "Don't mistake my words, Grandson. I like Lady Catherine. A great deal. But this is a time when practicality must rule, Jeremy. You must put your feelings for her aside and do what's best for this family. I'm begging you to wait until we have a better idea of the total amount of debt before you offer for the Crawford girl. Only then would you know if her dowry would be ample enough to make a difference.

"And only then can you decide if it's her—or you abandon thoughts of a union with her and search elsewhere."

His head told him that Cor was right but his heart wanted to secure a commitment from Catherine today. Still, a week or so wouldn't matter. He could bury his father and let the vultures come out. Once he had a handle on the debts, then he could speak with Lord Statham. If the earl did not provide a large enough dowry, Jeremy would withdraw his offer and never let Catherine know the two men had spoken. He only hoped that wouldn't be the case.

"All right. I won't speak of marriage today. I'd written her a note explaining why we wouldn't be able to come for tea this afternoon. I'll have it delivered so she won't think we forgot."

"Thank you for being reasonable, Jeremy," Cor said. "I know this is a heavy burden for you to bear."

He left her and found the note had vanished from the table in the foyer. Finding Barton, the butler told him that he'd seen it sitting there and had one of the footmen deliver it. Relieved that the letter had already been sent, Jeremy decided to take a walk to clear his head and think about the future.

As he left the house, he spied one of their footman coming down the street, what looked like a folded letter in his hand. Jeremy called to him.

"Did Barton send you to deliver a note to Lady Catherine Crawford?" he inquired, wondering if Catherine had sent a reply. If so, he was eager to read it.

"Yes, Your Grace," the servant said. "She won't get it, though, I'm afraid."

Jeremy's pulse quickened. "What do you mean?"

The footman shook his head and handed Jeremy's original letter back to him. "It was a bad business all around. A mourning wreath graced the door when I arrived."

He gripped the letter. "What happened?" he demanded.

"I didn't know if I should ring the bell or not," the footman said. "You know, with the family in mourning. Then the door opened and two men came out. One carried a surgeon's bag. I asked him what happened. He told me the family had been in a carriage accident on their way home last night. The earl was in a bad way. I asked about the lady and the surgeon told me she didn't survive. They pulled her dead from the coach."

Jeremy's jaw dropped. He staggered back.

Catherine . . . was *dead*?

He closed his eyes and could feel her in his arms. Smell her perfume. Hear her rich laugh.

"Your Grace? Are you well?"

Jeremy reluctantly opened his eyes, seeing a world without Catherine in it. He pushed past the footman.

And wanted to die himself.

Chapter Ten

"Give me the crutches, Tilly. I am determined to see Papa. And Mama."

"You're still weak, Lady Catherine."

"I don't care!" she shouted and immediately regretted her harsh words when the maid burst into tears.

Tilly retrieved the crutches that Rowney, Mr. Jones' assistant, had brought by this morning, to aid her in getting around. He reminded Catherine that the surgeon advised her to keep off the leg as much as possibly for the first two weeks to promote maximum healing. The cast could come off after six weeks.

She swung her legs off the bed, the one encased in the cast sticking straight out. Though weak, she reached for the crutches Tilly held and placed one under each arm.

"Stay near me," she advised her maid. "If I start to fall, catch me."

The servant nervously bobbed her head up and down.

Catherine pushed herself to her feet, keeping all weight off her right leg. She placed the tips of both crutches slightly in front of her and then swung her body toward them. Gradually, she made her way across the room. Though exhausted, she was determined to see her father. It took nearly a quarter-hour of starts and stops before she arrived at her parents' bedchamber. Beads of sweat covered her brow.

"Open it," she commanded.

Tilly did as asked and swung the door open.

Catherine hobbled into the large, airy room and saw Leah sitting on the edge of the bed, stroking her father's hand. Strong, her father's valet, stood in the corner, his face grim. A tall, thin man with an air of efficiency about him stood next to the bed. He looked at her, frowning, as she made her way toward the bed.

"I take it you are Doctor Crane," she said. "My mother mentioned your name a few times over the years. You helped deliver Leah, if I remember correctly."

For a moment, he looked flustered and then said, "Hello, Lady Catherine. Yes, I am Doctor Crane. I would advise you to return to your own bed. You shouldn't be up and about on that broken limb."

"Not until I see Papa," she said as she painstakingly moved to where the earl lay.

She stopped when she reached the bedside and leaned heavily on the crutches. As she looked down, she blinked back tears of despair and sorrow.

The sleeping man who lay flat on the bed looked nothing like the robust man she had known all her life. His skin was ashen. Cuts and bruises covered his face and hands, the only skin visible. He wheezed with each breath. Though almost six feet in height, somehow, it seemed as if he'd shrunk overnight.

"What is his prognosis?"

"I really can't say," Doctor Crane said vaguely.

She glared at him. "Because you don't know or because I'm a female and might become hysterical?"

"Both," the physician admitted.

"Leah and I are all he has left. Please, tell me what I need to know. Will he live? Or do we need to prepare ourselves to lose another parent?"

Crane sighed. "The earl is stable. He has a chance to live, possibly a few more years, but it will be on very different terms." His tone softened. "Your father is paralyzed, my lady. From the chest down, the best I can tell. His spinal cord was severed in the carriage accident. He will never walk again. Never even sit up. The remainder of his life will be spent prone, in his bed."

Catherine gripped the crutches tightly. She braced herself for the tears she thought would come and found her eyes suddenly dry. It was as if she'd known the news Doctor Crane gave her would be the worst possible and that she must not only accept it—but be strong for both her father and Leah.

"I see." She thought a moment. "Can he be moved?"

"I'd advise against doing so."

"Would he feel any pain?" she prodded.

"No," Crane admitted. "He's beyond discomfort."

"Then we will return to Statham Manor," she proclaimed. "Papa has always enjoyed the country far more than London. If his time is limited, then he should be where he's been happiest."

The physician nodded. "I can understand your reasoning. The country air would be far better for him. If you'd like, I can speak to your servants on the best way to transport him. Where is your family's estate?"

"We live in Kent. From London, it's just over fifty miles to Statham Manor. Canterbury is the nearest city, though the local village is only two miles from the manor." She paused. "I want to take him home as soon as possible. Mama will need to be buried."

Crane nodded. "I extend my deepest sympathy to you, Lady Catherine. If you'll excuse me, I will speak to your servants and then compose a letter for you to share with your local doctor, informing him of the particulars of Lord Statham's case."

"Thank you," she said graciously. "Tilly, send Jervis to me. I must speak to him at once."

"Yes, my lady." The maid left with the doctor.

Only then did Leah speak. "I'm glad we're going home, Catherine."

"I am, too. Would you be a love and get me a chair?"

Leah eased off the bed and dragged one over. She helped Catherine into it and then brought another one over. Lifting her sister's leg, she placed it in the chair.

"That's ever so much better. Thank you, Leah."

"I've seen Mama. She looks different." Her mouth began trembling.

Catherine took her hand. "It's not really Mama anymore. Mama's soul has gone to heaven. What's left behind is not her."

A knock sounded at the door and Catherine called, "Come."

Jervis entered. The butler had been with the Crawford family since her father had been a small boy. Catherine looked upon him with great fondness.

"We are taking Mama and Papa home, Jervis. Mama is to be buried there and Papa will want to be close to her."

"The earl has never particularly cared for London, my lady. I think it's best."

She told him she wished to leave London in the morning. She asked him to handle all of the details regarding the closing of the house and told him she doubted they would return. He was to let the town servants go, with references and a month's pay, and see the furniture was draped and the house firmly secured.

"I'll pen a note to my uncle now. He should be informed of what's occurred."

She rose, dreading the long walk back to her room.

"Might I carry you, Lady Catherine?" Jervis asked. "Of course, it wouldn't quite be like in the olden days," he said with a smile.

She returned the smile, remembering how he toted her around piggyback when she was a child.

"I would appreciate the help, Jervis. Leah, bring my crutches, please. Strong, if you would stay with Papa?"

"Certainly, my lady."

"Let me, Jervis," Strong said to the older man. The valet stepped forward and scooped Catherine up, Jervis leading the way.

Once she was settled in her room, Jervis promised to make all the necessary arrangements. She told Leah to inform her governess of their departure and sent Strong back to sit with her father.

Her note to her uncle was brief, asking him to come at once and revealing it was urgent. She would explain everything to him when he arrived. Giving the letter to Tilly, she told her to have a footman deliver it to Uncle Edward in person.

"If he's not at home, he'll be at his club. Make sure the footman understands my uncle is to return with him."

"I will."

After Tilly left, Catherine's thoughts finally turned to Jeremy St. Clair and the visit that should have occurred yesterday afternoon. She assumed when they arrived that Jervis informed the St. Clairs of the accident that killed her mother and injured both her and her father. Unfortunately, there would be no rescheduling of their teatime. The Season was over for Catherine. Life as she'd known it would never be the same. She would return to Kent and care for her father, while the Marquess of Sather would be free to pursue other friendships.

And find a wife.

For just a moment, Catherine let herself think of what it had been like to be dancing in his strong arms. There would be no dancing in her future. Even if her leg healed, she would not be returning to London to look for a husband. Papa would need her constant care, as would Leah. Her dreams of forming an attachment with the marquess would dissipate. By this time next year, Jeremy St. Clair wouldn't even remember their one night together.

While Catherine would never forget it—for it would be all she would ever have of him.

An hour later, Uncle Edward and Cousin Martin arrived. Catherine didn't think it would do for her to receive them in her room so she'd had Tilly ask for Jervis and Strong to help her downstairs. Strong, built as solidly as his name, easily carried her as Jervis brought the crutches.

When they reached the bottom floor, she asked that she be allowed to spend a few moments with her mother. Strong brought her to her mother's sitting room, where the countess had been laid out. She thanked the valet and took the crutches from Jervis. Both servants promised they'd be waiting outside the door when she finished.

After they left, she eased toward her mother, who was resting in a pine box, her hands folded over her heart. She was dressed in a soft lilac gown, one of her favorites. The pungent odor of the freshly-cut wood filled her nostrils. Catherine would never smell the scent again without thinking of death and the deep ache in her heart. As she stared at the woman who'd given birth to her, she understood what Leah had referred to. It was her mama lying there—but it wasn't. The sparkle that was an inherent part of the Countess of Statham had departed. Only an empty shell remained.

Still, Catherine placed both crutches against the table and leaned over so she could place a hand atop her mother's. The other stroked the dead woman's hair.

"Oh, Mama, I am going to miss you so very much. I think of all the things that we would have talked about over the years to come and it saddens me to know those are conversations we'll never have. I give you my solemn oath that I will care for Papa the best I can. Know when we lay you to rest, that one day he will be by your side in death as he was in life."

She bent and kissed the cold, lifeless cheek and then slid the crutches under her arms again and slowly made her way to the door. Strong lifted her again and carried her to the parlor so she could receive her uncle. Catherine had already given instructions for Jervis to send word to Statham Manor so they would know what to expect.

When they saw the coaches coming up the lane, they were to send for Doctor Patterson, the family physician. She wanted him to supervise the servants as they moved the earl into the manor and then she would let the physician read the letter from Doctor Crane regarding Papa's care.

The butler entered the room. "The Honorable Edward Crawford and Mr. Martin Crawford, my lady."

"Send them in, Jervis."

Immediately, her uncle pushed his way into the room. Martin strolled in after his father, looking bored as usual.

"My dear, how are you? You look dreadful. Whatever has happened? We saw the mourning wreath." He knelt and took her hands in his.

In that moment, Catherine glimpsed behind the curtain of her uncle's eyes. He'd always been obsequious to his older brother and extremely attentive and polite to the rest of the family. What she saw for a brief instant was a hunger that needed satisfying and she realized Edward Crawford hoped that it was his brother who had passed.

Because he would become the new Earl of Statham.

"We were in a carriage accident last night, Uncle. Very close to home. Mama did not survive the impact. It is her death we are mourning."

Uncle Edward released her hands and rose. "I am very sorry to hear that. It looks as if your leg is broken." He paused. "How does my brother fare?"

"He is alive," she confirmed and saw the shadow of disappointment that crossed her uncle's face.

"Well, that is good news, indeed," he proclaimed, his smile wide—and to her eyes, insincere. "I would hate for anything serious to have happened to keep him from his duties, either here in London or at Statham Manor. Managing an estate and a family's investments takes quite a bit of stamina." He paused. "Of course, I would be willing to step in and lend a hand for as long as needed to help my beloved brother."

Catherine wasn't sure how much she wanted to tell these two men about her father's condition. Something told her not to reveal everything at this time.

"Can we see Uncle?" Martin asked, stepping toward her. "Father is right, you know. Both of us are willing to do whatever is necessary, Cousin Catherine. If Uncle's injuries are severe, we would be happy to handle all of his affairs until such time when he is able to do so himself.'"

Martin's words, coupled with both men's eagerness to get their hands on the family fortune, chilled her. Based upon her suspicions and their forwardness, Catherine decided not to reveal the extent of her father's injuries.

"Papa is sleeping at the moment," she said. "Not only is he quite bruised from the coach having turned upside down, but he broke his wrist, which has caused him some pain. Doctor Crane came last night and stopped by again this morning. He gave Papa something for the pain less than an hour ago and told me Papa would sleep most of the day."

She smiled sweetly. "Other than that minor inconvenience, he was quite well and perfectly capable of continuing to manage everything. It was kind of you both to offer your help, though. Papa will appreciate hearing that."

Both men appeared disgruntled by her words.

"We both are out of sorts," Catherine added. "My leg will be in this cast for a good six weeks or more." She paused, letting that sink in before adding, "We are leaving for Statham Manor in the morning. As you can guess, Papa has had enough of London and only wishes to go home."

Uncle Edward nodded sagely. "Of course. I completely understand." He turned to his son. "Martin, we must let Catherine get her rest. Do let us know if there's anything I can do for you, my dear."

"I wish you a speedy recovery, Cousin Catherine," Martin said perfunctorily.

Both men bid her goodbye and quit the room. It was only after they left that she realized neither had offered condolences regarding her mother's death, much less made mention of attending the Countess of Statham's funeral. As far as Catherine was concerned, she hoped to never see either of them again.

Chapter Eleven

London—June, 1806

JEREMY WAITED FOR Luke and Rachel to finish eating. He didn't want either of them to hear his conversation with Cor. Already, it was hard to put a smile on his face and act as if nothing were wrong.

When everything was.

Luke had been stoic during their father's funeral, only later admitting to Jeremy the same feelings Rachel had confided. His brother had rarely seen, much less spoken to, his father. Jeremy suspected the lack of parental attention might have had something to do with Luke's occasionally outrageous behavior. He'd told the boy in no uncertain terms he would never treat him the way their father had. At the same time, he wanted Luke's word that he would not only do his best regarding his studies but behave at all times as a gentleman should. In the three weeks since the funeral, his brother hadn't given anyone a bit of trouble. It helped that Jeremy included Luke on the daily morning rides he took with Rachel and that he recommended books for Luke to read, which they discussed in-depth in the evenings.

Finally, the two children finished their meal. Rachel's governess had a botany lesson planned and was taking Rachel to Hyde Park. Luke had volunteered to go along since he had a keen interest in science. Jeremy told them he would see them late that afternoon, as he had business to attend to.

"You're always doing business," Rachel noted. "I'm glad I'll never be a duke."

"You'll have your own business to run one day," Cor said. "When you wed, you will manage a great household."

The girl sniffed haughtily. "I may never marry, Cor. You know I don't like being bossed around. The vows say you must obey a husband. I'm not quite sure if I would agree to that."

Luke laughed as he stood and placed his napkin on his chair. "I feel the same, Rachel. Marriage is overrated, in my opinion. Besides, Jeremy's the heir. He's the one who needs to marry."

"But you are now Earl of Mayfield," Jeremy pointed out. "You'll need a son to succeed you one day as the new earl."

What he left out was Luke's inheritance—Fairhaven. If Jeremy couldn't conquer the mountain of debt soon, he would be forced to sell Fairhaven. Though the property belonged to Luke, he was only fifteen. Because of his age, Jeremy managed and made all decisions regarding their late father's holdings, which had now transferred to his second son. It was one of the many things he desperately needed to talk over with Cor.

The children excused themselves, leaving him with her.

"What's on your mind, Grandson?" Cor asked.

Jeremy blew out a long breath. "Too many things," he said honestly. "After multiple meetings with Father's solicitor and banker—coupled with Matthew's astute advice—I've listed four properties. Two have already sold and a third buyer is deep into talks. It may come down to selling Fairhaven, though."

Displeasure flitted across her face. "Is that necessary?"

"It may be. Unless I wed rather quickly. Even then, it may take selling Fairhaven and then buying it back. Or purchasing another property for Luke once we're solvent again." He paused. "Have you met with the Patronesses?"

The Patronesses ruled Almack's with an iron fist, granting vouchers to the assembly rooms to a select few, based upon their family name and connections. Because of that, the Patronesses knew everything about everyone in society. Cor was good friends with two of these women and he'd tasked her with learning which young ladies bore the largest dowries.

"I met with both Lady Jersey and Countess Lieven." She removed a folded sheet from under her plate and passed it across to him. "This list contains the names of eligible ladies who hold both a large dowry and haven't accepted any offers yet. Lady Jersey told me you'd need to act quickly if you wish to claim anyone on this list. The Season will be over soon and she believes all of the names will commit to a gentleman by then."

Jeremy skimmed the list of six women. He recognized all of the names but one and could attach a face to two of the ones present.

"Be glad tonight is Wednesday, the only night Almack's is open," Cor said. "I obtained a voucher for you. The countess told me every girl on the list will be present tonight. If you're going to find a wife, it must be tonight, Jeremy."

"Do you think I'll be judged harshly because I should be in mourning for the next six months?" he asked.

"I, of course, will go to no events until next Season," Cor said. "It's different for a man. Especially a duke. Because of the level of society you've attained with your new title, you may write your own rules, Grandson."

He stared at the wall for a moment. The thought of dancing with anyone other than Catherine sickened him. Since his return to London after burying his father, he hadn't been to his club, much less any ball or the theatre, thanks to being swamped with information about his father's estate and the crushing debts he owed. Still, he owed it to the family to pull them from the quagmire Stephen St. Clair had sunk them into.

That meant going to Almack's tonight—and finding a suitable bride.

"Do you have any advice on what I should look for in a wife? Other than her extravagant dowry."

Cor thought a moment. "The younger, the better. That way, she'll easily be swept off her feet. You can be quite charming when you choose, Jeremy, and you'll need every bit of your charm present if you're to convince a young lady that you've fallen instantly in love with her after a single dance."

He frowned. "I have to *say* that—that I'm in love?"

"Not in so many words," she demurred. "Merely remark you are quite taken with her. How she's from a good family and that you're looking for the perfect woman to become your duchess. Tell her you're eager to start a family. All girls think about having babies with handsome men. Especially if they are dukes."

A family was the last thing he wanted. Thinking of putting his wife through childbirth turned his stomach.

"Remember, once you've made your selection, you must wrap it up quickly. Seek out her father. Make an appointment with him for tomorrow morning. Remain mysterious but know he should have every indication that, since you've danced with his daughter and you're the new Duke of Everton, you're looking for a bride." Cor paused. "If anyone has any worries, assure them that I will be present to guide the new duchess in her tasks. As I said, younger is better because she will be more easily trained."

Resigned to his fate, Jeremy said, "I will return from Almack's tonight with a name from this list, Cor. You may count on it."

JEREMY ARRIVED AT Almack's and presented his voucher, feeling foolish dressed in the knee-breeches the Patronesses required instead of his usual trousers. Someone called his name. Turning, he saw Neville headed toward him.

"Fancy seeing you here," his friend said and then he grew contrite. "Terribly sorry to hear about your father."

He shrugged. "Father wasn't in good health." He left it at that, knowing Neville and all of the *ton* had figured out that though Stephen St. Clair may have died from apoplexy, in truth, he drank himself to death.

"I'm a bit surprised to see you out and about so quickly," Neville continued, "unless you're here for what I think you are—to browse the Marriage Mart for a bride."

"I am," he confirmed. "Cor thinks taking a wife will help me settle into my new responsibilities. She also tells me she isn't getting any younger and wants a hand in training the next Duchess of Everton."

"Cor is a wise woman. She will make you proud in shaping the new duchess," Neville agreed. "Do you have anyone in mind?"

Jeremy had only one person in mind.

The one woman he could never have.

The viscount must have read something on his face. "I remember the last time we met. At the Wethersby ball. You seemed to really enjoy yourself that night, Everton. I was sorry to hear about . . . the situation . . . with Lady Catherine."

"Lady Catherine isn't here tonight," he said brusquely. "I am here to find a suitable bride. Come, Neville."

They entered the assembly rooms and stood to the side. Jeremy glanced about, spying two names from the list. He would need to find out what the other four looked like in order to be able to ask them to dance.

"Beg pardon, Your Grace, but the Countess of Lieven wishes to speak with you."

He turned and saw a servant at his elbow. "Take me to her."

The man led Jeremy to a row of women seated in a prime viewing spot and he knew these must be the famous Patronesses. Dorothea Lieven, the Russian ambassador's wife, sat on the left end. He greeted her with a bow and swift kiss to her hand. Magically, a chair appeared next to her and she indicated he should sit.

"How are you this evening, Everton?"

"Better now that I've met you, Countess."

"Cor asked me to point out a few ladies to you. Which ones do you already know?"

Jeremy knew she referred to the list that had been drawn up and provided her with the names of the women he would recognize. Over the next fifteen minutes, she showed him the remaining four as they arrived. In the meantime, they discussed politics. She seemed quite knowledgeable, most likely because of her husband's occupation.

Once the last name had been identified, the countess said, "I wish you the best of luck in your search tonight, Everton. I understand speed is of the essence. Remember, though you are in a hurry, act anything but. When you make your choice, nod to me. I will confirm if I think it's an apt one."

He rose and kissed her hand again. "Thank you, Countess. Your help in this delicate matter has been invaluable."

With that, he went and asked three of the six women to reserve a dance for him. If a choice had to be made, it would be easier with fewer candidates to consider. Signing each *programme du bal*, he realized, by tomorrow, he would be engaged to one of them.

Jeremy made sure the first two he danced with received compliments on their gowns. He made small talk with them as they danced and then he returned them to the sidelines.

The third woman, Lady Mary Mowbray, was by far the shyest of the three and on the plain side. She was blond and petite and he wondered if he was drawn to her simply because she didn't possess Catherine Crawford's height or rich, auburn hair. She seemed the opposite of Catherine in every way and that appealed to him. By the end of their dance, he'd made up his mind.

As he escorted her from the dance floor, he said, "Lady Mary, I wondered if you are engaged for the supper dance?" When he'd signed her card, she'd had many blank spaces still available.

She consulted her programme and said, "N-no. I am not. D-do you wish f-for us to dance again, Your Gr-grace?" Her round eyes told of her surprise at his request.

"I would. Very much." Jeremy lifted the card, ignoring the stutter which had suddenly emerged. He supposed he made the girl nervous and had good enough manners not to call attention to it. "I see you have a few other dances available. Would you save one more of them for me?"

To dance twice with a woman during an evening told the *ton* of his interest in her. To dance thrice practically called for the banns to be read.

She smiled and it almost made her pretty. "I w-would like that. Very much."

He lifted her gloved hand and kissed it. "I will return for you when it's the supper dance."

Jeremy looked to Countess Lieven and saw she watched them with interest. She nodded.

After a few minutes, he made his way in the direction of the Patronesses. When he reached the ambassador's wife, she motioned for him to come close.

"Lady Mary is a sweet girl. A bit on the nervous side but I'm sure you will make her feel welcomed into the St. Clair family, Everton."

"Thank you for your help, Countess. Would you be so kind as to point out Lady Mary's father to me?"

Her eyes swept across the room and stopped. "There. In the group of three men to the left of that doorway."

"The thin one on the left?" he ventured, seeing the daughter was a replica of the father, only female.

"Yes, that's the Earl of Seabrooke. He lost his wife several years ago. Lady Mary is his only child." She looked at him steadily. "That should make your task easier, Everton. The earl will want the daughter he dotes on settled, especially since his title will pass to his nephew upon his death."

Jeremy nodded. "Thank you for your help in this venture, Countess."

"Even if it's a small wedding, I expect to be invited to it," she replied.

"As Cor's good friend, you should expect an invitation. Soon."

CHAPTER TWELVE

Jeremy scrawled his name on the special license and then the minister indicated for Lady Mary to do the same. No, not Lady Mary.

The Duchess of Everton.

They'd barely known each other for two weeks. He'd proclaimed his sudden, undying affection for her. Charmed both her and her father. Purchased the special license so they could wed as soon as they wished. And now, they were husband and wife.

He would have preferred the wedding occur at Eversleigh. When Mary expressed an interest in holding the ceremony at her family home, only twenty miles from the Scottish border, Cor had smoothly convinced the eighteen-year-old girl that a smart London wedding would be more memorable, as well as convenient for others to attend. Mary tended to agree with everything Cor suggested, the dowager duchess already subtly shaping his new bride.

At least she hadn't stuttered through her vows. He realized the stutter came when she was nervous or flustered. He'd gone over every aspect of the ceremony with her for the past several days to make her comfortable with the order of events. In turn, she'd bored him to tears with every detail of her wedding finery. The lace on her dress. The gloves she'd ordered. The bouquet of blossoms she would carry.

Jeremy didn't care a whit for any of it. As cruel as it sounded, all he was interested in was the dowry Mary Mowbray brought. It made him like every other titled gentleman in England, who first looked to bolstering their coffers when they wed. England's great families had mixed together in marriage for hundreds of years. The bottom line came down to whether or not the union strengthened and empowered the new husband and his family. In this case, the St. Clairs received a huge fortune in Mary's dowry, one that would keep them from sinking into poverty. In return, she received a far loftier title than she and her father had ever dreamed she would attain, thus satisfying all parties. Jeremy would protect Mary. He would be courteous to her. He would help her become comfortable within the St. Clair family.

But he could never love her.

Jeremy hadn't thought he could ever love. Even now, he didn't know if he'd actually loved Catherine Crawford. He'd certainly been attracted to her beauty and wit. In time, he did think he would have grown to love her. Offered for her. Built a life with her. Yet in death, he'd idealized her to the point where he practically worshipped her. No other woman would have ever stood up to how he viewed Catherine.

And like Timothy before her, no one of his acquaintance spoke Catherine's name. No one—save for Cor—had any inkling of the feelings he carried in his heart for the dead beauty. Even then, he doubted Cor could understand the extent of his feelings for a woman he'd only spent a single night with.

He looked to Rachel, talking animatedly with the Countess of Lieven, and wondered how Catherine's sister, Leah, had reacted to her sister's death. Jeremy knew the two had been close. He supposed within a handful of years, Rachel and Leah would meet when they made their come-out together, since they were of the same age. Catherine hadn't told him what her sister looked like, only that she was inquisitive and friendly. He wondered if Leah resembled Catherine—and how he would react when he finally saw her. The fact that Rachel and Leah might one day be friends tore at his heart.

Pushing his morbid thoughts aside, he went to claim his bride.

"I think it's time we went in for the wedding breakfast."

Mary looked up at him with worshipful eyes. "Certainly, Your Grace."

"Jeremy. Remember?"

Worry filled her face. "I think it best if I call you Everton or Your Grace unless we are alone." That thought made her swallow hard. "If that is all right with you, of course."

"Whatever you wish." He tucked her hand through the crook of his arm and led her into the dining room. He'd decided to try to please her in small ways when he could, hoping to assuage the guilt that filled him because he'd only married her for her money.

Their guests followed them inside. Only a handful had been invited, including Morefield and Neville. Jeremy had asked Morefield to stand with him for the ceremony and his friend had agreed.

Morefield, as best man, now made a toast to the happy couple and the wedding breakfast was served. Jeremy ate, tasting nothing, dreading the time when everyone left and he would be alone with Mary in the carriage as they traveled to Eversleigh. He forced himself to pay attention to her. The more she spoke, the more he realized how truly immature she was. Cor reminded him that Mary was still young and, with the proper guidance, she would become a true duchess.

They cut their cake and another round of toasts occurred, one from the Earl of Seabrooke and another from Luke. Jeremy looked on with brotherly pride as Luke spoke eloquently. Matthew Proctor had told him about Luke coming to him for help in composing a toast. Jeremy assumed much of the wording came from Matthew. Still, Luke spoke the heartfelt words and those gathered applauded him soundly.

Finishing his champagne, he asked Mary if she wished for more.

"N-no, thank you, Everton. Cor has told me to always have a single glass lest I get tipsy and embarrass myself or you."

"Then I would stick with Cor's advice," he said gently. "She's the wisest woman I know."

"I . . . should go upstairs. To get ready."

"I will make your goodbyes for you. Once everyone has gone, I'll also change and we can leave directly for Eversleigh."

He had told her he preferred to return home for a short honeymoon rather than stay in London, knowing no good memories were here. He would need to make new ones with his bride. After a week, they'd return to London so he could begin to use his new fortune to straighten out his financial affairs.

Mary slipped away, Cor and Rachel accompanying her since she had no mother. Jeremy made the rounds, accepting good wishes from all. Finally, he came to Morefield and Neville.

"Thank you for coming," he told them. "I was glad to share this day with you."

"I'm getting married myself," Morefield revealed. "Got engaged last night."

Jeremy slapped him on the back. "You sly fox. My heartiest congratulations." He offered his hand. "Who is the unlucky lady?" he teased, thinking it would be Amanda.

"You met her the night of the Wethersby ball. Lady Charlotte."

His heart flooded with an ache he decided would never leave. "Ah, I do recall her. She was friends with Lady Amanda. And Lady Catherine, I believe."

Morefield's head bobbed up and down. "Yes, that's right. Charlotte and Lady Catherine are very close friends." He paused. "I know you're married now, Jeremy, but I must say that your choice surprised me. Especially when I saw how taken you were with Lady Catherine."

"Same here," Neville seconded. "I thought if any woman led you to the altar, it would be that one."

Jeremy felt his face flush with anger. "Why would you bring her up?" he demanded quietly, so as not to draw attention. "I'll admit I was enamored with Catherine Crawford. But I needed to wed swiftly, thanks to the debts my father left me. Marrying a dead woman wasn't an option."

Morefield and Neville looked at him blankly.

Finally, Neville said, "Why do you think she's dead, Everton?"

He gritted his teeth. "You yourself told me not two weeks ago at Almack's that you were sorry about . . . the situation."

Neville frowned. "I did. And I am. What does that have to do with you believing Lady Catherine to be dead?"

Jeremy couldn't understand why his friends tormented him. "I sent a footman with a message to her house the morning after the Wethersby ball," he ground out. "He returned and told me of the mourning wreath on their door. How there'd been a terrible carriage accident and the earl was severely injured." He swallowed. "And how Lady Catherine was pulled dead from the coach."

He turned away, not wanting anyone present to see how upset he was.

Morefield touched his arm. "Jeremy, it was Lady Catherine's mother who died at the scene. Not Catherine."

Numbness filled him. "But . . ." No other words came.

Could he have misunderstood what the footman said?

He looked to his two friends, speechless.

"I thought you knew," Neville said. "At Almack's. I was referring to Lady Catherine being in mourning."

Jeremy's heart hammered wildly in his chest. He'd gone home to Eversleigh and buried his father. Then he'd returned to London and become absorbed with his financial situation. He'd seen no friends. Attended no *ton* events. Spoken to no one about Catherine.

And hadn't known she was alive.

"It's not common knowledge, but I know from Charlotte that the Earl of Statham was paralyzed that night," Morefield added. "Lady Catherine wrote to Charlotte and told her how she has retired from society in order to care for her father."

A low keening erupted from Jeremy. His knees buckled. Both friends grasped an elbow and led him from the room into the nearby study.

Once inside, he collapsed to the carpet, the pounding in his chest so painful he thought it might explode.

He had married the wrong woman—and would spend a lifetime in regret.

AFTER THREE SNIFTERS of brandy to dull his pain, Jeremy told his friends to leave. As they started to the door, he called out, "Stop."

Both men turned, sympathy evident in their eyes.

"Not a word to anyone of this. Especially you, Morefield. I beg you. Say nothing to Charlotte. Catherine must never learn of my feelings for her."

"You have my solemn oath," his friend replied. "Charlotte would feel obligated to tell Lady Catherine of your affection for her. No good could come of her knowing, especially since you are now wed to Lady Mary."

"Thank you," Jeremy said hoarsely.

He watched them leave and then composed himself. Leaving the study, he saw the only guests that remained were Countess Lieven and the bride's father. They were deep in conversation. Jeremy decided to step outside a moment, hoping the fresh air would clear his head.

Waiting at the curb was the Everton carriage and matching team to convey him and Mary to Eversleigh. He recognized one of the two footman as the man who'd delivered the note to Catherine and motioned him over.

When he approached, Jeremy asked, "Do you remember taking a letter to the Earl of Statham's residence a few weeks ago?"

"I do, Your Grace. That was the house where the lady had died.

Remember, I returned the note to you. I can read a few words," the footman confided. "One of them is *lady*, which I saw on the front. That's why when I was told of the carriage accident and the earl lingering between life and death, I thought to ask how about the lady's health, as well. When they told me she'd passed, I knew I shouldn't trouble the family in such a time of sorrow and brought the letter back to you." He paused. "Did I do something wrong, Your Grace?" he asked earnestly.

Jeremy hadn't the heart to tell the footman that his innocent mistake had changed the course of his employer's life.

"No. Not at all. Thank you."

He returned inside the Seabrooke mansion and decide he should change his clothes. Manfry was there to help him, unhappy that he was being left in London for the week.

"I think I can manage to dress myself for a few days at Eversleigh," Jeremy told the disgruntled servant.

Leaving the bedchamber, he ventured downstairs. Immediately, Mary followed. She kissed her father goodbye while he did the same with Cor. He told Luke and Rachel to do as Cor asked while he was gone. Shaking hands with the earl, he promised to look after the man's daughter.

They went to the carriage as a servant loaded Mary's trunk on top. Since they would only be in the country for a week, Jeremy had told her to leave the majority of her clothes in London. Cor would see that her wardrobe was moved from Seabrooke's residence to her new home.

He sat next to her, afraid if he faced her that he wouldn't be able to conceal his misery. They rode in silence from London. Though he hated that their shoulders occasionally brushed against one another's, he took his bride's hand, knowing it was the least he could do. She seemed to relax with that simple gesture and begin chattering happily. He tuned out the noise and let his despondent thoughts engulf him for most of the trip.

Until they reached Eversleigh.

Jeremy gave himself permission during those hours to mourn the loss of Catherine all over again. He'd remembered her every feature. Recalled every word of their conversation. Each smile she had bestowed upon him. Thought about how happy they could have made one another.

Once they reached his home, he decided it would be unfair to himself and to Mary to continually focus on what might have been. With a last, loving thought as he recalled their searing kiss on the terrace, Jeremy pushed Catherine Crawford to the far recesses of his mind and locked her away. He would never forget her but he couldn't live with the anguish that filled him. He would cut off all feeling. Keep a tight rein on his emotions.

And refuse to look back.

Mrs. Talley, their housekeeper, met the carriage. "I have all the servants lined up to receive the new duchess, Your Grace," she informed him. She looked to Mary. "It is an honor to meet you, Your Grace. Don't be alarmed when you see the number of those waiting to greet you. It will take time but you'll learn the names of those you need to."

"And remember that others, such as Barton, will accompany us in the future," Jeremy added.

Mary clung to his arm as he led her inside. Servants lined both sides of the foyer, curiosity on their faces to see what their new mistress looked like.

They moved down one side of the line and then the other, Mrs. Talley providing the names and positions of each. He could see how overwhelmed Mary was becoming and squeezed her hand. She gave him a grateful smile.

Jeremy dismissed the lot and said, "Mrs. Talley, we are in need of sustenance after our journey. Would you have a light supper brought to the winter parlor? And would you be so good as to unpack for Her Grace while we dine? We left her lady's maid in London since we'll only be here a short while."

"Of course, Your Grace."

Turning to his new wife, he said, "Let me show you to your rooms."

He led her upstairs, past the rooms that had once been his father's, ones that now belonged to him, and opened the door for her. Her trunk had already been placed inside the chamber.

"Mrs. Talley will be an immense help to you. She is a kind woman. Feel free to ask her any question regarding the house."

"Where are your r-rooms?" Mary asked nervously.

Jeremy pointed to the connecting door between their suites. "You may come through there if you have need of me. You'll pass your dressing room and then mine before you reach my bedchamber."

A knock sounded and he bid them come. A maid brought hot water.

"Here. Wash the stains of travel from you. Change clothes if you wish. I'll be back in half an hour to escort you to the winter parlor. It's small and intimate, a perfect setting for the two of us to eat something."

He went through the connecting door and closed it behind him, venturing through both dressing rooms. When he stepped inside the massive bedchamber, he couldn't help but think he was pretending to be the new duke. That his father would breeze through the doorway, his face flushed, laughing at something that had amused him.

Opening the wardrobe, he saw the clothes he'd left at Eversleigh when he'd gone to town had been moved here. He glanced around and saw nothing of his father's remained behind and idly wondered where it all had gone. Quickly, he washed and changed clothes and then returned for Mary. He escorted her to the parlor and made small talk as they ate.

"Tomorrow, we'll ride the estate so that you may see your new home. Mrs. Talley can also take you on a tour of the house."

"It's so large. I fear I will continue to get lost for the next year."

"You'll be surprised how quickly you learn your way around."

"I hope." She yawned. "F-forgive me. My maid had me up long before d-dawn in order to prepare my hair for the ceremony."

He placed his hand over hers. "You looked lovely today, Mary. It's been a long day for both of us. Let me take you upstairs so you can get a good night's sleep."

His bride's eyes widened. "Y-you . . . don't wish . . . to . . ." Her voice trailed off as her cheeks pinkened.

Jeremy smiled reassuringly. "I think you will enjoy yourself more when you aren't so exhausted."

Relief filled her face. "Thank you. You are a very thoughtful husband."

He led her to her room and placed his hands on her shoulders. Pressing a kiss to her brow, he said, "Goodnight, Mary. I hope you will be happy at Eversleigh. And with me."

She smiled shyly. "I'm sure I will, Jeremy."

He left her and went to his own room.

And wept.

Chapter Thirteen

Five years later . . .

CATHERINE PLACED THE wet washcloth she'd used to bath her father in the basin of water as Strong dried the earl's useless limbs. Together, it took some minutes to dress him. She recalled how long the process lasted when she'd first brought him home to Statham Manor after the accident. She and Strong had learned much together as they'd cared for the man they both loved.

Strong combed the earl's sparse hair, smoothing it down. They'd long ago abandoned the notion of shaving him. It proved too difficult and seemed unnecessary since he never had visitors beyond Doctor Patterson. Edward Crawford had come only once. When he'd seen the state his brother was in, her uncle told her he couldn't bear to see his flesh and blood that way, so helpless. No longer a man.

His words infuriated Catherine and she'd ordered her uncle out. She'd apologized profusely to her father for his own kin's harsh words. The earl, who rarely spoke, had wept in silence.

She handed the basin to Strong. "Thank you for your help."

"It's my pleasure, Lady Catherine. The earl's been good to me since I was a boy. I intend to always be good to him."

The cheerful valet left and Catherine tidied up things as her father dozed. She finally seated herself in the armchair by the window and picked up her pencil. She chewed on the end as she envisioned the next scene, closing her eyes several times to let it play out in her mind.

When she had everything worked out, she reached for paper and began writing.

Telling stories had always come as second nature to her. She'd entertained Leah for years with tales she made up on the spot. Some of them Leah begged for over and over and Catherine began writing them down, changing them slightly until both she and Leah were satisfied. Over the years, she'd amassed a large stack of stories. Though she had ample funds in which to run the estate, she found herself growing slightly bored with her quiet life in the country. Though she got out to do some charity work in the nearby village, the bulk of her time had been spent at her father's side in this bedchamber. He slept for much of the day and so she'd found ways to pass the time.

At first, it had been writing more children's stories and also reading everything in the downstairs library. She enjoyed going to another time and place since she rarely got out and saw so few others.

Then everything changed with the publication of *Sense and Sensibility*, written *By a Lady*. Catherine knew that society considered writing a degrading occupation for women, one that robbed them of their femininity. Any book published by a female was done so anonymously so as not to damage its author's reputation. No women would openly admit to wanting to become a so-called literary lioness.

When she'd first read *Sense and Sensibility*, it had been over a year since her mother's death and her father's incapacitation. Catherine had drunk up the story of Elinor and Marianne, the older Dashwood sisters, as they struggled with poverty and affairs of the heart. Their younger sister, Margaret, reminded her so much of Leah. Catherine had wept as Willoughby shredded poor Marianne's heart and how the secret engagement of Lucy Steele to the romantic Edward Ferrars prevented Elinor from ever finding happiness. Her heart ached at how Colonel Brandon loved Marianne from afar and Marianne's callous treatment of the military man. In the end, the author managed to turn Catherine's tears of sorrow into ones of great joy, with both Elinor and

Marianne finding lasting love.

After reading the grand love story, Catherine began one of her own.

She never admitted that she wrote of love because she would never have it for herself. Once, at that ball so many years ago, she'd fancied a time she might find love with Jeremy St. Clair. Fate had intervened, keeping her from pursuing a friendship—and possible romantic attachment—with him. She learned months later from Charlotte's letters that Jeremy wed the bashful, timid Lady Mary Mowbray before the end of the Season. While she couldn't picture the dashing marquess with such a shy creature, she knew it had been his choice to make. Charlotte also wrote to Catherine that Jeremy's father had passed and that he'd become the next Duke of Everton.

She doubted she would ever see him again—and so to try and heal her heavy heart, she wrote of Jeremy St. Clair. Even though the author of *Sense and Sensibility* went on to write new romances, Catherine stopped when she'd finished her single effort. Too many of her private thoughts were spilled onto the page, even if she did disguise the names. She allowed many bad things to occur to the couple in her book in order to make their story more interesting. If she let her couple meet and easily fall in love, where was the story? Instead, she brutally attacked her characters, putting them through misery before she allowed them to find their happily ever after with one another.

If only she had the same in her future.

She stopped after that one effort at romantic fiction and put it away in a box under her bed. Gathering her courage once again, she went back to her children's tales and decided she would try to become published under the pen name C. E. Lawford. She'd been christened Catherine Elizabeth, hence the C. E. She thought Lawford was close enough to Crawford without giving any clue to her real identity. Since married women in Britain couldn't legally sign a contract, that was her saving grace. Once she'd turned twenty-one, she was of age and signed with her publisher.

She was more fortunate than most would-be authors. She didn't have the option to sell via subscription, where a set group agreed to buy her book in advance. That only applied to well-known authors or those with a patron who recommended the book to friends. Instead, she had enough capital to publish on commission and agreed to take on the financial risk. Her publisher paid the costs of publication and then repaid himself as her books were sold, charging a ten-percent commission for each book which left the shelves.

After production costs were paid back, the rest of the profits fell to her. Thank goodness her books had sold well enough to recover the costs—and then some. Catherine kept the funds she earned in a separate account, knowing the day would come when her father passed and she and Leah would be at the mercy of her greedy uncle. Surprisingly, life hadn't worked out as she expected. Her father still lived, while Edward Crawford had actually been the first to die. She'd received word from her cousin last month of Uncle Edward's death. Since women didn't attend funerals, Catherine wrote a short note of condolence. Martin hadn't bothered to call at Statham Manor in five years. She didn't want any word from her to change the situation.

Taking up her pencil, she returned to her latest story about a brother and sister who discovered a magic broomstick.

Two hours later, she set aside her writing and stood, stretching her arms high above her head. She went to the bed and heard the usual wheezing from her father. His breathing had never been right since the carriage accident.

Seeing he was awake, she said, "Hello, Papa. I hope you feel nice and clean in your new nightshirt and fresh sheets."

"Cath . . . rine," he said, a faint smile on his lips.

"Yes, Papa. I'm here. Strong helped me bathe you. Do you need turning again?"

They'd learned from experience to move him to different positions for brief amounts of time to keep the bedsores away. Even then, some still formed. She was grateful he really couldn't feel them.

"I love . . . you."

She tenderly cupped his cheek. "I love you, too, Papa."

He coughed and then his breathing grew more labored. His eyes grew larger and then his breath came in rapid spurts.

"Should I have Strong fetch Doctor Patterson?" she asked anxiously.

"No," he rasped. "It's . . . time."

Catherine grasped his hand, knowing he couldn't feel her touch. Tears welled in her eyes. She'd known this day would come. Doctor Patterson thought it would occur shortly after she'd brought her father home but he'd continued to surprise them all by continuing to live.

"Nothing . . . you . . . can do." He smiled. "Your mother . . . waiting . . ."

She held her breath, even as the last one left his body. For several minutes, she sat, not moving, accepting that he was gone. Rising, she kissed his forehead.

After five years devoted to his care, her life—and Leah's—would now change radically. Martin Crawford would be thirty next year. The spoiled boy had become a spoiled, selfish man and would make for a terrible Earl of Statham. Still, everything would be his by law, from the title to this house to all of the land and investments. She gave thanks that she had the money from her books for she doubted Martin would provide much in the way for her and Leah. She could see him sticking them in a tumbling down cottage, the same way the half-brother in *Sense and Sensibility* had done to the Dashwood women.

Catherine realized she was on the shelf at twenty-three, even though she had a dowry guaranteed by her father. Her youth had passed her by and no man would want to become her husband. At least Leah would have a chance to find wedded bliss. Her dowry was also protected from Martin. Thank goodness Papa had made sure of that. At sixteen, her sister would need to wait a year—better two—before she made her come-out. Once Leah married, Catherine could be a devoted aunt to her sister's children. That would almost be as good as having ones of her own.

She released her father's hand and penned a brief letter to Martin Crawford in London, knowing he would come immediately to claim all that was his. Finishing it, she rang the bell and Strong appeared.

"Papa is gone," she told the faithful retainer. "I wanted to tell you how grateful I am to have had your help with him these last years. You are a good, kind man, Strong."

The valet mopped tears from his eyes. "I thought the world of the earl." He paused. "I wonder if the new earl will even have need of me."

"That, I cannot say. Cousin Martin may bring his own valet. It's up to him. If he discharges you, I will write a letter of reference."

He gave her a grateful smile. "Thank you, my lady. You have been a saint to care for the earl as you have."

She bowed her head a moment, overcome with emotion. Raising it, she said, "I've written to my cousin, informing him of Papa's death." She handed him the sealed letter.

"I will see to its delivery myself," Strong promised. "I'll leave for London once we've laid the earl out downstairs. He is already fresh from his earlier bath. Let me dress him a final time."

"Thank you." Catherine left to find Leah. Jervis informed her that Leah and her governess were out riding but should return within the hour. She told the retainer her father had passed and sent him upstairs to help Strong. She had their housekeeper gather the servants. Catherine addressed them regarding her father's death and said, while she could make no promises as to their future employment, she would put in a good word for each of them with the new Earl of Statham. Anyone not retained could expect a letter of reference from her.

Sadly, the servants dispersed. She knew the next time she saw them, each would wear the black armband signifying their grief at the earl's passing. She watched as Strong and Jervis carried her father downstairs and into the small parlor. Strong told her he would stop in the village to inform the vicar and Doctor Patterson of the earl's death before he made his way to London.

Needing some fresh air, Catherine left the house and walked slowly to the stables. When she drew near, she saw two riders approaching in the distance and steadied herself. As they rode into the yard, her eyes met Leah's. Her sister leaped from her horse and ran to Catherine, throwing her arms about her. No words were necessary as the sisters clung to one another, Leah's sobs the only sound. The governess dismounted and claimed the reins of Leah's horse, leading both mounts into the stable.

Leah pulled away. "That hateful cousin of ours will show up gloating by nightfall," she said.

"You remember Martin?"

Her sister's chin rose a notch. "I do. He is as vile as Uncle Edward was. I hate both of them."

Catherine stroked Leah's hair. "It doesn't matter what he is because he's the new Earl of Statham and will do whatever he wishes."

Fear showed in Leah's eyes. "What will happen to us, Catherine? Statham Manor is now his. Will Cousin Martin allow us to remain in our home? Or perhaps send us to London?"

"Your guess is as good as mine. Obviously, he doesn't value family much since we haven't seen him in a good while." She placed both hands on Leah's shoulders. "You will be fine. Before long, you will make your come-out. Papa reserved money for your gowns. You have a generous dowry. You will be able to choose a man to wed and never see Cousin Martin after that if you wish."

Leah looked relieved and then she bit her lip. "What of you, Catherine? Will you wed? Can I go with you when you do so or will Cousin Martin be my guardian?"

"We can talk about that later. Right now, let's go say our goodbyes to Papa."

Catherine led her sister back toward Statham Manor, wondering how long the place would remain their home.

Chapter Fourteen

As Leah predicted, Martin Crawford showed up just before nightfall. When Jervis came in to announce his arrival, Leah threw her hands in the air and stormed over to the French doors.

"I won't see him," she declared to Catherine. "Not tonight." With that, Leah opened the doors and hurried through them, closing them behind her.

She'd been gone only seconds when the new Earl of Statham entered the room. Catherine rose to greet him and he took her hands in his.

"My dear cousin. I'm sorry at Uncle's passing." Despite his kind words, his posture revealed he was full of himself, drunk on the idea of being the new earl.

"Thank you," she said stiffly. "Would you care to sit?"

She seated herself again on the settee and he took the chair nearby.

"May I offer you some refreshment?" she asked politely, masking her true feelings for him.

"No, nothing for me." He studied her a moment and cleared his throat. "Cousin, there are important matters that must be discussed."

Catherine frowned. "You do realize Papa passed only today? I realize there are things to talk over about the household here and the one in London we closed years ago. I can also speak at length with you about the servants. I'm sure you'll wish to meet with Papa's estate manager. I'll provide the names of Papa's solicitor and his banker in

London, as well. Can't all of that wait, Cousin Martin? At least until Papa is buried within the family vault with Mama."

"I'd prefer you address me as Statham."

Shock filled her. "Even when we are in private? We have known each other since we were children," though she didn't mention how he'd tormented her. He was a good six years older and yet had always threatened her and pushed her around, both with actions and words. Catherine decided he wasn't going to do it to her now. She'd been too young and frightened to fight back twenty years ago. After everything she'd experienced, she was no longer afraid of Martin Crawford—or anyone else.

"Quit being so full of yourself, Martin." His jaw dropped but she continued. "Yes, you're the new earl. It's your legal title. From now on, Mr. Crawford is Lord Statham. I understand that. I was hoping we would be on friendlier terms since we will occupy the same household."

His brows knit together and everything she'd feared would happen hung in the balance. Trying to placate him, she said, "Unless you'd prefer to remain in London while Leah and I stay at Statham Manor, that is."

He didn't speak for almost a minute, causing her mouth to go dry.

"The thing is, I will be coming back and forth between both places," he began. "I have a large group of friends and will certainly want to entertain them at house parties. I also plan to open the London residence immediately and do the same at it. You and your sister would be . . . an inconvenience."

His words took her aback. "Family is inconvenient? Where would you have us go, Martin? As the head of the Crawford family, it's your responsibility to look after Leah and me." She paused. "You wouldn't want the *ton* judging you for abandoning your cousins, would you? Especially since you now have the title, I'm sure you'll be searching for a wife with a large dowry."

His jaw tightened at her insolence.

"I'm prepared to give you two months to mourn Uncle," he finally said, barely containing his anger. "At that point, the Season will have begun. You will come to London, bringing Leah with you, and find yourself a husband. I'll be looking for a wife. At Season's end, I expect you to wed and be out of my household. I realize you're long in the tooth but Father already shared the name of Uncle's solicitor. I called on him before I rode to Statham Manor to get a clear picture of my financial situation. The man assured me Uncle had put aside funds for his daughters' dowries, money I can never touch. Surely, that will tempt some man to offer for you. Perhaps a widower in his thirties or forties who needs a second wife to raise the children from his first marriage."

She couldn't believe his audacity. "You're allowing two months for me to mourn Papa, the best man I ever knew."

"That's right. I don't intend to care for you—or your sister—beyond the summer. My obligation to you both will be fulfilled at that point."

It angered Catherine that Martin had gone straight to Papa's solicitor, much less that the man had agreed to meet with him so quickly. She supposed the lawyer knew where his bread would be buttered in the future. Still, it left a sour taste in her mouth. She would never recommend the man to anyone of her acquaintance.

"What if no one offers for me?" she challenged. "What then, Statham?"

He shrugged. "If you can't find a man to wed you and take Leah off my hands, then I will allow you to live off your dowry." His eyes narrowed. "If that becomes the case, Catherine, I must warn you to spend wisely for there will be no more coming your way."

"You'd throw out your own family?"

He looked at her steadily. "I'm the Earl of Statham. I can do anything I want now."

She shook her head in disgust. "How can you treat your blood relatives in such a shoddy manner?"

He laughed harshly. "We're not family, Catherine. Not in the way it counts." He gave her a sly smile.

She looked at him in confusion. "We are first cousins, Statham. How is that not family?"

He rubbed his chin in thought. "You really don't know, do you?"

"Know what?" she demanded.

Crossing his arms, he said, "Where do you think you got that horrid red hair? And why is Leah blond when both of your parents had dark hair?"

The question took Catherine aback. The thought had never occurred to her before. She never spent time on her looks, especially having been buried in the country with no social life for five years. She had worried about her auburn hair before, long ago, when she was barely old enough to have a governess. Papa had assured her the deep red shade was lovely, just as she was. She'd never given it a thought since then.

Martin smirked. "Neither you nor that brat sister of yours is a purebred Crawford. Your mama couldn't have children, Catherine. She tried, several times, and it almost killed her. The doctor told her there could be no children. Ever. That's when Uncle got creative. He retreated with her to the country for several months after he'd gotten some actress with child. That woman came to Statham Manor and delivered her child here.

"Your mother begged my uncle for a baby. *You* are the result of his liaison with a red-haired actress. Society never knew since they'd been in the country for so long. When they returned to London with you, no one questioned them."

Catherine sat, stunned, comprehending the words he spoke but not understanding that they applied to her.

Martin began pacing the room, talking with his hands. "They tried one last time for a child, wanting a son and heir to Statham. Your mama made it almost six months before losing the baby. She lay close to death for weeks."

Vaguely, she recalled when she was young how Mama had grown large and then taken ill. She'd been bedridden. Catherine had only been allowed to visit her once before Uncle Edward came and took her to London to stay so Mama could rest. When she returned to the country, Leah was here. Papa explained that Mama had needed peace and quiet in order to have Leah. That her little sister was a true miracle.

She looked at Martin, who wore an ugly smile.

"Leah is the daughter of another trollop. I think Father said some shopkeeper's daughter. She was paid well for her services and taken in as a servant afterward. Her name was Jane, I believe."

She drew in a sharp breath. Jane had been Mama's personal maid. She'd left to marry a boot black after Mama had been killed and seemed sad to go. A sick feeling washed over Catherine. She remembered how pretty Jane was and how much Leah resembled the woman, especially now, at sixteen.

Dully, she rose, afraid she was going to be sick.

Martin smiled triumphantly. "Finally, you understand. I don't consider you family at all. You may bear the Crawford name but your papa was foolish to do what he did in order to please his barren wife. I don't want you or your sister around my children. I will keep this secret from the *ton*—as long as you are gone from my sight by the end of the upcoming Season. Consider that my parting gift to you, *Cousin*."

Catherine clasped her hands together. Rising, she quit the room with as much dignity as she could muster. As she retreated to her bedchamber, she knew Leah must never learn what had been revealed this night.

Leah looked out the carriage window. "I see London!" she exclaimed. "It's been so long since we were here, Catherine."

She glanced out the window, unsure of how she felt returning to the city. Her last memories of London were of the carriage accident. Mama's death. Her broken leg. Though the bones had knit together, Catherine now walked with a slight limp when she was tired. She couldn't imagine what dancing would be like.

The thought of dancing made her think wistfully of Jeremy St. Clair. He'd been married for years now and must have children. She wondered if he and his wife ever came to *ton* events. If she would see him. If he would even recognize her. For a moment, her heart grew heavy, thinking of the young woman she'd been the night they met and how that woman no longer existed.

Leah sat back. "I still don't understand why we've come to London so soon after Papa's death. He was only buried a week ago and yet we're here. Is it because it was too hard to be where Statham is?"

Catherine hadn't told her sister anything regarding what the earl had revealed. Now, though, she needed to let her know why they were in London.

"First of all, there's much to be done to open the London townhome again," she began.

"You've already sent Jervis and two house maids to do that," Leah pointed out.

"I did. They will have removed the sheets from the furniture and aired out the place. Much more needs to be done. I need to see if any repairs are in order. There's staff to hire, including a cook."

"Jervis could do that."

"He has the authority to do so but it's best to come from me. I want to make sure everything is handled properly so that when Statham comes to town, he won't be disappointed."

"Who cares if he is?" Leah said sullenly. "I don't like him. Not one bit. He's a pompous ass."

"Leah!" Catherine exclaimed. "Wherever did you learn such language?"

"It fits him," her sister said stubbornly.

Catherine chuckled. "I agree. There are other things to consider, though." She paused. "I'm going to take part in the Season when it begins in six weeks."

Leah's jaw dropped. "What? We're in mourning, Catherine. You can't go to parties and balls!"

"I must. Statham has made his feelings known that he doesn't care for either of us. The sooner I can find a husband, the better."

"But . . . what about me?"

Catherine took Leah's hand. "Oh, dearest, you would go with me. Statham has no interest in being a guardian to you. I want us out from under his thumb. I'm sure I'll be able to find some nice gentleman to wed."

She'd given it a great deal of thought and decided to aim as low on the social ladder as possible. Her age alone would lessen her prospects to barons and possibly viscounts. She would hope a nice baron would take an interest in her. The fortune she would bring him would certainly help. By marrying a man without a lofty title, he wouldn't have as many connections in society and wouldn't be invited to as many prestigious *ton* events, lessening her chancing of being seen by Statham. Her idea was to blend into the woodwork and quietly settle into marriage.

And keep her secret safe.

When it came time for Leah's come-out, her sister would be young and fresh. With her fair looks and generous dowry, she would be able to wed a better title. Statham should be married himself by then and rarely present at all of the social gatherings since he'd already have a wife in hand. Catherine hoped Leah would marry well and, hopefully, find love.

"Think about it, Leah. Any gentleman that becomes interested in me will be getting two Crawford ladies and only have to wed one," she teased.

"I suppose. So, we came to London not only to manage the townhome but for you to prepare for the Season?"

"That's correct. I left all my party gowns behind when we left for Statham Manor. I'll need to comb through them and see if there's any I can still wear."

"Oh, Catherine, you can't do that. Years have passed. Those gowns will be sorely dated."

She hadn't the heart to reveal to Leah that Martin refused to pay for a new wardrobe for her. She'd written to their solicitor for an appointment and asked that he send his reply to their London home. She wanted to ask if she could use a small portion of her dowry on her wardrobe. If not, she'd need to find a good seamstress to help alter the gowns she had. Only then would she dip into her author savings and buy a gown or two.

The carriage slowed and Catherine glanced out the window again. Icy fear gripped her heart.

They were at the very corner where the accident occurred.

She looked quickly away, fussing with her reticule, swallowing the bile that threatened to erupt.

Finally, the carriage came to a halt. The door opened and Strong held out a hand to help her down. Statham refused to send any footmen to London with them, saying they wouldn't be needed until he arrived and used the coach on a regular basis. Though he'd decided to keep his valet, Catherine had talked him into letting Strong become their coach driver while in London. He would remain in that capacity even after Statham arrived. The valet had been grateful to her. If she were lucky enough to find a husband, she planned to ask him if he would hire Strong.

The door opened and Jervis greeted them as Strong brought in their luggage.

"I've placed Lady Catherine and Lady Leah in their former rooms," Jervis told Strong. Turning to her, he added, "I haven't cleared out the earl's and countess' wardrobes yet, my lady. I thought you and Lady Leah might want to go through them to see if there's anything of sentimental value that you wish to keep. Do you know when the earl is expected in London?"

"Not until the start of the Season. He has a shooting party planned this week and another social gathering two weeks afterward. It will give us plenty of time to make sure his rooms are ready. He does plan to take a wife soon. As we look through the house and note any repairs, we should leave the rooms designated for the countess alone. That way, she may redecorate them however she chooses."

"Very well, my lady. I'll have hot water sent up for both of you."

"Thank you. Have tea prepared, as well. I'd like to discuss with you everything that's been done so far. You will join us?"

"If you wish."

Catherine went to her bedchamber. It was like stepping back in time. Nothing had changed. The wallpaper and furniture were the same. Everything was arranged as it had been before. She glanced at the bed, recalling how she lay there in agony, with her aching leg and head. Her fingers went to her forehead and touched the scar that she artfully covered with her hair each morning. She wondered how women were wearing their hair these days and what the latest fashions were.

The only friend she'd remained in touch with had been Charlotte, who'd actually married Morefield. They wouldn't be in London until the start of the Season. She had written of her father's passing but not of coming to town. She would write Charlotte today and let her know she was in London. Knowing Charlotte, she would demand Morefield return them early.

Catherine couldn't wait to see their children. Charlotte had given birth to a boy four years ago. A little girl had arrived last spring. It made her wonder if she would be able to have children of her own. If some man might find her—or her dowry—appealing enough to offer for her. Would it be as Statham said and she'd become a stepmamma to motherless children? Would her new husband want more? Only time would tell.

She left a maid who unpacked for her and summoned Leah to tea. Jervis had made two hires and there were appointments tomorrow for maids and a cook. The butler led her through the house so she could inspect it. Together, they decided what tasks needed to be performed to bring the house up to date. Jervis would handle that portion.

As they finished their tour, the doorbell sounded. It surprised her to find their solicitor being admitted by a maid.

"Mr. Larson. This is a surprise. Won't you come in?" she offered, leading him into the parlor.

"You asked that I send my reply here. I knew that meant you were coming to town. Do you have time to see me now, Lady Catherine?"

"I do. Please, have a seat."

"I'm sure you have a few questions of me and that is why you requested an appointment."

"I do. First, I wanted to confirm that Leah and I still have a dowry. I will be participating in *ton* events this Season and, if the opportunity arises, I may choose to wed."

His eyes widened. "Lord Statham is scarcely in his grave, my lady. Surely, you wish to mourn your father."

Catherine's gaze bored into him. "I will mourn Papa's passing until the day I die. The new earl thinks it best, though, for me to . . . move on."

Larson's eyes narrowed. "I see. No further explanation is needed. Having met the new Lord Statham, I quite understand."

"I have a few questions. Can I access any of my dowry in order to have a new wardrobe made up? In five years of country living, I had no real need of new clothes. Under the circumstances, I must update my attire."

"I'm afraid that's not possible. The dowry can only be part of the marriage contracts and is to go to your future husband and his family."

Disappointment filled her. She hated wasting any of her writing money on frivolous clothes.

"So I take it to mean that if I do not marry, I cannot have access to the funds?"

The solicitor frowned. "There is a clause that if you do not wed, you would be able to draw from the funds. You would have to turn thirty before that could occur."

Catherine sighed. Another blow. "What about the possibility of merging my dowry with Leah's? In case no gentleman offers for me, I thought to put the two together. It would make Leah a most attractive candidate."

"I'm afraid that's not possible," he apologized. "It's either wed yourself or wait another seven years to claim the funds."

She smoothed her skirt. Rising, she said, "You've been most helpful, Mr. Larson."

He came to his feet, pity for her on his face. "I wish I had better news for you, Lady Catherine."

"I'll make the best of the situation. Thank you."

She rang for Jervis, who saw her visitor out. The pressure to marry was even greater than before. If she didn't, not only would Statham toss them onto the streets, but he would reveal the circumstances of their births. For Leah's sake, that must never happen.

Chapter Fifteen

Jeremy read through the morning papers while he breakfasted. Rachel quickly downed her meal and asked to be excused. He nodded in agreement, not looking up. Once he finished, he folded the last section and placed it on the top of the correspondence Cor shuffled through.

Rising, he said, "I will see you—"

"Sit," she commanded.

He did so without thinking and then eyed her warily. "You haven't used that tone with me in quite a while. Not since I became the Duke of Everton."

"We need to talk." Cor set aside the letter in her hand. "More than a year has passed since Mary's death. It's time you find another wife."

Jeremy stood. "We are not having this conversation."

Her steely gazed seemed to pierce his soul. "Oh, but we are, Grandson. Sit," she said firmly.

Once more, he returned to his chair.

"Your daughter needs a mother. And you need a woman who can provide you with an heir. A spare would also be nice."

"I'm too busy, Cor. You know that. Besides, Luke is my heir now."

"Jeremy, you have done the impossible. You paid off all of your father's debts. You put Mary's dowry to good use. You invested in businesses at the right time and made profits beyond what I could have imagined. The St. Clairs are now on firm financial footing and will be for generations to come." She paused. "I'm putting my foot down, though, as the matriarch of this family. I want to see you wed again before I'm gone. And I want more grandchildren from you."

"That's nonsense, Cor. You'll outlive us all."

She sniffed. "I wouldn't wish that on anyone. My bones creak every time I move. Too many of my friends have gone and died on me." Her gaze locked on his. "I'm getting old, Jeremy, whether you want to admit it or not. Please, do this for me. The Rutherfords are having a ball tonight to open the Season. Go. Find a wife. Make me—and yourself—happy."

She placed her hand over his. "You haven't had happiness in your life for years. Not since Timothy died. It's time you found some. Or someone."

"I'll go," he conceded. "If only to please you. Now, if you'll excuse me, I have matters to attend to."

He left the breakfast room and went to his study. Closing the door, he sat behind the large desk, covered in papers. Contracts. Files. Information about his competitors. Ignoring it all, he walked to the window and stared out at the April day.

Cor was right. He'd spent the last five years doing everything he could to pull the St. Clair name and fortune from the mire. He'd worked long days, sometimes twenty hours or more at a stretch. He'd made the right investments. Bought the right shares. Scooped up properties and sold them for three times their worth after making improvements. He knew *ton* gossips must discuss him with glee, dirtying his hands in business, but he'd kept his family from going under.

He was lonely, though. Not that Mary had been a witty companion. The poor girl never got over her initial shyness. He'd treated her with kindness. Given her all the pin money she desired. Even made love to her—and gotten her with child. After the first miscarriage, he was loath to touch her. After the second occurred, he didn't for several months. Finally, she'd begged him, telling him only a baby would satisfy the emptiness inside her.

She'd died in childbirth.

At least he had Jenny. Sweet, sweet Jenny. When he felt the black cloud descending upon him, he would take a trip to the nursery and spend time with his daughter. She was fourteen months now. Toddling about. Calling him Papa. She had Mary's blond hair and sweet disposition.

Cor was right. His daughter deserved a mother. Rachel, too, would need a feminine hand to guide her for her come-out in a couple of years. Cor might not be around by then. It was time for him to reenter society for their sakes. He needed to set the wagging tongues at rest and do what was right for Rachel and Jenny. Society would judge them by his actions and reputation. He wanted the best for them both.

He also wished for someone to share his life. Not some empty-headed miss straight from the schoolroom who'd bore him to the point of madness. Instead, Jeremy wanted a companion. A friend. A lover. He refused to have a woman bear his sons, though. Luke was maturing and would make an excellent duke someday.

Wistfully, his thoughts turned to Catherine Crawford and what had become of her. He knew she still cared for her invalid father at their country estate in Kent, near Canterbury, thanks to Charlotte. The two women corresponded on a regular basis and Charlotte would mention Catherine a few times a year. He never asked about her but eagerly took to heart any scraps of news that Charlotte shared. Anytime he traveled from London to Eversleigh, he thought of how they were no more than twenty miles apart—and yet a gulf wider than an ocean separated them.

Jeremy returned to his desk. He knew Morefield and Charlotte had returned to London two days ago since Morefield had sent a note informing him so. He hadn't seen them yet. Knowing how Charlotte still loved to dance, despite her widening waistline, he assumed they would be at the Rutherford ball tonight. He dashed off a note to Morefield, telling him that he would be at tonight's ball and rang for Barton.

"This is for Morefield."

"I'll see that it's delivered at once, Your Grace."

"And tell Manfry that I'll be attending a ball tonight."

The butler tried to hide his smile and failed. "Certainly, Your Grace. Manfry will be pleased at that news."

With that, Jeremy pushed aside thoughts of dancing and empty talk of the weather and picked up a contract to review.

CATHERINE SAT AT her dressing table while Leah arranged her hair. She hadn't hired a lady's maid for herself as she interviewed and put staff into place for Statham's London residence. He wouldn't have paid for one in any case. Because of that, Leah had spent the last week practicing on Catherine's hair, using both hot irons and paper curls, and varying the styles with different gowns.

She and Leah had also combed through their parents' wardrobes. She gave a few choice pieces to Barton and Strong and had Barton sell the rest of her father's clothes. Her mother had been three inches shorter and much smaller in her bosom and hips so none of her clothes fit Catherine. Instead, she'd found numerous pairs of gloves and several hats and reticules that looked almost new and would work for the Season.

After she'd found a reasonably priced dressmaker, Catherine had offered the woman the entire lot of her mother's clothes, knowing the woman could use much of the materials and trims in her work. The seamstress gladly bought everything, giving Catherine a generous sum, which she then used to commission two ball gowns and three day dresses. She wore one of those gowns tonight, knowing she had a short window to make a good impression amidst all of the young misses who made their come-out at the Rutherford ball. The seamstress had then reworked some of Catherine's old gowns. There had been magic in her needle for many of them looked as fashionable as anything currently seen on the streets of London.

She'd written Charlotte and told her of her intentions to return to society. Two days later, Lady Stanley, formerly Amanda Rutherford, had called on Catherine. She'd wed four years ago and was the mother of a two-year-old son she spoke of proudly. Amanda had offered to renew their acquaintance and said she hoped it turned into a friendship. She'd also told Catherine she would make sure her mother invited her to the Season's opening event and mention her to others. Because of that, several invitations had arrived in the mail. She thought half of them were sent in blatant curiosity and the others in pity. Still, it would give her entrance into society once again. She needed to make the most of every opportunity as she searched for a husband.

"There. What do you think?" Leah asked.

Catherine looked at her image in the mirror. Her sister had done a series of looping, rope-like twists that cascading into two loose braids. The effect was stunning.

"You've done better than any lady's maid, Leah. I almost look beautiful."

"You *are* beautiful, you silly goose. Men will flock to you tonight."

Catherine didn't think so. Dozens of younger women would have their pick of the choice gentlemen in attendance. Of those left over, some of them would have heard the gossip about her. How her father had recently died and she wasn't even bothering to mourn him. Still, she hoped a few names would be scribbled onto her dance card.

Leah lifted the sapphire necklace and placed it around Catherine's neck. She gazed at it in the mirror, remembering how proud Papa had been when he'd given it to her. She blinked several times, fighting the tears that threatened to fall.

"I have an idea. I'll be right back."

Leah hurried from the room and returned a minute later. She handed something to Catherine. When she looked down, she saw a pair of her mother's earrings resting in her palm.

"I shouldn't," she said. "These are Mama's. That means they now belong to Statham."

"They match the necklace perfectly. Wear them, Catherine. He'll never notice and you can return them to Mama's jewelry box later. You should go downstairs, though. Charlotte will be here soon." Leah frowned. "I still can't understand why Statham won't escort you. He's going to the same place."

"Leave Statham to his own business. I'd rather go with Charlotte and Morefield," Catherine replied.

Her cousin had arrived two days ago. She'd walked him through the townhouse, pointing out what work had been done and what was left to complete. She noted that she'd left the countess' suite alone in order for his bride to have the chance to decorate it as she wished. She'd also presented to him a list of the servants she'd hired. He seemed to ignore everything she had done. His only remark had been to inform her he would speak to her if he saw her at an event but he wouldn't go out of his way to engage her in conversation or introduce her to anyone. He also said he would need the carriage each evening and she would need to make other arrangements to be transported to the various events. Catherine bit her tongue, knowing no good would come if she upbraided him.

They went downstairs to the foyer. Jervis met them, approval in his eyes.

"Lady Catherine, you are a vision to behold," he complimented. "I hope you'll enjoy tonight's ball."

Moments later, Statham appeared at the top of the stairs and descended, looking her over carefully.

"You need to remove your jewels," he said casually.

"What?" Leah cried.

"Any jewels in this house belong to the estate." He looked pointedly at Leah. "That means they belong to me."

Catherine slipped off the earrings and handed them to him. She stepped back.

"And?" he prompted.

"The necklace is mine. It's not a part of the estate. Papa gave it to me for my eighteenth birthday." When she saw doubt on his face, she added, "You can ask Leah. Or Jervis. They'll tell you. Mr. Larson would say the same. A gift is just that and shouldn't be returned."

Her cousin frowned in displeasure as he slipped the earrings into his pocket. He turned to Jervis. "Is my coach ready?"

"Yes, my lord." Jervis went to the front door and opened it. He handed Statham his hat and cane. "Have a pleasant evening, my lord."

Statham walked out without a word.

The moment the butler closed the door, Leah said, "How petty of him. I hate him. More each day."

"Leah, watch your tongue," Catherine chided.

"I hope you have a lovely time." Her sister embraced her and fled up the stairs in a huff.

When she was out of sight, Jervis said, "She's young, my lady."

"I know. She still worries me, though. We already walk on eggshells around Statham as it is."

He gazed at her with sympathy.

The doorbell rang. One of Charlotte's footmen stood there. She left with him and allowed him to hand her into the carriage where Charlotte and Morefield waited, hoping she didn't betray how nervous she was.

"You look dazzling, Catherine," Charlotte declared. "You'll have to have Morefield beat gentlemen off with a stick." She frowned. "We saw Statham's coach pulling away as we arrived."

"I can't thank you enough for conveying me to the ball tonight."

"We're happy to do so," Morefield said.

"My husband has his instructions. He is to talk to his single friends and make sure they all dance with you."

"Please, don't go to any trouble on my part."

"It's no trouble at all," Morefield assured her. He looked to his wife and nodded.

Catherine knew something was up. Though she'd kept the secret of her birth from her friend, she had shared with Charlotte Statham's edict that she marry by Season's end. She'd also told Charlotte why she needed a way to tonight's ball.

"Morefield and I have talked things over," Charlotte began. "We've decided it might be easier if you came to stay with us during the Season. Leah, too, of course. It would be more practical, all of us leaving from our place, than coming for you each time."

The offer moved her. "Charlotte, that's most generous, but I'm afraid it might reflect poorly on Statham."

"What if it does? He's been horrid to you since becoming the earl. Your papa would be appalled at how derelict he is in providing for you and Leah."

"Statham wishes to make a match during the Season," she reminded her. "I'm sure there would be gossip if Leah and I left his household and came to stay with you."

"I don't think so, Lady Catherine," interjected Morefield. "Women seem to do this sort of thing all the time."

"May I consider it for a day or two? I might even mention it to Statham to sound him out."

Charlotte sniffed. "I'd think he be happy to see the both of you gone." She looked to Morefield.

He cleared his throat and then said, "We'd also like to extend our hospitality to you if you choose not to accept any offers. Once the

Season ends, that is. You may not find a suitable husband and Charlotte and I are concerned for you and your sister's welfares."

"I cannot have you take us in as charity cases," Catherine said firmly. "I'm determined to find someone to marry." She wondered if Morefield thought no one would offer for her. Doubt and insecurity filled her.

Morefield looked at her steadily. "The offer will remain open, Lady Catherine. You shouldn't have to rush into a marriage because of Statham's demands."

She remembered how her father had also told her to take her time. Unfortunately, she no longer had that luxury. "Thank you," she said graciously.

They fell silent until they arrived at the Rutherford townhouse. The footman handed them down and Morefield escorted them inside.

Catherine braced herself as they entered. Tonight, she might meet the man she would wed.

Chapter Sixteen

Catherine looked across the large foyer and into the ballroom beyond. Everything seemed the same—and yet so different. She now saw things through the eyes of someone years older, not a starry-eyed girl approaching her first Season. Glancing about at the women in the receiving line in front of them, she thought how young and fresh they all seemed compared to her. What if her attempt to land a husband failed?

She refused to believe that was possible. She couldn't let Leah down.

They moved through the receiving line, greeted first by Amanda, who introduced her husband to Catherine.

"I'm delighted to meet you, Lady Catherine," the handsome, fair-haired man said. "Amanda speaks fondly of you. Might you reserve the third dance for me? I've promised the first to my wife and the second to my mother-in-law."

"Of course, Lord Stanley." She flashed her friend a grateful look. At least one slot on her card would be filled tonight.

Amanda introduced her parents. It surprised Catherine when Lady Rutherford clasped her hand.

"It's so very good to meet you, my dear. Your parents were great favorites in society. They are missed."

Tears misted Catherine's eyes. "Thank you, Lady Rutherford."

Next, she met Viscount Aubrey. He was tall and lean, with the same dark blond hair as his sister, though his merry eyes were a startling blue.

"Amanda told me she had a new friend coming tonight. It's a pleasure to make your acquaintance, Lady Catherine." His eyes gleamed at her. "Might you have the first dance open?"

She swallowed. "I do, Lord Aubrey."

"I'll be stuck in the receiving line for a bit. Go ahead and mark my name down if you will. I wouldn't want to lose my spot and a chance to dance with you."

"Certainly," she said, sensing her cheeks pinkening due to his interest in her.

A servant met them as they left the line and handed them their *programme du bals*. Catherine paused to record Aubrey's name beside the first dance and Stanley's for the third.

Morefield took the card from her. "I'd like to partner with you, as well. Do you have a preference?"

"Dance with me first, Morefield, then with Catherine," Charlotte ordered.

He wrote his name in the second blank. "Done," and returned the card to her. "I will see both of you soon," he promised as he bowed and left them.

"We usually dance twice. The first one and the supper dance," Charlotte informed Catherine. "After that, Morefield goes to the card room and I sit with the matrons. Though I still love to dance, I find after having two children that it tires me after a while."

"I will sit with you and keep you company."

"You will do no such thing," her friend admonished. "I want you to dance as many numbers as you can. We won't leave until the last song has been played."

Two women paused in front of them. Catherine recognized both. Countess Lieven was one of the revered Patronesses at Almack's and wife to the Russian ambassador. Catherine couldn't recall the name of the other but remembered her mother hadn't cared for the woman.

"It's Lady Catherine Crawford, am I correct?" the woman asked sharply.

"Yes, ma'am." Catherine curtseyed, dismayed the woman didn't bother to introduce herself.

"I'm quite surprised to find you here tonight. Statham has only recently taken his title. That means *you* should be in mourning."

She'd known some would disapprove of her actions but Catherine hadn't expected to be confronted so boldly only moments after entering the ballroom. She wasn't letting Statham bully her and she would stand strong against this woman, as well.

"I have been in mourning for many years, my lady. Five to be precise. I lost both parents that night in the carriage accident. It merely took Papa longer to pass."

"I say!" The woman looked appalled and quickly turned away.

The countess remained behind and said, "Do not listen to her, Lady Catherine. She's old and spiteful. I, for one, am happy to see you here. How are you?"

"I am well, thank you."

"May I see your programme?"

Catherine handed it over and the ambassador's wife studied it. "I see you already have a few partners. Let's see if we can find you some more."

With a flick of her wrist, a dark-haired man with brown eyes appeared. She spoke quietly to him, so low that Catherine couldn't hear what was said. Then the man nodded abruptly and left.

"It's taken care of. You should not lack for partners tonight."

"You are optimistic, Countess Lieven. I realize I have several years on me, especially when compared to most of the young women present."

"I wouldn't worry, my dear. You're a beautiful woman among pretty girls. I know you gave years of your life to your father's care.

Nursing a loved one can take its toll. My advice is for you to relax and enjoy yourself tonight as you reenter society." The countess leaned close and touched her cheek to Catherine's. She whispered, "If you need anything while in London, let me know."

Astounded, she said, "Thank you."

After that, a stream of gentlemen came her way, quickly filling her dance card. As each gentleman left, Charlotte told her exactly who he was and his position in society. Dumbfounded by the list of prominent gentlemen who'd agreed to partner with her, Catherine was at a loss for words.

Clasping her elbow, Charlotte said, "You're already a success, Catherine, and the first song hasn't even played yet. You will have your choice of husbands. I'm sure of it."

She glanced about the crowded room and heard the orchestra tuning up and then saw Lord Aubrey making his way toward her.

He bowed and offered his hand. Leading her to the center of the ballroom, he said, "Thank you for helping me open the ball."

"What?" she asked, noticing that no other couples joined them.

"Ah, I see you've never been to a Rutherford ball. My parents and siblings always start off the proceedings and dance the first measures before others step in."

Catherine stopped in her tracks. "I . . . I didn't know. I . . . I haven't danced in several years." She thought of her slight limp and how that would translate to dancing—especially with so many eyes on her.

Aubrey smiled. "I'm considered an excellent dancer, Lady Catherine. Follow my lead and all will be well."

He encouraged her to keep moving and they came to the center of the room. By now, Lord and Lady Rutherford were there and Amanda and Stanley joined them. Aubrey took her right hand in his and placed an arm snuggly about her. The musicians awaited their cue. Catherine saw Lord Rutherford nod to them and the music began.

Jeremy tapped his cane on the roof of the carriage and his driver stopped. He hopped out.

"We're still three blocks away, Your Grace."

"And the road all the way there is clogged. I'll walk from here. Stay nearby."

He headed toward the Rutherford townhouse. By the time he reached it, the receiving line was so long, he decided to avoid it. He moved toward the ballroom, anxiety filling him as his eyes passed over so many women embarking upon their come-out. They'd looked young to him five years ago when he'd chosen Mary as his bride. At twenty-eight now, he felt ancient because they looked barely out of the schoolroom.

The dancing wouldn't begin until the receiving line died down, so he decided to get a drink. He weaved through bunches of women and their protective mamas who eyed him with speculation. By the time he returned from the card room to ask a few partners to dance, he was sure the news of the Duke of Everton's presence would have spread like wildfire.

He entered the card room and accepted a drink from a servant. As he sipped it, he made his way around the room, visiting with a few old friends and other acquaintances from his business ventures. When he thought enough time had passed, he set down his empty tumbler in order to return to the ballroom. As he ventured there, he spied Morefield and raised a hand in greeting.

His friend rushed up, clearly out of breath. "I've been looking everywhere for you, Everton. I was gone all day. Looking at new horseflesh. I only received your note after I dressed for this evening."

"That's quite all right. I wasn't expecting a reply. I merely wanted you to know I would be in attendance tonight. It's Cor's idea. She thinks it high time I took a new wife so that Jenny will have a mother.

With Rachel's come-out in the near future, I thought it best to begin attending Season events again and try to get into the good graces of society."

"Will you stop talking?" Morefield demanded.

Jeremy frowned, noticing his friend's agitation. "What's wrong?"

"Nothing's wrong. I merely need to tell you something." He paused. "Lady Catherine is here."

His heart lurched in his chest and then began pounding wildly. "Catherine—is here?"

"Yes." Morefield pulled him aside, next to a large potted plant in a corner. "She came in the carriage with us. Statham passed and she is reentering society."

A warm rush ran through Jeremy. If he put a name to it, he might have called it joy.

"Charlotte's tasked me to help fill Catherine's dance card."

He smiled broadly. "I will take every available dance."

Morefield shook his head. "You don't understand. Countess Lieven spoke to Lady Catherine a few moments ago. Suddenly, men flocked to her. I'm sure her card is filled by now. You're too late."

"What!" He eyed his friend. "Then give me your spot. I'm sure you are one of her partners."

"I'll be happy to, Everton. It's the second of the evening."

He placed a hand on Morefield's shoulder. "Thank you."

"Good luck, Jeremy. I know . . . what she meant to you."

The orchestra began tuning their instruments and Morefield flashed him a smile and departed. Exhilaration filled him. He was free. Free to dance with Catherine. Free to ask for her hand. He paused. It wouldn't do to get ahead of himself. While she'd crept into his thoughts daily over the years, he had no idea if she still possessed any interest or feelings toward him.

How could she not? He still remembered that wonderful supper conversation. Their time together on the terrace. The feel of her in his arms as he held her, her perfume wafting in the air.

Their kiss.

She had to remember him. She had to.

Jeremy stepped into the ballroom, his eyes sweeping across the floor. Only three couples stood in the center and he recalled the Rutherford custom of family opening the ball before others joined in. He spied Amanda and her husband, Stanley. She still retained her figure despite having given birth to a son. Lord and Lady Rutherford stood in the center and the earl nodded brusquely, causing the music to strike up. Aubrey faced Jeremy's direction and he regretted their friendship had gone by the wayside.

Then his jaw dropped as Aubrey twirled with his partner. He was dancing with a beautiful redhead. Her deep, auburn hair gleamed and her rich, sapphire dress hugged every curve.

It was Catherine Crawford.

Jeremy took three steps toward the dance floor and forced himself to stop. He couldn't charge across a ballroom full of guests and claim Catherine in the middle of a dance. He was trying to avoid scandal and repair his reputation, not add fuel to the fire. Stepping back, he watched the couple with envy as they conversed while they danced. The years had only added to Catherine's poise. She was more beautiful now than she'd been as that young woman he'd met the day he'd returned from his Grand Tour.

He waited patiently for the music to end. Minutes from now, he would hold the woman he'd loved for years in his arms.

Finally.

Chapter Seventeen

Lord Aubrey smiled down at her. "You have told me an untruth, Lady Catherine." His blue eyes twinkled at her. "You are a marvelous dancer."

Her cheeks heated at the compliment. "I used to love to dance. I broke my leg, though, several years ago. I haven't danced since then. Though it mended, when I am tired it causes me to limp."

"I'm sorry that happened. Amanda told me of the accident. My condolences to you. I can't imagine losing both of my parents."

"It was . . . difficult."

"Would you like to take a walk in the park with me tomorrow afternoon?" he asked as he swept her into a turn. "Or if your leg tires easily, we can drive."

He was being far too kind to her. She knew Amanda had instructed him to spend time with her but asking her to the park tomorrow was unnecessary. "Lord Aubrey, you have more than done your duty tonight. I know your sister asked you to dance with me."

"She did," he admitted. "But *I* am the one asking you to accompany me to the park tomorrow."

"Why?" she asked, bewildered that he would want to be in her company.

"Why?" He laughed. "Because I am interested in you, Lady Catherine."

She felt her blush deepening. "My lord, look around your ballroom. There are dozens of young ladies here for you to choose from. Why would you ask me and not one of them? You know how the *ton* is. Once you're seen paying attention to a woman outside a scheduled event, tongues will wag. You don't need your name coupled with mine when there are so many eligible women for you to pursue this Season."

His intent gaze almost caused her to stop dancing. Catherine swallowed, her mouth dry.

"I see I'm not making myself clear. I *am* interested in you. I *want* to see you tomorrow." He tightened his hand around hers. "The question is, are you interested in being seen with me?"

"That . . . would be nice," she said primly.

Aubrey laughed. "I want to get to know you better, Lady Catherine. None of these young misses have anything on you. Already, we've had more conversation between us than I'll have the rest of the evening."

She laughed. "You mean you might tire of talking of the weather or contemplating if the lemonade is too tart or too sweet?"

"Exactly."

The music ended and he escorted her from the dance floor. As he did, he asked, "Do you have any more dances available tonight?"

"I'm afraid not," she said with regret.

"Who is your partner for the supper dance?"

Catherine consulted her programme. "Lord Burleigh."

"Burleigh? He'll bore you to death over supper. Leave it to me. I'll tell him you're an old friend of the family and Mother wishes you to sit with the family. In fact, I'll make sure to claim you for the supper dance and lead you to our table."

"You can't do that," she insisted.

"My parents are hosting this ball. Tonight, I can do as I please." He took her hand and kissed her fingers and bowed. "Till later."

As he retreated, Morefield brought Charlotte to Catherine's side.

"Aubrey certainly seemed interested in you," her friend remarked. "You talked almost the entire dance."

"He asked me to drive with him in the park tomorrow."

Charlotte's eyes lit with glee. "I'm so happy for you."

Catherine frowned. "I have no lady's maid, though. No one to chaperone us. If I ask a maid to accompany me, it would anger Statham."

"An even better reason for you to move in with us during the Season." Charlotte looked to her husband. "Morefield, you must speak to Statham tonight. Man to man. He would probably turn Catherine's request down out of spite. Coming from you, though, he will see the advantage to having his cousins under someone else's roof." She smiled at her husband. "Morefield can be quite persuasive."

He raised his wife's hand and kissed it. "Then I am a man on a mission. If you'll excuse me."

As he walked off, Charlotte said, "That won't do. He's to dance the second dance with you. Morefield!" she called out.

"Good evening, ladies," a deep voice said.

As Catherine turned, Charlotte said, "Oh, hello, Everton. Would you go and fetch Morefield? The music's about to start and he was to partner with Catherine."

Her heart slammed against her ribs as Jeremy St. Clair's eyes met hers. "I arranged with Morefield to claim this particular dance." He offered his arm. "Lady Catherine?"

He was here. After all this time. Not a day had gone by that she hadn't thought of this man. She remembered between worrying about her own injuries and her father's how Lord Sather was supposed to call on her that day after the ball. Catherine never learned if he had. Their servants had presented no note from him. No flowers. With everything that had occurred and her insisting they return immediately to Statham Manor, none of the servants had mentioned the marquess at all. She'd been swallowed up in caring for her father and by the time she'd thought to ask, it was too late.

She assumed he knew what had happened to her family. After all, he was friends with Morefield. Charlotte had mentioned Sather a few times in her letters. How he'd become the Duke of Everton. That he'd wed. But Catherine knew nothing beyond that. She didn't want to.

Yet here he stood in front of her, looking even more handsome and distinguished than he had when she'd first met him. She realized he was one of those men who would only grow better looking with age.

When she hesitated, he took her hand and placed it on his forearm and led her to the dance floor.

As they moved to its center, he said, "You may not remember me." His arm went about her as he took her hand in his. "But I remember everything about that night."

"I do, too," she said softly and the music began.

They danced the first measures without speaking. She inhaled the clean, masculine scent that she'd never forgotten as she drank him in. She could see motion and color swirling about them but she focused solely on him. The solid feel of his shoulder as her fingers rested upon it. His hand splayed across the small of her back. Yet what good could come of this? He was married. Catherine almost wished Jeremy St. Clair hadn't come back into her life for already her heart ached more than it had since losing Papa.

"I'm sorry about the accident," he said. "I would have called to see how you were but my own father passed away that same night. By the time I returned from Eversleigh and the funeral, you were gone." A shadow crossed his face. "I've regretted that ever since."

"I'm sorry for your loss." She paused, deciding to address what stood between them. "Charlotte and I correspond every month. She told me you've wed. Is your duchess here? I would enjoy meeting her."

An odd look crossed his face. "Mary is gone," he informed her, his voice void of emotion. "She gave birth to our daughter over a year ago and was lost in childbirth."

Catherine thought she might faint and clutched his shoulder. "My deepest sympathies, Your Grace. As hard as it was for me to lose Mama and Papa, I cannot imagine losing a beloved spouse."

His gaze locked on her. "I'm not here to talk about Mary, Catherine. I'm here to talk about us."

"Us?"

"I have never felt a stronger connection with anyone than I did with you that night at the Wethersby ball. I tried to put you out of my mind but it was impossible. Tell me you've thought of me, Catherine. Tell me I'm not alone in my feelings for you."

The dance ended. Reluctantly, he released her.

"I have thought of you often," she admitted as they left the dance floor. "But years have passed, Your Grace. We are two very different people now."

Everything he'd said thrilled her. It was as if all her dreams were coming true. Yet Catherine was aware of something that she hadn't know all those years ago when he'd kissed her in the moonlight.

The circumstances of her birth.

It was the reason she wanted to marry a low-ranking gentleman. If Jeremy St. Clair pursued her, she was certain it would end in an offer of marriage. One she could never accept. How could she marry into one of England's oldest, most noble families? She was illegitimate. A bastard of her father's by some unknown actress. It didn't matter that her parents had passed her off to society as their own offspring. She knew the truth. And if it came out after she wed Jeremy, it would destroy him. Catherine couldn't risk the scandal. She had Leah's future to think of, even more than her own.

They reached the edge of the dance floor and he said, "I agree that our experiences have changed us. What has not changed are my feelings for you, Catherine. Nothing could ever change them."

She refused to destroy him and his family's good name. She would have to put an end to this.

"I was a very young woman when we met, Your Grace. I'm afraid we no longer suit one another."

He grabbed her programme and struck through the name written beside the next dance.

She gasped. "You can't do that."

He gave her a wicked grin. "I'm a duke. I make my own rules."

JEREMY DIDN'T BELIEVE Catherine. She'd told him they wouldn't suit.

She was lying. The question was, why?

Lord Stanley, the partner whose name he'd crossed out, approached them. Jeremy excused himself and stepped away from Catherine in order to meet Amanda's husband in private.

"You had the next dance with Lady Catherine, I believe."

Stanley nodded agreeable. "I do."

"I plan to marry her," he said bluntly. "She will dance the next number with me."

The viscount eyed him interest. "I understand, Your Grace." He nodded and left.

Jeremy rejoined Catherine, who frowned as Stanley walked away.

"Amanda arranged for me to dance with her husband. What did you say to him to make him turn away?"

"Wouldn't you like to know?" he responded. "Come."

He took her hand, longing to strip the glove from it so he could kiss his way up the tender flesh of her bare arm. Instead, he guided her back to the dance floor. The music began again and he took her in his arms.

She glared at him. "You can't run off all of my partners."

"I agree."

Already, he could see his actions had caught the eye of several people present. He remembered that his purpose tonight had been not only to begin searching for a new wife but to clean his tarnished reputation by behaving impeccably before the *ton*. Rachel and Jenny's future depended upon him. He'd restored the St. Clairs' financial position and now he must remedy the social aspects.

"I wish I could claim all of your dances," he said. "I know that's not possible. I merely wished for us to finish our conversation."

She sniffed. "Nothing needs to be finished, Your Grace. I've told you that we no longer suit."

He gazed at her steadily. "I don't believe you."

Catherine gasped. "You . . . you . . . no gentlemen would say that to a lady. You're calling me a . . . liar?"

Jeremy grinned. "I am."

She huffed. "Then why would you even be interested in being with me?"

"Because you're different from every other woman on the Marriage Mart tonight. You have a grace and beauty that none of the others possess. The years have strengthen your confidence. You have a maturity about you that I find quite appealing.

"And because I've longed for you ever since the night we met. You are the woman I should have married, Catherine. It's always been you."

She stiffened in his arms. Tears welled in her eyes.

"Don't cry," he said softly. "Unless they are tears of happiness."

"Make no mistake, Your Grace. I'm not happy," she ground out, her blue eyes darkening. "I'm furious at you. I tried to politely tell you that I have no desire to be your duchess. You've accused me of lying. I would never want to be with a man who thought so little of me." Catherine paused, her eyes growing wintry. "Besides, you already have a daughter. I'm not interested in being a mother to another woman's child."

His hold tightened on her. Nothing she could have said would have surprised him more—or cut him to the quick. He adored Jenny. There was nothing he wouldn't do for his sweet daughter.

"Thank you for making your opinion known to me," he said curtly.

They finished their dance without further conversation. Jeremy returned her to where Charlotte stood and bowed.

"I wish you a good evening," he said tersely and walked away.

Chapter Eighteen

Catherine's throat grew thick with unshed tears as Jeremy strode away. A part of her went with him. This man would always hold her heart. He could never know how she truly felt about him. She'd needed to hurt him in order to push him away. Obviously, he cared for his daughter a great deal and her cruel words had done the trick.

"Excuse me," she told Charlotte. "I must go to the retiring room."

Catherine fled the ballroom, her eyes downcast. Hopefully, Charlotte would wait to tell her next partner where she was. She entered the room and was grateful no one was in it, which didn't surprise her because it was so early in the evening. She went to a basin and splashed cool water on her face, drying it with a handkerchief she removed from her reticule.

She refused to cry. After the accident, she'd learned tears did no good. They didn't make her leg ache less or help it heal more quickly. They didn't bring Mama back. They certainly didn't cure Papa's paralysis. She'd learned to make the best of things, locking away her emotions. She greeted everyone with a smile and, above all, she never let her father see how difficult it was to care for him. Walking into his room each day with him lying immobile in his bed ripped at her heart.

Pushing Jeremy away now had hurt the most of all. Catherine told herself it was for the best. She'd seen the passion in his eyes. He'd revealed how he'd longed for her all of these years. He would have married her without question. Knowing what a blackguard Statham was, it wouldn't have surprised her if her cousin had tried to blackmail her after the wedding so that he would keep her secrets. She wouldn't put herself in that position and she certainly would never put the St. Clair family at risk.

As it was, she'd already gained the attention of Lord Aubrey. He would be an earl someday. That still might tempt Statham to extort money from her. He'd proven so mercenary that Catherine must not only find a husband soon but watch whom she wed. Her original plan of marrying the lowest ranking gentleman was sound. She only needed to find one that fit the bill.

Two giggling girls entered and she decided she better return and find her partner. She did, apologizing for missing part of their dance. The baron was in his mid-thirties, with a round, red face and thinning hairline. Before the music ended, she already knew he had three very active little boys and wanted a new wife to take charge of them. Physically, he didn't appeal to her in the slightest but Catherine added his name as the first to the list she would keep of possible suitors.

She danced several more times, making sure to keep her eyes on her partner and not scouring the ballroom for a glimpse of the Duke of Everton. It was almost impossible to do for she felt drawn to him as a magnet. She must never seek him out and knew never to be alone with him, else her resolve would crumble.

Finally, the supper dance arrived and Lord Aubrey returned to her side.

As they danced, he asked, "How has your evening been so far? Is it a good start to the Season?"

"I have met some very nice people and renewed a few old acquaintances."

"I saw you danced twice with Everton," he remarked.

"We did." She left it at that.

"We were friends as boys," he finally said. "He and his brother,

Timothy, came home often with me from Eton. I also visited Eversleigh." Aubrey paused. "The brother died. It somehow killed the friendship between us. I suppose I reminded Jeremy of Timothy and all the times we'd spent together."

"I see."

"Did he ask to call upon you?" he asked casually.

"No. Why would he?"

Aubrey seemed to relax. The song ended and he led her into supper. They went straight to a table where Lord and Lady Rutherford already sat. Amanda and Stanley joined them.

"I'll bring you a plate, Lady Catherine," Aubrey said, as the other men at the table rose and followed him to the buffet line.

"How has tonight gone?" Amanda asked. "I saw Countess Lieven speaking with you."

"Her influence must spread far and wide. My programme was filled minutes after she stopped by and greeted me."

"She takes to certain people," Amanda confided. "If she supports you, you will easily find a husband this Season."

As the men returned with plates heaping with food, Catherine saw Jeremy cross the room. He seated himself next to a fair-haired young woman with eyes as wide as a doll's. Catherine turned away and did her best to eat, though it was hard to swallow. Twice, she glanced their way and saw them speaking animatedly.

Lady Rutherford was kind and engaged her in conversation. Amanda mentioned she was holding a garden party the day after tomorrow and insisted that Catherine attend. Aubrey immediately asked to escort her. In front of his family, she didn't have the heart to tell him no and quietly agreed.

Lord Rutherford excused himself and returned to the card room. Lady Rutherford told Amanda and Aubrey that they needed to come and meet one of her girlhood friends.

That left Catherine sitting with Lord Stanley.

"I want to apologize for missing our dance," she began.

His mouth twitched in amusement. "Oh, that's quite all right. It gave me a chance to have a drink." He took a sip of his wine. "I was under the impression that you didn't know many people in London."

"I haven't been here in years. I came to town recently and am staying at my cousin's house, Lord Statham. I'm hoping to meet new people and renew former acquaintances during the Season."

"At least you don't have to worry about being paraded about the Marriage Mart. Not many women can say they managed to land a husband the day the Season begins."

His words shocked her. "I beg your pardon?"

Stanley studied her a moment. "I see I've spoken out of turn. Forgive me, Lady Catherine." He rose.

She did the same and placed a hand on his forearm. "Please, don't leave. Tell me what you mean."

He indicated for her to sit and she did. He took his seat and leaned close. "I'm sure he will say something to you soon. Do me a favor and act surprised if you can." He hesitated. "Everton told me he planned to marry you. That's how he chased me away earlier."

Catherine gripped the table's edge. Nausea swelled within her. She grew woozy.

And then she fainted.

JEREMY LAUGHED AT something his companion said. He couldn't remember her name, only that it was her second Season, so she wasn't as green as a few of the other women he'd danced with. He'd actually enjoyed dancing with her and she'd been quite pleasant over supper.

But she was no Catherine Crawford.

Fresh hurt oozed through him as he wondered why Catherine had pushed him away. She had a kind heart so her cutting remark had seemed totally out of character. He'd sensed the spark still between them and she'd admitted she'd thought about him as he had her.

What action drove her to push him away as she had?

He'd positioned himself at a table so he could see her and Aubrey, her supper companion, taming the jealousy he felt against his old friend. He watched them surreptitiously while still actively participating in conversation at this table. Some influential people of the *ton* sat here and he still wanted to win his way back into their good graces.

The blond touched his forearm gently. "If you will excuse me, Your Grace, I wish to visit the retiring room."

"Of course."

He rose and helped her from her seat. Two other young ladies at the table accompanied her.

After she left, he turned to his right, where Countess Lieven sat. He'd greeted her when he'd first sat but he'd been occupied by those across and seated to his left.

"You seem to be enjoying yourself, Everton."

"Yes, I am." He glanced over and saw Catherine smiling at something Aubrey said.

"I see you're keeping your eye on Lady Catherine Crawford."

He cut his eyes back to his companion. "Is it that obvious?"

Her tinkling laughter sounded. "Not to a casual observer. Most here are too busy with those around them to notice."

"Except you."

She nodded. "Except me. It's a particular talent of mine. I know I helped you once before."

"And I am most grateful for that, Countess."

"I noticed you danced with her twice in a row. So did others."

When he didn't reply, she said, "I approve. Of you and Lady Catherine. She has an air about her. It would be well worth your time to pursue her."

He frowned. "I can't. The lady informed me earlier this evening that she has no interest in me."

Countess Lieven clucked her tongue. "Then persuade her, Everton. You can be most charming when you choose to be."

"I'm no longer interested in her either," he lied.

"Then why do you keep staring at her?"

"I can't help it," he admitted. Jeremy sighed. "My family is what's most important to me, Countess. First in my heart is my daughter, Jenny, who's just over a year old. Lady Catherine told me she didn't want to mother another woman's child. I can't seriously consider wedding a woman who'd treat my own flesh and blood like an outcast."

She pursed her lips in displeasure. "And you believed that? A woman who selflessly nursed her father for years? Lady Catherine has strength of character. There is some other, hidden reason why she turned you away, Everton. You should discover it. Ask to call upon her tomorrow. Take her for a drive in the park."

Bitterness filled him. "Aubrey already beat me to that. He's taking her for a drive tomorrow."

Jeremy glanced again at the Rutherford table and saw Lady Rutherford, Amanda, and Aubrey stepping away, leaving only Stanley and Catherine present. Lord Rutherford had already left some minutes earlier. Seeing the pair rise, he assumed they were returning to the ballroom.

He stood. "I will take your advice, Countess."

She smiled. "Then I wish you the best of luck, Everton."

As he crossed the room he saw the pair sit again. Catherine's face lost all color. She began slumping and Jeremy raced the rest of the way to her, catching her before she hit the floor. Unfortunately, she clasped the tablecloth in her hands and as she slid from her chair, she took it with her. The moment he scooped her up, dishes crashed to the floor. Every head in the room turned in their direction and several began rushing over to her aid as others gasped.

Stanley stood and loudly said, "Lady Catherine grew overheated and told me she needed some fresh air." He stepped in front of Jeremy, who held the unconscious Catherine in his arms. "Don't worry. Her fiancé will care for her." He nudged Jeremy's shoulder and said, "Follow me."

Stanley helped him push through the buzzing crowd and said, "Take her to the study."

Only as they left the supper room did he realize what Stanley had said. Jeremy remembered telling him he was going to marry Catherine—and now everyone in the *ton* thought they were engaged.

He wondered what she would think when she awoke and found herself pledged to him.

Jeremy had been inside the study many times before when he used to visit the Rutherfords with Timothy. He followed Stanley there now and waited for him to throw open the door. Once he did, Jeremy entered and went to the settee. He sat, leaving Catherine's head and shoulders in his lap. Some of her hairpins fell out, loosening her hair. He slipped a curl between his thumb and forefinger and rubbed it, marveling at the silky texture.

"Is she all right?" Charlotte cried as she rushed into the room, Morefield following closely behind her.

Before he could reply, Amanda appeared. "How is she?" Aubrey and Lady Rutherford were on her heels.

"She's fine, as I stated," Stanley said. "She grew warm and was merely going to seek some fresh air when she became weak. You can see she's in good hands."

"Are you engaged?" demanded Charlotte. Morefield, standing behind his wife, shrugged helplessly at him, a huge grin on his face.

"Everton said he was going to marry her," Stanley volunteered.

"I did say that," Jeremy admitted to the group. "However, I had not yet asked Lady Catherine for her hand."

Amanda laughed. "So everyone in the *ton* knows—except for the bride-to-be. How delightful!"

He caught Aubrey frowning at him.

"Should we send for smelling salts?" a worried Lady Rutherford asked.

"No," he said firmly. "It's a nasty way to awaken. She'll rouse shortly."

"We don't want to overwhelm her," Amanda said. "Come, everyone. Let's leave them." She took Stanley's arm and then her mother's. "We should see to our guests."

The three left. Aubrey glared at Jeremy before following them out.

"I think we should stay," Charlotte said. "It might frighten Catherine to awaken alone with Everton." She took a seat and motioned for her husband to sit next to her.

Moments later, he felt Catherine begin to stir. Her eyelids fluttered a few times and then opened. Those bright, blue eyes focused on him and, for a moment, her guard was down. Jeremy saw the longing in her eyes.

And knew he still had a chance.

Chapter Nineteen

Catherine closed her eyes again. The dream seemed all too real. She could smell Jeremy. Feel the heat from his palm as his hand cupped her face. She felt utterly content. And safe. She couldn't remember the last time she wasn't worried about something. In his arms, though, she knew nothing bad could ever happen to her.

"Is she awake?" Charlotte asked.

She frowned. *How did Charlotte get in her dream?*

Catherine mumbled, "Go away," hoping to sink once more into the luxury of being held by a man who was everything she'd ever wanted.

"Catherine? Wake up," Charlotte insisted.

Reluctantly, she opened her eyes—and found herself looking into Jeremy St. Clair's emerald ones.

She tried to bolt up but he held her in place.

"Be still," he said soothingly. "You fainted."

She realized he held her in his lap and smoothed her hair in comfort. Butterflies exploded in her stomach, making her feel faint again.

Charlotte knelt next to her. "Everything is fine, Catherine. You were too hot. Did the dancing tire you too much? How is your leg? Does it pain you?"

Morefield appeared and eased his wife away. "She's fine. Let's give them time together."

"At least tell her about Statham," Charlotte said.

Morefield gazed down at her. "I spoke to Statham about the convenience of having you and Leah stay with us during the Season. He thought it a splendid idea. I'll send our carriage over at noon tomorrow. Have your things packed up by the maids so you and your sister can return to us."

Catherine's eyes followed the couple as they left the room. She looked around it, having no idea where she might be.

Suddenly, she remembered why she'd fainted. Stanley told her that Everton was going to marry her. She struggled to sit upright but he held her firmly in place.

"Be still a few more minutes," he urged. "You don't want to sit up too quickly or you'll grow lightheaded again."

Catherine moistened her lips. "We are alone," she said. "It's most improper. How am I to find a husband if I'm compromised?"

He chuckled. "I believe you've already found one. After you fainted, I carried you from the buffet room. Stanley told everyone not to worry because your fiancé had everything in hand."

"What?"

Catherine shot straight up, hitting his jaw. She pushed away from him, eyeing him warily as he held it.

"I'm sorry," she offered, seeing that he looked in pain. "Did I hurt you?"

"I bit my tongue. It may bleed a little."

He took her hand and she froze. A delicious warmth spread through her with the contact. No, she couldn't give in, despite what Stanley had said.

"You'll have to explain that Stanley misspoke," she said.

"I'm afraid it's impossible to un-ring a bell," Jeremy remarked. "The only way we won't be engaged is if you break our engagement."

"But there *is* no engagement," Catherine insisted. "You never asked me to marry you."

"Then I will remedy that now."

He slipped from the settee to one knee and took both her hands in his. Sincerity shone in his eyes as he said, "Catherine Crawford, meeting you changed my life. If fate hadn't intervened, I believe we would have wed years ago." His grip tightened. "We are both free now. I have never forgotten you, nor you, me. There's something between us, which is more than most couples have before they wed. I want to make you my wife. Say you'll be mine, Catherine. Mine alone. No others between us."

She wanted this man more than anyone else. She could wed a thousand men over the years and none would stir the feelings within her that Jeremy St. Clair did. Remembering her birth mother, though, she knew she couldn't wed him. Complete honesty was important to her. If they couldn't share everything, it wouldn't be fair.

And if she told him her ugly secret, he would never want her.

When she didn't reply, his eyes darkened. Suddenly, he stood and yanked her to her feet, his mouth crushed to hers. He released her hands and wrapped his arms about her, imprisoning her. Catherine struggled to free herself and failed miserably, realizing she didn't want to be free.

Instead, she gave in to the kiss—and what a kiss it was.

Unlike their kiss long ago when his lips softly brushed hers and then teased her mouth open, this kiss had no gentleness in it. It was harsh. Demanding. Possessive. Thrilling. His tongue swept inside her mouth and assaulted it like an invading army. His aim was to conquer—and he did. Her knees buckled but he held her upright, pressing her tightly against him, her breasts crushed against his broad chest.

Her blood stirred and began to sing in her veins. She answered his kiss, her tongue waging war with his, fighting for him. For her.

For them.

She moaned. He growled. She fought to breathe. He stole it from her. Her body molded to his until she didn't know where she ended and he began.

And still he kissed her.

She had no sense of time. Rational thought became impossible. Only Jeremy St. Clair's demanding kisses existed, one ending as another began.

Gradually, his hold on her lessened but he did not release her. Instead, he broke the kiss, his lips hovering just above hers.

"You've given me your answer, Catherine. Your kiss can't hide the way you feel about me." Those green eyes glowed. "You're mine."

He kissed her again, deeply. Lovingly. Longingly. His mouth parted from hers once again.

"I'll purchase a special license tomorrow. We'll wed by next week."

His words left no room for opposition. His kisses had broken her resolve. She would marry this magnificent man.

Even if her secret ate away until nothing was left of her.

"I have one request," she managed to say, her breath ragged.

He nuzzled her throat, causing her pulse to jump. "Anything. I can deny you nothing."

"My sister. Leah. She must come with me. I cannot leave her with Statham."

Jeremy smiled at her. "I always wanted your sister to meet mine. Now, Rachel will have the sister she always wanted." He kissed her again, softly, reverently.

Catherine thought this must be what heaven was like.

"No, PLEASE FOLD the garment this way," Catherine demonstrated to the maid who was helping her pack. She hid her frustration, knowing a downstairs maid had none of the skills that a lady's maid possessed and that she was lucky she had any help at all.

A knock sounded and she turned to see Jervis standing in the open doorway.

"Yes, Jervis?"

"Lord Statham wishes to see you at once, Lady Catherine. He is in the study."

She turned to the maid. "Remember when you finish to go assist Lady Leah."

"Yes, my lady."

Catherine stepped into the corridor with Jervis. "Did he say what he wanted?" she asked anxiously. She hadn't seen him this morning and had hoped to leave the house before he even rose.

"No."

"Thank you for sending the maid to help. I want to be ready to leave the minute Morefield's coach arrives." She placed a hand on the butler's arm. "I know you have been with the Crawfords for years, Jervis, but if you wish, I'll see if Everton has a place for you."

"I would be most grateful, Lady Catherine."

She was already planning to take Strong with her and Leah and hoped Jeremy would find a place for him. Now, she added Jervis to the growing list.

The door to the study was closed so she knocked and heard her cousin bid her to enter. Catherine went inside, pushing aside memories of her father sitting at that very desk.

"Have a seat." It was more a command than invitation.

"Thank you," she said graciously.

He pushed aside the page in front of him. "How did you manage it? Becoming engaged on the first day of the Season?"

She clasped her hands in her lap. "I renewed my acquaintance with Everton. We had been friendly during my come-out. If the accident hadn't taken me away from London, there's a strong possibility he would have asked Papa for my hand."

Statham snorted. "Why didn't he ask me?"

"It wasn't necessary. I am of age, Statham. There was no need to inconvenience you. You aren't my guardian." She thought of Jeremy on bended knee, asking to marry her.

And of those endless kisses that set her afire.

"I will provide him with the name of the family solicitor and they can discuss the dowry," she continued. "I hoped you would be pleased that I will soon be off your hands. As it is, I'm moving to Charlotte's house today with Leah. The London townhome will be available for you to entertain as you see fit."

"Does Everton have any sisters?" he asked abruptly.

Catherine wondered why he would ask that. "One. She is Leah's age."

"I see."

She waited for him to speak further but silence hung over the room. Finally, she stood. "I will see to the rest of the packing. If you'll excuse me."

"When is the wedding? Is it here?" he demanded, a sour look on his face.

"I'm not certain of the exact date. Everton's purchasing the special license today. He wants us to be wed by next week. Of course, I will let you know the time and place." To placate him, she said, "I was hoping you would give me away. As for the breakfast, Charlotte begged to host it and I could not turn down her request."

Her friend hadn't—but Statham didn't need to know that. Catherine knew he wouldn't want the expense of hosting the wedding breakfast himself.

He lifted a sheet from his desk and began reading it so she supposed she'd been dismissed. She returned upstairs and found that her things were now packed away so she went to Leah's room. The maid fastened the lock on the trunk.

"I'll have a footman come and bring the trunks downstairs, my lady," the maid said.

After the servant left, Leah threw her arms around Catherine. "I'm so relieved we'll be leaving Statham."

"Have a seat," Catherine advised. "There's much more to tell you." She led Leah to the bed and the sisters sat.

"We'll only be at Charlotte's a short while." Before Leah could protest, she added, "I'm getting married. You will come to live with me and Everton."

"Who's Everton?" her sister asked, a puzzled look on her face. "Oh, Catherine, don't tell me you accepted the first man you danced with merely to get away from Statham."

"No, I didn't." She decided to let her happiness show.

"Then why . . ." Leah's voice trailed off. "You're blushing. And you're smiling. Good heavens, you're radiant! Who is this Everton?"

"He's the Duke of Everton. Jeremy St. Clair."

"A duke?" squealed Leah. "Catherine!" She hugged Catherine hard. "Tell me."

"I knew him many years ago. During my come-out. Lord Sather was to call on me the next day after a ball. He insisted upon bringing his sister, Rachel, who is your same age. He thought you might become good friends. And his grandmamma was also coming to tea." Catherine paused. "But his father died that night after he reached home. And our carriage crashed."

Leah took Catherine's hands. "Oh, my goodness."

"Everton became the duke and married. He has a daughter. She's a little over a year old. Her mama died giving birth to her. So, I am to be both a new wife and mother."

"You look so happy."

"I am, Leah. Having Jeremy ask to marry me is what I always wanted."

"Do you love him?"

"I think so."

Leah's eyes lit with mischief. "Have you kissed him?"

Catherine felt her face flame. "I have."

Her sister hugged her again. "This is the best of news. You sacrificed so many years caring for Papa and me. It's time you claim some happiness of your own."

A footman knocked at the door. "I'm to bring the trunks down." He stepped into the room and handed Catherine a letter. "This came for you, my lady."

"Thank you. These two trunks go as well as the three in my room."

"Very well."

Catherine saw her name boldly scrawled on the front and knew it had to be Jeremy's hand. She turned it over and studied the seal, which would soon be her family seal. A twinge of guilt ran through her. Deceiving Jeremy was the last thing she wanted to do. A part of her itched to reveal her past but seeing Leah's happiness and feeling her own made her push it aside.

She read the note quickly and turned to her sister. "You and I, as well as Charlotte and Morefield, have been invited to tea at Everton's this afternoon. He wants you and Rachel to become acquainted and for us to meet Cor, his grandmamma."

"What an odd name."

"I know. I'm sure there's some significance behind it. I'm going to send a reply before we leave for Morefield's."

Catherine returned to her room and read the message once more. Her eyes lingered over the last line.

I'm counting the hours until I see you, my love.

Jeremy had called her *my love*.

Chapter Twenty

Jeremy paced across the room, stopping occasionally to look out the window.

"Will you sit?" Cor asked, clearly irritated.

Rachel merely looked at him as if he'd lost his mind.

After he'd returned from buying the special license, he'd informed both women that he'd asked for Catherine Crawford's hand in marriage and that she was coming with her sister and the Morefields to tea today. Rachel plied him with a thousand questions. Cor merely nodded her approval.

He took a seat, his heel tapping rhythmically, causing his knee to bounce up and down.

"You must really care for Lady Catherine if you're so nervous," Rachel pointed out.

"I do," he snapped, wishing she and the others would arrive.

"Of course, he does, Rachel," Cor said soothingly. "Your brother has always made careful decisions where his family is concerned. I've already met her and approve of the match."

"You've met her, Cor?" Rachel asked. "Tell me everything about her," she enthused.

"She's beautiful. Charming. Intelligent. She will make for a wonderful duchess. Do you have anything to add, Grandson?"

Only that he might die if he didn't see her—didn't kiss her—in the next few minutes.

"No. You've described her well," he said. "She lost her mother several years ago and has been caring for her invalid father. He recently passed."

Hearing a noise, he hurried to the window. "They're here," he said, his voice steady but his heart racing with anticipation.

Without a word, he bounded out of the drawing room to go meet her, hearing Rachel ask, "Where on earth is he going, Cor?"

He raced down the stairs and threw open the front door. One footman opened the coach door as another set down the steps for the party to descend from the carriage. Jeremy took a deep breath, hoping to calm himself.

Morefield climbed out first and nodded to him before assisting his wife. A petite blond followed. Her green eyes immediately found him and she grinned unabashedly. She had to be Leah Crawford. Jeremy nodded politely and stepped forward, easing the footman out of the way so he could accept the hand Catherine held out. When his fingers closed around hers, serenity filled him. Their eyes met and she gave him a radiant smile.

He handed her down, refusing to release her hand. They drank in one another.

"I quite like him, Catherine."

Jeremy turned. "I like you, too, Lady Leah." He tucked Catherine's hand into the crook of his arm and offered the other to her sister. "May I escort you inside?"

Leah took it. "Thank you, Your Grace." She glanced at Morefield. "Were you as batty over Charlotte as Everton is over Catherine?"

Morefield laughed as he took his wife's arm. "Probably so."

Leah sighed. "I hope when I have my come-out that I will find a gentleman who adores me in exactly the same way."

Jeremy said, "You and Rachel will make your come-out together. The two of you will take London by storm in a couple of years."

"Then by all means, let me meet your sister so we can begin

strategizing how to conquer the *ton*."

He looked up and saw that Rachel had come out from the house, as well. She now tugged Leah away from him.

"I'm Rachel St. Clair. Jeremy has told me we'll be fast friends. I rather like the idea of plotting how to navigate the *ton*. Come meet Cor."

The two girls hurried inside and the couples followed them. Cor awaited them in the drawing room.

"I've rung for tea," she said. "Come see me, Lady Catherine."

Catherine went and greeted Cor. Jeremy watched as Cor kissed his fiancée's cheek. He'd never seen her show any type of affection toward Mary.

"And you must be Lady Leah."

Leah went to the dowager duchess and curtseyed. "I am. Why are you called Cor? I find that name most unusual."

The old woman laughed. "My, you are as inquisitive as Rachel. Sit, everyone."

Once they all had settled in, the tea cart arrived. After everyone had a cup of tea and plates filled with sandwiches and sweets, Cor said, "It's a very simple story, Lady Leah."

"I've never heard any grandmammas called that," Leah said.

"My given name is Cordelia," she explained. "My brother, who was older by three years, couldn't get out that mouthful. He only managed to say Cor. As I grew up, everyone in my family called me by that name. Why, I believe I was six—no, seven—before I actually learned my Christian name was Cordelia. I decided that sounded much too pretentious. All of my friends also called me Cor. Though my children called me "Mama", Jeremy here is the one who started calling me Cor."

He took up the story. "I don't remember how old I was. I think at some point Cor tried to teach me to say Grandmamma."

"Jeremy ran before he walked," Cor said. "He was always in motion. It took him forever to speak. I think calling me Grandmamma was too much for him to bother with since he was always in a hurry. He toddled in once when I was entertaining friends, having escaped his nanny. One of them called me Cor and told me how delightful he was. His little face lit up and he ran toward me, his arms spread wide, shouting Cor."

"Luke and Rachel followed suit," he said. "She will always be Cor to us all."

They spent a pleasant hour conversing. He'd deliberately led Catherine to a small settee and seated himself beside her, his thigh and hip wedged against her. He liked how easily she laughed and how well she and Leah fit in. Soon, Rachel and Leah left to tour the house. They already seemed as thick as thieves.

As Morefield entertained Cor with some outrageous story, Jeremy turned to Catherine. "Would you care to go up to the nursery?"

His heart beat fast, wondering what her answer would be. Last night, she'd offended him with her remarks about not wishing to mother another woman's child. That was before their kiss. He knew he'd won her over with it, but she still might have reservations about Jenny. If they were truly to have a marriage, she must be accepting of his daughter.

He need not have worried. Her face lit up. "I would very much enjoy meeting your daughter."

"If you'll excuse us, we're going to the nursery," he informed the others.

For a moment, it looked as if Charlotte would ask to join them. He frowned at her and she sat back.

Jeremy led Catherine from the drawing room and to the stairs. They climbed to the top floor where the nursery and schoolroom lay, along with bedrooms for a nanny, governess, and other servants. Opening the door, he saw that Jenny was being rocked by Sara, her nanny.

They stepped inside and Sara rose. "Good afternoon, Your Grace."

"Hello, Sara. This is Lady Catherine, my fiancée. I wanted her to meet Jenny." Jeremy turned and saw Catherine glowed as she looked at the baby.

"May I hold her?" she asked.

"Of course, my lady." Sara handed the sleepy girl over and Catherine went to the rocker and sat. She slowly rocked and begin talking to Jenny, telling her how glad she was to meet her and how she hoped to be a good stepmamma to her. Then she began to sing a lullaby, her voice low and soothing.

Tears welled in his eyes, seeing them together. He blinked rapidly.

When Jenny fell asleep, Catherine rose. Sara motioned her over to the crib and Catherine eased the baby into it.

"Thank you," she told Sara. "I hope you won't mind if once His Grace and I are wed that I spend time in the nursery each day."

"Not at all, my lady. You'll always be welcome."

Catherine turned to him. In that moment, if he hadn't known before, he knew now.

He was in love with her.

Leading her from the nursery, he took her across the hall and opened the door. "This is the schoolroom." He brought her inside and closed the door. "Timothy and I met with our tutor here before we went off to Eton."

Catherine began wandering about. "I imagine generations of St. Clairs have spent time within these walls." She paused and looked out the window.

Jeremy followed her, slipping his arms around her from behind and holding her against him. His lips touched her neck. A sigh escaped her and her head fell to the side, granting him better access. He licked and nipped as she squirmed, little sighs coming from her. But he needed more. Spinning her quickly so she faced him, his mouth came down on hers. She opened readily, eagerly, and he took his fill.

Minutes later, he stopped. His hands itched to wander to her breasts and hips. He would remain a gentleman. For now. As far as Jeremy was concerned, their wedding couldn't come soon enough.

MOREFIELD ESCORTED THEM home, except for Leah. She begged to stay longer and Catherine said she could. It pleased her that the girls had hit it off so well. Matthew Proctor, Jeremy's secretary, had come in as they were about to leave. He promised to escort Leah home after the girls talked themselves out.

"That will never happen, Matthew," warned Rachel. "I finally have the sister I've always dreamed of. Two brothers were plenty to put up with all of these years. Leah and I have decided to share a room. We already have so many things in common." She put her arm around Leah. "And we will make our come-out together."

Catherine kissed Leah goodbye and returned with Charlotte and Morefield to their townhouse. She would see Jeremy at the Billingsley ball later that evening.

"I do like Cor," Charlotte said in the carriage. "She will be quite an ally to have. What do you think, Morefield?"

"I've known Cor over twenty years. She never changes. She is hospitable. Dependable. And a fierce protector of Everton and his siblings."

"What are you going to wear tonight, Catherine?" Charlotte asked. "You know every eye will be on you. I'm sure tongues have wagged all over town all day at the earl's daughter who captured the heart of a duke at the opening ball of the Season."

She only had one other decent ball gown to wear. The others had been made over. "I'll wear lavender tonight. Do you think you might spare your lady's maid for a few minutes to help me with my hair?"

Charlotte clasped her hand. "Of course. That dreadful Statham, stranding you without one. I thought your hair looked lovely last night."

"Leah did it. She practiced on me for a couple of weeks."

"When is the wedding?" Morefield asked.

"Everton hasn't said. He only wants it soon. He mentioned next week."

"Next week? That's hardly time to put anything together," Charlotte complained. "I'm assuming Statham won't be hosting the breakfast?"

Catherine grinned. "I told him you were. He was delighted to have it somewhere else."

She watched the couple exchange a look and then Morefield said, "The breakfast will definitely be our gift to you."

They arrived home and Catherine relaxed in a hot bath before dressing for the evening. Someone had pressed all of her clothes and hung them in the wardrobe. A maid arrived to dress her and then Charlotte's personal maid came and arranged Catherine's hair in a simple coiffure that complimented both her dress and face.

Nerves shot through her as she left the bedchamber. Charlotte was right. As the first engaged couple of the Season, she and Jeremy would likely draw attention tonight. She knew she wasn't any different from the person she'd been her entire life, but ever since Statham had told her of her origins, she felt as if she would make some horrible mistake in front of the *ton*. Do or say something that would be seen as unpardonable.

Descending the staircase, her pulse sped up when she saw Jeremy waited at the foot of the stairs. He looked marvelous in his snow white shirt and black waistcoat and coat. His dark hair gleamed and his eyes told her how much he appreciated her efforts.

He took her hands in his. "You look ravishing." His lips brushed her cheek. "I have half a mind to skip the Billingsley ball and find a clergyman who would marry us tonight."

"You'll do no such thing, Everton," Charlotte warned. "It'll be a proper wedding and breakfast for Catherine."

Jeremy winked at Catherine. "I am your humble servant, Charlotte."

"When is the wedding? Morefield and I are hosting the breakfast."

"When is convenient for you?" he asked. "I'd like it as soon as possible."

"Next Thursday will do," she replied. "That's a week away. Where will the ceremony take place?"

Her fiancé turned to her. "Where would you like it?"

"Could we have it here, Charlotte?" Catherine asked. "I don't want a huge church filled with people I barely know. I'd prefer something small and intimate."

"I'll make it happen," her friend proclaimed as her husband slid his arm about her waist.

"We'll see you there," Jeremy said and led her outside to his coach. The ducal seal graced its doors and a team of the finest horseflesh stood ready to carry them across London.

Once inside the carriage, she said, "I know I've already asked a favor of you. To let Leah come live with us."

He chuckled as he pulled her into his lap and kissed her. "Rachel is the happiest I've seen her."

Catherine looped her arms around his neck. "It will be nice to help them prepare together for their come-out. We can hire a single dancing master. The same seamstress can make their gowns. How old is Luke?"

"He's twenty and at university now."

"He will be a perfect escort for them and I'm sure he'll be able to introduce them to many of his friends. Of course, I'll expect we'll also keep an eye on both of them. They're both high-spirited girls."

"I'd rather keep an eye on you."

He kissed her again, this time longer.

"Don't ruin my hair," she pleaded. "I'm already nervous enough as it is. The *ton* will be watching us closely tonight."

"Let them," he said, nipping at her lips.

Catherine gave over to the kiss, relishing the taste of him and the clean, spicy cologne he wore.

He broke the kiss and slid her from his lap to sit next to him. "You better stay there or I can't be held responsible for what you might look like when you alight from this carriage." He paused. "Did you have another favor to ask of me?"

"Yes," she said breathlessly. "Papa had two retainers I wish to bring with me. Neither is happy with Statham. These men are like family to me, Jeremy. Jervis is the butler at Statham Manor and has been with our family since Papa was a boy. He is almost a second father to me. Jervis is wise and capable and simply wonderful."

"And the other servant?" he asked.

Catherine smiled. "I adore Strong. He was Papa's valet. I know all men have a valet but Strong did everything for my father, especially after the carriage accident paralyzed him. Strong bathed Papa. Turned him to prevent bedsores from occurring. Spent hours and hours at his bedside, talking to him and telling him about everything occurring on the estate. Strong made Papa still feel as if he were a part of everything and not so isolated. Frankly, I don't know how I could have managed without Strong during all those years. Both men are extremely loyal to me. If you could find a position for them, I would be so grateful. Jervis wouldn't have to be a butler. He would thrive wherever you placed him. Strong is no longer a valet since Statham brought his own with him. Strong serves as a driver for the earl."

She looked at him hopefully, knowing how much she wanted to help Strong and Jervis, but not knowing how her husband-to-be would react to her request.

"I have numerous estates. Finding two men a place won't be a hard task. Once you're familiar with my holdings, you can help me decide where Jervis and Strong should be employed."

Relief filled Catherine as he slipped off her glove and raised her wrist to his lips, pressing a hot kiss along it. "I've told you. I can deny you nothing."

Waves of heat rippled through her. Her breasts grew heavy. "Thank you."

Jeremy placed the glove on her hand again, smoothing it up her arm.

They arrived at the ball and, as Catherine expected, she felt every eye on them as they stood in the receiving line and then entered the ballroom.

"The countess wishes to speak to us," Jeremy said, escorting her to the far side of the room.

Countess Lieven kissed both her and Jeremy. "Well done," she said. "When is the wedding?"

"Next Thursday," he replied smoothly. "You should receive your invitation tomorrow."

"Dance with Everton no more than three times," she instructed Catherine. "It's obvious he's smitten with you but you need to come to know more of those in society."

They circulated about, meeting some people she knew and many she did not. Jeremy signed his name to her dance card, reserving the first and last dance and the supper dance in the middle. The rest of her programme filled quickly.

What surprised her most was when Statham claimed a dance. She gave it to him readily, wondering why he wished to be seen with her. She decided it was because Jeremy was a duke and her cousin might wish to trade on her soon-to-be status as a duchess.

When Statham returned her to Jeremy for the final dance of the evening, her suspicions were confirmed.

"Here's your fiancée, Everton. Cousin Catherine is a wonderful girl. We spent many good times together growing up. I look forward to getting to know you and your family."

Statham left and immense relief filled her. Jeremy took her the dance floor and she tried to lose herself in the music.

Catherine couldn't help but notice that Statham sat out the dance—and watched them from the sidelines. Unease filled her. She had held up her end of their bargain by finding a husband.

Would Statham hold up his and keep her secret safe?

Chapter Twenty-One

CATHERINE DECIDED THAT if she must keep the knowledge of her and Leah's mothers from Jeremy that she would be open in every other regard. Because of that, she asked her publisher to tea. She'd already invited him to their wedding but wanted her fiancé to know exactly who John Bellows was. She told Mr. Bellows she wanted her fiancé to know about her children's stories.

Luke, Jeremy's brother, had come down from Cambridge for the wedding. Catherine was enjoying getting to know the middle St. Clair sibling. Like his brother and sister, he had the St. Clair emerald eyes and midnight black hair. He also was a terrible flirt and teased her unmercifully. Not having had a brother, Catherine relished their banter. She hoped not only would she give Jeremy daughters but sons, as well. She imagined a household filled with children who loved one another and never hid their affection as they enjoyed one another's company.

She'd asked that tea be at the St. Clairs'. As usual, Luke was giving both her and Rachel a hard time about how women primped. He also couldn't understand the fuss over the wedding. Even though it was to be a small affair, there were many details to attend to and he'd become exasperated at all of the wedding talk.

"If I ever think of marrying, I'll merely elope to Gretna Green," Luke said.

"You'll do no such thing," Cor warned.

Barton announced their visitor and John Bellows entered. He was a jovial man, with a baldpate and blue eyes that twinkled, and as wide as he was tall.

"Thank you for coming, Mr. Bellows. I particularly wanted you to meet my fiancé." She introduced him to Jeremy and then Cor, Luke, and Rachel. Leah had already met Bellows and knew what Catherine intended today.

As they waited for tea to arrive, Catherine said, "Mr. Bellows holds a special place in my heart. He is not only my friend but we do business together."

She saw a puzzled expression appear on Jeremy's face. Rachel sat up, suddenly more interested in their visitor.

Luke said, "Ah, this should be interesting. Catherine's in business, Jeremy. I wonder what it involves. Should a duchess do business?" he asked, stirring the pot.

Cor gave Luke a look that immediately silenced him.

Catherine smiled. "I have always enjoyed creating stories. I did so when I was young in order to entertain myself. When Leah came along, she became my audience of one."

Leah chimed in to show her support. "Catherine made up the most fantastic stories. They had adventure and romance. I begged for a new one each day."

"Sometimes, I would alter stories I'd told Leah. I would tweak them until I was satisfied. Leah is the one who put into my head that I should try to publish them so other children could enjoy reading them." She smiled. "That is where Mr. Bellows came in."

All eyes turned to their visitor. "Lady Catherine sent me a letter several years ago. I run a publishing house. In it, she included a short story about a pig and a frog who become friends. I was quite charmed by it and wrote back, asking if she had written any more. We corresponded over several months and I started publishing her stories. Eventually, I put a group together and sold them as one volume."

Rachel clapped her hands in delight. "I have a copy of it." She gave Catherine an approving smile. "You're quite talented."

"I had time on my hands in the country," Catherine continued. "Even though I was nursing Papa, he slept for long periods of time. While I sat at his bedside, I would write. Mr. Bellows eventually came to visit us at Statham Manor."

The publisher chuckled. "I had to meet the author who'd entertained both me and my seven grandchildren. Every time I saw one of them, they clamored for another C. E. Lawford tale. Imagine my surprise when I discovered C. E. was a female."

"My name is Catherine Elizabeth," she explained. "I didn't think I would have a chance of being published unless I masked my identity. Initials indicate a male. Hence, I became C.E."

Jeremy threaded his fingers through hers and smiled warmly at her. "Who knew I was marrying such a talented author?"

"Will you continue to write your stories once you wed Everton?" Leah asked hopefully.

Before she could respond, Cor said," Of course, she will." Looking at Catherine, she said, "I would think you might sell even more copies if you wrote as the Duchess of Everton."

"I would like to continue writing. As long as it doesn't interfere with my duties once I marry Everton," she said. "When we have children, I'm sure I'll be quite busy."

She sensed tension run through him. "Would you rather I stopped writing?" she asked softly.

"No," he said firmly. "You should continue. We can't have Mr. Bellows' grandchildren disappointed, can we?"

Her publisher beamed. She knew he was glad the duke would allow her to continue since her books were some of the most popular in England.

Luke held up a teacup. "To Catherine—a future St. Clair who continues to surprise us all."

The others lifted their cups in response. "To Catherine."

After Mr. Bellows left, Jeremy walked her back to Morefield's. She didn't see the point of getting the carriage out when there were only a few blocks between the two residences.

"Are you disappointed to hear that I am an author?" she asked.

"Not in the least. In fact, I'm bursting with pride."

Catherine decided she'd imagined the tension she thought she'd detected in him.

"I've thought we should go to Eversleigh after the wedding. Just for the week. I still have duties with Parliament in session but I'd like to show you your new country estate."

"I would love to see it. Where is it?"

"Near the coast. Just outside Dover. I've spoken to Cor. She will remain in London with Rachel and Leah, while Luke heads back to finish his term at Cambridge."

"You're certain you don't mind Leah moving in?"

Jeremy grinned. "If I didn't allow Leah to move in with us, I'm sure Rachel would pack her bags and show up on Morefield's doorstep, demanding to be let in so she could select her new bedchamber."

"They have become good friends rather quickly," she said. "I'm so pleased. And grateful to you for taking Leah in, along with me. And Strong and Jervis."

He stopped. "If I had to take in every servant and relative you had, it would be worth it, Catherine," he said huskily. "And if we weren't on this busy square, I would kiss you thoroughly to let you know how much I mean it."

Her heart filled with love for him. He hadn't said the words to her—nor she to him—but Catherine knew this man did love her and would tell her in his own time.

CATHERINE LOOKED DOWN at the slim wedding band resting on her finger.

She was a married woman.

Looking across the room, she caught Jeremy's eyes. He smiled at her and a frisson of pleasure rippled through her. Soon, they would be man and wife in every way possible. She looked forward to seeing where his drugging kisses would lead.

She turned back to Mr. Bellows and Countess Lieven, who were animatedly discussing Bonaparte. This would be the perfect time to slip away and change from her wedding gown to more practical traveling clothes. Strong would drive them to Eversleigh once the wedding breakfast concluded. He'd given notice to Statham a week ago and her cousin had dismissed him on the spot. Jervis was waiting until she returned from her stay in the country and then he, too, would end his association with the earl.

Catherine left the sunny room and went to the staircase. She'd reached the first landing when she heard someone call her name. She saw Statham hurrying up the steps. Unease filled her. She'd let her cousin give her away today, hoping to smooth over the hard feelings between them, but she wished she could cut all ties with him. It wouldn't be possible, though. If she angered him, he could still reveal her secret.

He reached the landing and drew her to the far wall so anyone passing below wouldn't see them.

"We must talk now that you're wed."

"I did as you asked, Statham," she said bluntly. "I found a husband. I've removed Leah from your household. We won't trouble you anymore. You can entertain to your heart's delight. Find a wife. Be happy."

"I've decided to wait on marrying," he informed her. "I do plan to get close to your husband, though. A duke runs in the highest of circles. Being friends with Everton will grant me entrance into any event I choose."

"Everton makes his own friends. I don't have anything to do with that."

"Oh, Catherine, you're his duchess now. You wield a great deal of influence with him and society as a whole. If I have both of your approvals and you make it known, I will be able to achieve everything I want."

"What do you want, Statham? I've kept to our bargain. Are you going to be a gentleman and hold up your end?" she demanded.

He gave her a sly smile. "I've decided to change the terms of our agreement."

Her stomach tightened. "To what?"

"First, your affection for your sister will work in my favor. Leah is to remain with me."

"What?" she hissed. "You don't want her."

"I am her guardian by law. Not Everton. She will go where I tell her to."

"No!"

Statham gripped her elbow painfully. "Yes, Catherine. Leah will reside with me. You can tell her once you and Everton return to London. I will make all decisions regarding her welfare. To see her, you will have to see me. I expect to be invited to both Eversleigh and Everton's London residence on a regular basis. I know how much you love the girl."

"And you would use that love to control me?"

"Yes. Because if you fight me on this, I will tell the *ton* that the two of you are bastards. You're a St. Clair now. You don't want to hurt your husband and your new family. Can you imagine what society would say about the bastard who hoodwinked a duke into marrying her? His name would be dragged through the mud. He might even have a case that you defrauded him and he could annul the marriage and set you aside. Of course, you would never find another husband in society again. Leah's chances would also be ruined."

Nausea filled Catherine. She knew Statham would do exactly as he said if she didn't go along with his plans.

"There's something else," he continued.

The gleam in his eyes sent a chill through her.

"I've decided to wait two years before I wed. And when I do, I want my bride to be Rachel St. Clair."

"No," she moaned. "Please, Statham, no. Don't do this."

"I won't have to. If you cooperate. Just think, in two years' time, you could already have borne Everton a child. What if it's a boy? He would be the heir apparent. I know you wouldn't risk Leah's future, as well as your own child's. Do as I say and everything will be fine."

"How will I get Rachel to agree to wed someone twice her age?"

His deadly stare caused her to tremble. "You have two more Seasons to figure that out, Catherine. Plenty of time."

With that, he turned and descended the stairs.

She gripped the banister, feeling faint, and knew she had to get to her room. Once there, she rushed to the chamber pot and vomited. The sour taste filled her mouth.

What was she going to do?

She couldn't let her secrets be exposed. It would ruin her and Leah, not to mention bring shame to the St. Clairs.

But when would the blackmail stop? Already, Statham wanted to weasel his way into Jeremy's circle of friends. And how could Catherine let Rachel's life be ruined by convincing her to wed a monster?

It became clear that she would have to cut ties now. Statham would never let up. Sooner or later, he would spill what he knew to the *ton*. Ruin was inevitable. It would merely depend upon when he made the secrets known as to how many lives would be destroyed.

She still wasn't truly married yet. She and Jeremy hadn't consummated their union. If they didn't, he could sue for an annulment. Once they separated, she knew Statham would gleefully make known the circumstances of her birth, and Leah's. At least by then, Jeremy would be rid of her. While the gossips might rake him and his family over the coals for a short while, they would eventually sympathize with him for being duped by a fraud. After all, he was a duke. There would be enough eager mamas pushing their unmarried daughters toward him. In the long run, he would suffer only for a short amount of time.

It would mean utter ruin for her, though. She would never be able to hold her head up in society again. Leah's chances of a match within the *ton* would also vanish. Still, the rising merchant class could offer her sister a chance to wed within it. It wouldn't be possible for her to marry a man with a title but, with her beauty, Leah could marry someone with quite a bit of money and be very comfortable.

Or they could go to America. The colonies prided themselves on being a classless society. She could take her earnings from her books and they could sail for Boston or New York and begin again. No one would care who their mothers had been. Maybe the both of them could find husbands and leave this disaster behind. Catherine decided that would be the best course of action. A clean break with England and everyone involved.

And no possibility of ever running into Jeremy on the street.

No matter what the outcome, Catherine knew her heart would never heal. She'd given it to Jeremy St. Clair many years ago. No man would ever bring her the joy and passion that he did.

She heard a quiet knock at the door and Charlotte came in.

"I thought I would help you—oh, Catherine, you look as if you'd seen a ghost!" Charlotte rushed to her and took her hands and then gave her a knowing smile. "I know what ails you."

"You do?" She didn't think anyone could have overheard her conversation with Statham.

"Without a mother to speak to you, I'm sure you're worried sick about your wedding night with Everton. Never fear. I'll admit that the first time you couple, it will hurt somewhat. He must breach your maidenhead."

Charlotte smiled. "After that, things can be quite pleasurable. At least they are with Morefield. I'm sure Everton will be no exception."

Catherine swallowed. "Thank you for sharing with me, Charlotte."

"Here, left me help you undress."

She gave herself over to her friend and allowed her to ready her for the trip to Eversleigh. Catherine decided she would wait until they were there in order to speak to Jeremy in private and tell him she couldn't consummate the marriage.

As she accompanied Charlotte downstairs again, Catherine spied her new husband. He'd already changed from his wedding finery and now hurried toward her and kissed her cheek.

"Are you ready?"

She nodded, not trusting herself to speak.

They said their goodbyes and went outside to their coach. Jeremy saw her safely inside and then sat next to her, putting his arm about her shoulder. Catherine leaned into him, savoring what would be their last hours together in peace.

Before she ripped his world apart.

CHAPTER TWENTY-TWO

JEREMY KNEW THE moment Catherine fell asleep against him. The tension which had blanketed her melted away. He looked down at her, the long lashes resting against her porcelain cheeks.

His duchess. His wife.

His life.

Guilt coursed through him. He'd married her under false pretenses. He had no intentions of letting her get with child. He'd seen too many women in his family die from childbirth.

Catherine would not be one of them.

He knew it would hurt her because of what he'd already seen of her and Jenny together. Catherine was a natural mother and had handled the baby with ease. She would long for children of her own.

And he could never let that happen.

Jeremy admitted to himself that he was a selfish bastard. He'd rather have an unhappy, childless Catherine in his life than see her swell with a child inside her and then watch as her life drained away after birthing it. He'd spent too many years without her and wasn't willing to sacrifice her in an attempt to produce an heir. Luke would make for a fine Duke of Everton someday.

He didn't know how to break the news to her, though. He had yet to tell her he loved her. It had to be obvious, though. He doted on her. He couldn't stop kissing her when they were alone. He only hoped he would be enough for her.

She awoke after an hour and tried to pull away from him. He tightened his arm about her.

"You're not going anywhere, Your Grace," he teased, pressing a kiss against her temple.

She stiffened. "I'm hot," she declared and scooted away from him.

Her behavior puzzled him. Twice when they'd been alone in a coach together, he was afraid he would break down and make love to her, knowing she'd be a willing participant. Now, though, she seemed a stranger who rode in his carriage, looking out the window.

Reaching for her hand, she shook him off. "Not now," she murmured and continued to stare at the passing countryside.

Where was the passionate woman he'd married?

They arrived at Eversleigh. Mrs. Talley met them and greeted Catherine as Jeremy instructed Strong where to take the carriage.

"The servants are ready to meet you, Your Grace," the housekeeper said.

Jeremy remembered the last time he'd seen the lot of them lined up. It was when he'd brought Mary home.

Catherine moved through the group of servants listlessly, none of her usual vitality present.

Once he dismissed the lot, he asked, "Are you well?" noticing how pale she seemed.

"I'm so tired," she admitted. "I think the whirlwind of the past week of activities has finally caught up to me."

"Are you hungry? Mrs. Talley can have food brought upstairs to us."

She looked away. "No. Go ahead and eat without me."

Jeremy took her arm. "Here, let me take you to your rooms."

He escorted her upstairs, pointing out her suite and his and the connecting door that lay between them.

Though it hadn't been the case with Mary, he enveloped her in his arms and said, "I'm sure your bedroom won't be used often. I plan for you to sleep with me each night. At least, we'll try to sleep," he teased, hoping to lift her dark mood.

Anguish filled her face and she cast her eyes downward. "I am weary, Jeremy. Could we . . . is it possible to discuss this tomorrow?"

He drew her to him, her head resting against his chest as he stroked her hair. "Of course, darling. The wedding and travel have tired you. You'll feel better in the morning." He kissed the top of her head and she shuddered.

Withdrawing his arms, she moved away.

"Here's Her Grace's trunk," a voice called from the open doorway and Strong came in, setting it on the floor. He glanced at the couple and then left without another word.

"Shall I have a maid come and unpack for you?" Jeremy asked.

"No," Catherine said listlessly. "I'll deal with it tomorrow." Finally, her gaze met his. "I will see you in the morning."

Lifting her hand, he kissed her fingers. "Goodnight."

He withdrew from the room and went to his own. As he undressed, he couldn't fathom what he'd done to make her behave in such an odd fashion. He tossed his clothes on a nearby chair and shrugged into a dressing gown. Pouring himself a drink, he sipped as he contemplated what had occurred during the day. The wedding had gone off without a problem. The guests enjoyed the breakfast. Even Statham, whom Catherine had an odd relationship with, acted graciously.

Then it hit him. She must be terrified about coupling with him. She had no mother to tell her what was to come. Nerves had probably overtaken her.

Worse, her husband hadn't yet told her that he loved her. He already knew Catherine loved him. She couldn't easily hide her feelings. With ever look, every kiss, every touch, she told him how she felt about him. Yet she, too, had not uttered the words.

He was a fool. She was waiting on him to make his feelings

known. She was worried. Fearful. And he hadn't comforted her, much less told her of his love for her. That could be easily remedied. He would march in and convince her how much he loved her—and then make love to her all night. Going to his chest, he opened it and optimistically withdrew three French letters, placing them in the pocket of his dressing gown.

Jeremy went to the connecting door, relieved that he'd figured out what ailed his bride. He turned the handle and pushed but the door didn't budge.

Catherine had locked him out.

CATHERINE SPENT A sleepless night. She tossed and turned, wishing she'd come out and told Jeremy she could never be a true wife to him. When the time came, though, she'd lost her courage.

She knew he'd tried to come to her last night because she'd heard the doorknob turn in the silence. Putting the bolt into place had been a last minute thought and she was glad she'd done so. She rose and went to the door now and turned the lock. She would dress and then visit him. As she stepped away, the door flew open immediately.

Jeremy stood before her in a dressing gown of deep burgundy. Dark stubble covered his face, making him look rough and dangerous. His bloodshot eyes told of his lack of sleep. He stormed into the room and latched on to her upper arms. His mouth came down on hers and he kissed her hungrily. She reached to shove him away and her fingers touched hot, smooth flesh. He crushed her to him.

There was no escape.

She tried not to respond. Tried not to feel the burning need for him within her.

And failed miserably.

Catherine began kissing him back, thinking she would only do that. One last time to enjoy his kisses. His taste. One more time to remember his touch.

Before she knew it, they were on the bed. He tore the front of her nightgown, baring her breasts. He kneaded them, his thumbnail raking across the raised nipple. She cried out at the delicious sensation. His mouth fastened on one breast, his tongue teasing its nipple. She began writhing under him as he awakened something new within her.

He moved to her other breast even as his hand slid down the curve of her hip. Hovering over her, his hand swept across her stomach and downward. One finger eased inside her and she cried out his name in shock. He lifted his head and moved to her mouth, his tongue plunging deep inside, even as his finger did the same below. He stroked her and something built within her, something dark and deep and wonderful.

A second finger joined the first and Catherine moaned in pleasure. Then a tide swept across her so quickly, she didn't have time to catch her breath. Wave after wave of pleasure exploded from her, taking her to the heavens above.

Gradually, her tremors calmed. Jeremy slipped his hand from her and broke the kiss. Despondency filled her. They'd made love. She was trapped—and would ruin him.

"I made a horrible mistake, my love." His green eyes gleamed at her. "I didn't tell you I loved you. I should have. I promise I will, every day of our lives. In the morning when we awaken. While we dress. When we eat. When we make love. When your eyes grow weary and sleep is at your doorstep."

His gaze grew tender. "I love you, Catherine St. Clair. I think I did from that very first night. I pined for you all those years in-between. I cannot believe that we are together now. That we're finally man and wife. I'm sorry I never said the words but they've always been in my heart. I know you've wanted to hear them." He grinned. "You'll probably grow tired of hearing them so much but I'll say them all the same."

Jeremy reached and withdrew something from his dressing gown that he'd tossed onto the bed. Catherine could barely move, much less think.

He loved her. She'd always known it in her heart. She longed to tell him the same but couldn't. And she'd made a mess of things now that they'd consummated their marriage.

He opened something and begin sheathing his manhood.

"What is that?"

"It's a French letter." He rolled it over the entire length and then placed his hands on either side of her head. "It will keep us from making a baby."

"You mean . . . what we did before . . ."

He laughed. "That was merely a way to pleasure you, sweetheart. Now, I will make love to you."

She put her palms against his bare chest. "Wait. So we haven't consummated our union yet?"

"No. But give me a moment."

"Wait," she said again, this time more firmly. "Why do you need a French letter?"

"I told you. It helps prevent a baby from coming." His eyes shifted a fraction. "I thought we could enjoy being a couple for a while."

Catherine knew him well enough by now. She said, "You're lying."

He looked startled. "Why do you say that?"

She took a risk and said, "Then make love to me without it."

Anguish filled his face. "I can't." He tried to kiss her but she turned her head away.

"Jeremy, I want the truth."

"I don't want you to have a child." He moved away from her, rolling to her side.

"Why?" she asked, curious as to his reason. "Jenny is a girl. Surely, you need an heir."

He took her hand and entwined their fingers. "My mother died in childbirth. I never knew her. I watched Father marry two more wives. Both Luke's and Rachel's mothers died in childbirth. Then I foolishly got Mary with child and she died after birthing Jenny."

Jeremy touched her cheek. "I can't lose you, Catherine," he said hoarsely. "Not after all those years apart. Besides, Luke can be my heir. You don't ever have to risk your health in order to give me a son. I won't let you."

Catherine saw this was a way to get out of her marriage. It wouldn't hide the ugly truth that would come out later. If anything, she could trust Statham to publicly divulge what he knew. But by then, she and Leah could be far away.

She braced herself for she knew her words would wound him deeper than any knife.

"Let me? *Let* me? You let me marry you, thinking I would become a mother, what I've wanted my entire life."

"You can be a mother," he said stubbornly. "To Jenny. She needs you. Mothering her should satisfy your maternal instincts."

"I want children of my own as well, Jeremy," she said angrily. "I assumed I wanted your children. Now that I know how deeply you deceived me, you are the last person I'd ever couple with. You are not the man I thought you were."

Catherine paused before her voice broke and then softly said, "If you refuse me in this, then I don't wish to be wed to you."

"What?" He sat up quickly. "No, you don't mean that, Catherine. You couldn't."

She swallowed. "I do. I want a child. Many of them. I can't imagine my life—or our marriage—without children. My mother only had Leah and me and I always wished I could have had several more brothers and sisters. Children are what give a marriage purpose. They're everything I've dreamed of for as long as I can recall."

"I love you, Catherine," he said, determination filling his face. "I'm not prepared to fill your belly with my seed and then see you perish when we can live and love and be happy together."

She slowly shook her head. "You don't seem to understand. If you won't give me children, then I entered this marriage under false pretenses. I'm not willing to stay wed to a man who denies me the very thing I want most in life."

Jeremy cradled her face in his large hands. "I love you, Catherine. I know you love me. Can we not be enough for each other?" Misery filled his face.

Catherine divorced herself of every feeling she had for this man. To save him, she must lose him.

"No, Jeremy. I want an annulment."

Chapter Twenty-Three

CATHERINE SAT ALONE in the Everton carriage as it made its way back to London. She had traveled this same road less than a day ago. Now, she returned with a heavy heart.

Jeremy chose not to ride with her. Instead, he'd claimed a horse from the stables and rode ahead of the coach. Every now and then as they made their away around a bend, she caught a glimpse of him and fresh sorrow blossomed within her.

She wanted to die. It would be easier if she did. She'd wronged the man she loved, even if she did it for the right reasons.

When London came into sight, she leaned partly out the window and saw her husband ride off. Even knowing how badly she'd hurt him, he'd still accompanied her to the city, protecting her from any harm on the road. Catherine closed her eyes. Every breath she took brought further misery. She didn't know if she could survive. She had to, though. She had Leah to think of. She couldn't leave her sister in the hands of Statham. Catherine must get both of them out of England, far from his conniving grasp.

Strong didn't head to the St. Clair townhouse. Instead, she had instructed him to go to her solicitor's office. She'd found a new one when she and Leah had first come to London from Statham Manor since she no longer trusted Larson, who served as Statham's legal representative.

They arrived at his office and Strong helped her down.

"Once I've concluded my business here, we'll go to Mr. Bellows' office."

He nodded. Strong hadn't made his opinions known. For that, she was grateful.

Catherine entered the offices and spoke with the clerk, telling him she needed to speak with Mr. Davidson at once. He asked her to wait and then after talking with Davidson, the clerk returned and escorted her to him.

Davidson rose. "Your Grace, I hadn't expected to see you."

He knew of her recent marriage since Catherine arranged to have her dowry transferred to his control. Larson hadn't been able to stop her but he did keep Leah's, saying Statham, as guardian, had the final say on it. Davidson had met with Jeremy two days before the wedding. Catherine was here to find out if the monies had already been transferred to Jeremy.

"I have some unfortunate news, Mr. Davidson."

"Please, have a seat."

She took it and composed herself. "Everton and I are not suited. You are to draw up annulment papers."

Shock caused his face to turn ashen. "Your Grace, I –"

"Has my dowry been forwarded to Everton's estate?"

"I was going to do that this afternoon."

"Then keep it. Draw up the papers as soon as possible. I'd like to sign them by tomorrow morning. Can you manage that?"

"I can," he said, uncertainty on his face.

"Then I will return here at nine o'clock tomorrow morning. Do we both need to be present when we sign?"

"No."

"Good. I will sign and then you may contact Everton and let him know that he can sign." She rose.

He did the same. "Forgive me, Your Grace, but I'll need to know the circumstances." Davidson hesitated. "To obtain an annulment, only three categories are available."

"What are they?"

"Fraud. Incompetence. Or . . . impotence." He blushed profusely.

Catherine had been the one to misrepresent herself and she succinctly said, "Fraud," knowing Jeremy would think she'd charged him with it because of not wanting to have any children with her. By the time the truth came out, he would know she was the one to blame. She decided she would write a letter to him and give it to Davidson once Statham began the rumors. She would confirm she'd kept her true identity from her fiancé and his family and that she was the one who had committed fraud. The annulment fell squarely on her shoulders.

"Very well," the solicitor said.

"I will see you in the morning, Mr. Davidson."

Catherine left the office and Strong drove her to her publisher's office. Once again, she entered and spoke with a clerk, apologizing for not having an appointment, but stressing the urgency of her business. She was immediately granted access to Bellows.

He greeted her, shaking her hand warmly, and closing the door.

"This is an unexpected pleasure, Your Grace."

"Events have changed my circumstances," she revealed. "I will be moving to America."

"America? Whatever for?"

"I'd like that to remain personal for now, Mr. Bellows."

"Of course, Your Grace. What can I do for you?"

"Would you consider continuing our arrangement and publishing my work?"

He smiled nervously. "If His Grace approves, I don't see why not."

"His Grace has nothing to do with it. We are seeking an annulment."

The man's jaw dropped. Quickly, he closed it, obviously flustered.

"I have many more children's stories in my head. I would prefer to publish them with you but I can always go elsewhere."

"No, Your Grace, I'd be happy to publish them. As a matter of fact, I've been exploring the possibility of partnering with a publisher in America. If I'm able to work it out and you're agreeable, your work could be released both here and there."

Knowing she would be the sole source of income for her and Leah, she said, "The idea appeals to me greatly."

"When do you leave?"

"Very soon." Catherine rose and offered her hand. "You've been a good friend to me, Mr. Bellows. I will write to you from America and give you my new address. Most likely, Leah and I will settle in Boston or New York."

"I would recommend Boston, Your Grace. It's smaller than New York and it has a thriving community of artists and authors. My cousin moved there over a decade ago and seems quite happy."

She smiled. "Then Boston it is. Good day."

Catherine returned to the coach and had Strong take her to her bank. There, she withdrew everything in her account and closed it. Her reticule felt heavy with the bank notes she carried.

"Where next, Your Grace?"

"Don't call me that anymore, Strong. Everton and I are getting an annulment."

To his benefit, he merely nodded, taking the news in stride.

"Do you know anything about ships to America?"

Surprise filled his face. "I suppose. A few merchant ships leave from London. Those carrying passengers depart from Bristol or Liverpool, though."

"Hmm. Liverpool is a good distance away. How far is it to Bristol?"

Strong thought a moment. "I'd say a good hundred miles." He hesitated. "Are you planning to go to America, Lady Catherine?"

She nodded. "I think it's for the best under the circumstances."

"You'll need someone to look after you," he said, determination filling his lined face.

Catherine saw where this was leading. "No, Strong. You're to stay here. I can't have you going across an ocean with Leah and me."

He gave her a dejected look. "Where else would I go, my lady? Despite you being gentry, you're all the family I've got."

She realized that was true. The former valet was the one link to her past.

"Are you really interested in leaving England?"

He shrugged. "Not much here for me."

"Then I would be happy to have you come along with us to Boston." She thought a moment. "We can take a mail coach to Bristol. I'd rather leave from there than London."

Strong grew pensive. "In case the duke tries to change your mind about the annulment?"

"Even if he attempted to—which I doubt after what's passed between us—I can't stay."

"It's because of your mother, isn't it? And Lady Leah's."

Catherine sucked in a quick breath. "You . . . know?"

Strong nodded. "I was valet to the earl, my lady. With him every day."

"Then you met my mother, I suppose?"

"I did. She was a lovely woman, my lady."

"Would you tell me about her? Just a little?" she asked.

"She was very beautiful. You resemble her a great deal. You have her auburn hair and the same bright, blue eyes she possessed, though you're a little taller than she was. She acted on the stage. Mostly in small roles. I was the one who brought her to the country and visited her every day, making sure she had what she needed as she increased. She was very grateful for my visits. Always had a kind smile and word for me. She liked to sing and she knitted you caps and sewed many outfits that you wore when you were a baby. I think you would have liked her very much."

Catherine closed her eyes, imagining the woman. Though Mama would always be her true mother, it was nice to hear that the one who gave her life was kind.

She opened her eyes. There would be time for her to think more about this woman. Time to ask Strong more about what he could recall of her. For now, Catherine must focus on a quick departure.

"Thank you for sharing those memories with me, Strong. Now, we need to act quickly and leave London as soon as possible."

His face darkened. "It's the new Lord Statham, isn't it? He's threatened to expose you." She saw understanding dawn on his face. "You're trying to protect His Grace and the St. Clairs."

Tears welled in her eyes. "Yes. Statham is blackmailing me. He's asked me to arrange for him to marry Everton's sister in two years. I can't see her life ruined. And if I don't comply, my cousin will tell the *ton* that Leah and I are bastards, passed off to the *ton* as purebred Crawfords. That's why I seek the annulment, Strong. The St. Clairs will be embarrassed for a short while but society is more forgiving of a wronged duke. By the time the scandal breaks, Leah and I will be far away."

"I see." He rubbed his chin thoughtfully. "Several mail coaches run from London to Bristol each day. Once we reach Bristol, we can book passage on a packet ship."

"What is that?" she asked, having no knowledge of ships that sailed on the seas.

"It carries mail, cargo, and passengers. Will you be able to afford a stateroom for yourself and your sister? Traveling in steerage wouldn't be advisable for two ladies."

"I have funds from my books that we can use for passage and to start our new lives."

"Good. The staterooms are tiny but you'll have a bed with linens and a washbasin."

"Should we arrange for tickets today on one of tomorrow's mail coaches?"

"I can take care of that."

Catherine reached into her reticule and handed over some bank notes. "Is that enough for the three of us to have tickets?"

Strong laughed. "More than enough." He grew serious. "What about Lady Leah?"

"She's still at Everton's. Statham told me I'd be the one to inform her she was moving back under his care for the next two years since he is her legal guardian. It's another way he aims to control me. I've got to find a way to get her from Everton's without him or Statham knowing."

He thought a moment. "I made friends with one of the upstairs maids when I got to the duke's townhouse. I knew a younger brother of hers years ago. I could get her to pack a valise for Lady Leah while she's at dinner tonight and sneak it down to me."

"That's wonderful, Strong. I'll write Leah and tell her I need to see her. That she's to keep it a secret. Once I sign the annulment papers, we can pick her up and leave London."

"My lady, I've got to return the duke's carriage," Strong pointed out.

"Oh, dear. Can you rent something so that we both can take our trunks with us?"

"I can. You gave me enough money to do so. I'll pick you up tomorrow morning and take you to your solicitor and then allow you to meet your sister." He paused. "Where will you go now?"

"Obviously, I can't go to Everton's. I don't think I should involve Charlotte in this." She thought. "I have an idea." She gave him an address and he helped her into the carriage.

Half an hour later, they pulled up in an exclusive square. Catherine instructed Strong to wait until she knew if she would be given refuge for the night.

With trepidation, she rang the doorbell. A most intimidating butler answered the door. She looked him directly in the eye and asked to speak with Countess Lieven, offering the butler her card.

"I have not had time to have new ones printed," she said with calm dignity.

He glanced over her shoulder to where the ducal coach stood. "If you'll follow me, Your Grace."

She swept past him. He led her to a small parlor and left. Minutes passed. Her nerves grew more frayed.

And then the Countess of Lieven entered the room.

She kissed both of Catherine's cheeks. "My dear, it is so good to see you, though I must say I'm quite surprised. I thought you were supposed to be at Eversleigh."

"I hope you don't think me impudent but I need a tremendous favor from you."

The countess studied her. "If you came to me, you must need something important."

"May I stay the night with you?"

She frowned. "Have you quarreled with Everton?"

"Much worse," Catherine confirmed. "We plan to annul our marriage."

A long moment passed. "I see."

"I can't chance seeing him. I would go to Charlotte's but I'm afraid he would find me there. I thought about an inn but I wasn't comfortable with the thought of staying in one." She swallowed. "I have nowhere to go."

"Not even to Statham?" the countess inquired.

"Especially not Statham," she said vehemently.

The countess placed a hand over Catherine's. "You are more than welcome to stay with us. I am going out tonight, though. I hate to leave you alone."

"Don't worry about me. I'm truly grateful," she said. "May I have my driver bring in my trunk? And I would ask for ink and paper. I need to write to Everton and my sister."

"Of course."

Catherine was shown to a large, airy bedchamber. Strong arrived shortly afterward with her trunk.

"Should I wait for you to write to Lady Leah?" he asked.

"No. She's grown so close to Rachel that if I send her a message tonight, she might reveal the contents. I'd rather have you deliver it in the morning. Please have your friend pack a few of Leah's things, though, so that the valise will be ready by the time we arrive."

Catherine stopped. "I can't thank you enough for what you're doing, Strong."

"No thanks are necessary, my lady."

He left and a servant brought her a tray with food, as well as pen and paper. Catherine hadn't eaten all day and found herself famished. Once she'd eaten, she wrote a brief note to Leah, asking her sister to meet her outside for a quick errand. She stressed not to tell anyone in the household where she was going. Catherine only hoped Leah would do as she asked and not let Rachel or Cor know, much less Jeremy. She wondered how he had explained his sudden arrival back home—and why his wife didn't accompany him.

The letter to her husband took much longer. As a writer who found words usually came easily to her, Catherine struggled to complete the letter. Once she finished, she read it over.

Jeremy –

You will soon hear rumors about me that will prove to be true. I am the one—not you—who entered into our marriage under false pretenses. I only learned the true circumstances of my birth after my father's death. After discovering my delicate situation, I realize I never should have accepted your offer, much less married you without telling you who I really am. I was afraid if I did, you wouldn't marry me. I regret being so selfish because of the pain it has caused you.

I've come to my senses and understand what an embarrassment I am to your family. That is why I sought the annulment. I hope you'll understand our parting is for the best. It will give you a chance to find a more suitable wife to be your duchess and a mother to Jenny.

I'm sorry I hurt you.

Catherine

She'd decided not to go into detail. By the time he read her letter, he would already know what was being said about her and Leah. She refrained from telling him she loved him because it would be cruel to wound him even more than she already had.

Catherine sealed the letter and wrote his name on the front. She would leave it with Mr. Davidson tomorrow and tell him to deliver it to the St. Clair residence in one week's time. By then, Statham would know of her betrayal and would, undoubtedly, spread his gossip. Jeremy would already have the signed annulment in hand and be able to get on with his life.

Chapter Twenty-Four

Jeremy couldn't go home. He and Catherine weren't expected for a full week. For him to arrive a day after his wedding—without his bride—would lead to too many questions.

Questions he couldn't answer.

He thought of going to Morefield's but decided Catherine would head there for refuge. He couldn't see her going to his London residence and facing him after their last conversation. It wouldn't be fair to keep her from Charlotte.

Though he hadn't been in several weeks, he decided to retreat to his club. He'd begun going regularly to White's and other clubs after he got back on his feet financially. The club was the best place to discover which businesses members were investing in and how their profits and losses stacked up. He'd gleaned valuable information merely from spending time there, playing a few hands of cards or reading a newspaper, idly talking with others who came in and out.

Today, it would be his sanctuary.

He stabled his horse a few blocks away and walked to St. James' Street. Entering White's, he consulted the betting book, where members placed bets on the most trivial of matters. Usually, the wagers recorded amused him. In his current mood, he only found them childish.

Grabbing a newssheet lying on a table, he settled into a chair and rested it in his lap. Try as he may, he couldn't read a line on it. Every time he tried to focus on the print, all he could see was Catherine's face. The deep hurt that he'd put on that beautiful face, denying her the chance to become a mother.

Jeremy stopped a waiter and ordered a glass of port. He sipped on it, pretending to read, as he listened to the conversations of others who sat near him. He signaled for another drink and then another. After that, he lost track. He was determined to dull the ache within him, as physical a pain as if he'd been run through with a sword.

Someone was shaking him. Blearily, he opened his eyes and recognized the fair hair and blue eyes. "Morefield."

His friend bent close. "What are you doing here, Everton? You're supposed to be at Eversleigh with your wife."

"Doesn't want me," he said sullenly.

"What?" Morefield hissed. He glanced around. "You're coming with me."

Somehow, Morefield got him out of the chair and urged him through the club and out the doors. Darkness had fallen. Jeremy tottered about unsteadily as a wave of nausea hit him and he vomited in the street.

"Lean against this," Morefield instructed, pushing him against a brick wall before marching off.

Minutes later, he returned with another man and they assisted him to a hackney. The rolling motion made him sick to his stomach and he placed his head in his hands.

"Tell me before we get home what has happened," Morefield demanded.

"I've lost her," Jeremy said, his words void of emotion.

"I don't understand, Everton."

"She wants an annulment," he said bluntly.

"Catherine . . . wants . . . what did you say?"

"You heard me. I did something. Awful. She doesn't want me anymore." He plunged his face back into his hands.

Morefield peppered him with questions but Jeremy waved them away. "I don't want to talk about it."

They arrived and Morefield got him out of the hackney. He sank to the ground as his friend paid the driver. Together, the two men yanked him to his feet and took him safely inside.

Morefield's valet took over from there, scooping Jeremy up and slinging him over his shoulder. The man carried him up and up, Jeremy bouncing with each step, his stomach curdling, until he was tossed upon a bed.

"I won't try to talk to you anymore tonight, Everton, because you're too inebriated. But you will give me answers in the morning. If you don't, I'll turn Charlotte loose on you."

Jeremy groaned. "Not that."

"Yes, most definitely that. She is my secret weapon. Strip him," Morefield ordered the valet. "Make sure his clothes are cleaned and he's had a bath when he comes down in the morning."

JEREMY AWAKENED TO a pounding headache. He opened his eyes and the light streaming in from the window blinded him. He closed them and tried to roll over but hadn't the strength to move.

"Awake, Your Grace?" a voice asked.

Opening one eye, he saw Morefield's valet hovering over him.

The servant tried to help him from the bed but Jeremy tossed off the arm. He rose shakily. The room swayed. His stomach lurched.

"The chamber pot is here, Your Grace."

He vomited into it and then pissed.

This time, the valet latched on to him and didn't let go.

"Drink this." A cup with some murky liquid was thrust at him.

He drank the vile concoction just to spite the man.

"Very good, Your Grace. Believe it or not, you will feel better for having drunk it. I've drawn a bath for you."

He found himself in a tub being roughly scrubbed and then shaved. He was too tired to protest. Finally, the valet rinsed him and managed to get him out of the tub, drying him off as if he were a small child. Jeremy stepped back into his clothes, all cleaned and brushed.

"Getting dressed is half the battle, Your Grace. Do you need assistance going downstairs to the breakfast room?"

"No," he growled.

Making his way down the stairs took longer than he expected because they seemed to move every time he reached out and took another step. He held a death grip on the banister, cursing Morefield for putting him up on such a high floor. By the time he reached the breakfast room, he was sweating profusely.

Morefield awaited him, sipping tea as he went through the morning's mail.

"Have a seat, Everton. I'll get you something to eat and drink. You don't look in any shape to attempt the buffet."

His friend placed a full plate in front of him, along with a cup of tea.

"Drink it black. And eat everything on your plate. You're going to need your strength."

Jeremy didn't attempt conversation as he concentrated on the meal. As he kept the food down and the hot tea warmed his belly, he began to feel human again. His jumbled thoughts began to clear.

His problems were still the same.

He had a wife who no longer wished to be his wife. He was madly in love with the said wife. And he'd been a fool to lose her over something so ridiculous. Not every woman died in childbirth. If by some ungodly reason Catherine did, he would treasure whatever time he'd had with her—and love their child to pieces. That baby would be a part of her he would always have.

"I've been a damned imbecile," he finally said.

Morefield nodded. "I assumed the falling out was your fault."

"It was."

"Are you going to do something about it?"

"I am." The pounding in his head had lessened to a dull, steady thumping. "Is she here?"

"Catherine? No. Not to my knowledge. I escorted Charlotte to the opera last night. She came home afterward and I went to White's—where I found you. Unless Catherine arrived before we did, I doubt she's here. None of the servants have mentioned her this morning. I'm sure my butler would have informed me if we had additional guests beyond you."

"I didn't think she'd go home. Of course, Cor will take Catherine's side. She should." Jeremy looked around. "Where's Charlotte?" he asked warily.

"She rarely comes to breakfast. She prefers to eat sparingly and sip her hot chocolate in her room."

"Don't tell her I was here."

"I won't," Morefield promised. "Have you worked everything out with yourself?"

"I know I was wrong. I'll admit as much and then beg for her to take me back."

His friend smiled widely. "You've already discovered the secret of marriage. It only took you one day. I wish I could have learned the lesson so quickly."

"You and Charlotte argue?"

Morefield chuckled. "All the time. In the end, I apologize. It doesn't matter if I'm right or wrong. She accepts it and we go back to being happy."

"I'll be damned."

"Try it with Catherine. I'm sure it will work, Everton." He grew serious. "It's obvious to everyone you're meant to be together."

Jeremy's throat grew thick. "Thank you. For everything."

"Shall I summon my driver to take you home?"

"No. It's a short walk. That will probably do me some good."

"I hope you can work things out, Everton."

"I do, too."

He left and stepped out into the pale sunshine. The light still bothered his eyes some. As he walked, Jeremy swore he would never drink so much again. He would also take the lesson he'd learned to heart and never be so foolish. A marriage might survive a husband driving his wife away once. He doubted it could survive the same thing twice.

As he arrived home, he thought he glimpsed Leah walking a block away. She turned and got into a carriage. He pushed the thought aside, knowing she and Rachel were inseparable. Where one went, the other would be.

Jeremy entered his townhouse and went straight to the breakfast room, hoping to find Catherine there. Instead, only Cor sat. Her eyes widened as he came in and took a seat.

"Why on earth are you here, Grandson? You're supposed to be at Eversleigh."

His heart sank. "Then Catherine is not here?"

"No. Why would she be?" Cor's gaze bored into him.

Jeremy looked into the eyes of the woman who had raised him, ashamed of what he had to share. "I've made a mess of things, Cor. I won't bore you with the details. I know what I need to do, though. First, I must find my wife and grovel."

Her gaze softened. "It's hard when we love, isn't it?"

"I couldn't agree more."

"What are you going to do to win her back?"

"Whatever it takes." He sighed. "Have Rachel and Leah already breakfasted? I'd like to talk with Leah to see if Catherine's contacted her."

"Rachel had a headache last night, poor girl. She's sleeping in this morning. Leah came downstairs to eat but she left a quarter of an hour ago." Cor paused. "She did have a note delivered to her, though. She's been waiting for a book to arrive at the bookstore. I supposed it was from the bookseller."

His gut tightened. "Or not. I thought I saw her getting into a carriage a block west of here when I arrived. She might be going to meet Catherine. Do you know if she took the note with her?"

"I don't know, Jeremy."

Barton appeared. "Your Grace, this just came for you." He brought over a letter on a silver tray.

Jeremy grabbed it eagerly and tore it open, scanning the contents. He dropped it on the table, thinking he might be sick again. Cor looked at him expectantly.

"It's from Catherine's solicitor," he said dully. "At her request, I'm to go and sign the annulment papers immediately."

Chapter Twenty-Five

Catherine waited for Strong to return with Leah's valise. He had parked their rented carriage a block away from the St. Clairs' London townhouse. She didn't want to take any chances and be seen by any of the family or servants.

She leaned against the seat back, a deep weariness piercing her to the bone. Sleep again had evaded her. Even the countess had remarked upon the deep shadows under Catherine's eyes. She'd thanked the woman for extending her hospitality and left when Strong arrived with the rented transportation. They'd gone directly to Davidson's office, where he presented her with the annulment papers. Her hand shook as she signed them but it had to be done. She'd instructed him to write to Everton once she left and deliver the message promptly, telling the duke the papers awaited his immediate signature. The sooner he signed, the more protection his reputation would have.

She'd also left the letter to Jeremy with Davidson, telling him to keep it for a week and then send it to the duke. He agreed, his eyes sad. The solicitor asked what she would do next and Catherine had said she would be traveling. If and when she ever wed again, she would contact him regarding her dowry. She didn't suppose American wives presented dowries to their husbands but if she married one, she would certainly claim the money Papa had designated. If she didn't wed, she would claim it once she turned thirty. It would be more than enough to live on for years to come.

The carriage door swung open and Strong set a valise inside.

"I went around back, Lady Catherine. The maid had it waiting for me."

"And the message to Leah?"

"I found a boy passing by and gave him a shilling to deliver it now. Hopefully, Lady Leah will be coming in the next few minutes. I'll wait outside for her."

She touched his arm. "Thank you, Strong."

He tipped his cap and exited the vehicle.

Catherine prepared herself for what would come next. Leah was a high-spirited girl. She wouldn't take well to the news they were leaving England. Catherine had decided full transparency was in order. She would keep nothing from her sister. Once Leah knew the entire story and the consequences, she would have to go along, though Catherine expected a hurricane of emotions to be unleashed from Leah.

The door opened and Leah climbed inside the coach. Strong quickly shut the door and moments after Leah seated herself, the carriage took off.

"What is going on, Catherine? Why on earth are you even back in London? And where is Jeremy? It's not like you to be so secretive, much less demand it from me."

"You didn't tell Rachel you were meeting me? Or Cor?"

"No," Leah said, sounding annoyed. "Rachel had a headache and didn't come to breakfast. I didn't say anything to Cor."

"And Jeremy?" Catherine asked softly.

"He wasn't there either," Leah said, now perplexed. "Why would he be? Oh! You've quarreled."

"Much worse than that. We are annulling the marriage. I've already signed the papers this morning. Jeremy will do the same within the next hour or two."

The color drained from Leah's face. "What?" She grabbed Catherine's hands. "Tell me. Please. I want to help."

She looked deeply into her sister's eyes. "You aren't an adult, Leah, but I'm going to have to treat you as one. What I tell you will only be spoken of inside this carriage the one time. We will never mention it again. I do promise to tell you the unvarnished truth so you will understand why we are leaving England for America."

Leah jerked away. "What? You can't mean it. Any of it. Catherine, you *love* Jeremy. You can't leave him." She crossed her arms. "I certainly don't plan to be a part of this. I won't move to America on some whim."

"Do you think I would do anything on a whim?" she asked, her voice low and serious. "Listen to me, Leah. Do not interrupt." She hesitated and decided the best course was to plunge in.

"You and I are bastards."

Her sister gasped. Catherine dared her to speak.

When she knew Leah would remain quiet, she told the girl the truth. Leah wept through most of it. By the end, Catherine had an arm about her sister, trying to comfort her.

"Remember what is most important—that Mama and Papa loved us dearly—and they loved one another."

Leah sniffed. "But . . . but what does this have to do with us now? Did you *tell* Jeremy this? Is that why he seeks an annulment?"

"No," Catherine said quietly. "Statham is the rat who will divulge our birth origins to the *ton*."

"Statham?"

"He is the one who revealed the circumstances surrounding our births to me. Statham wanted you to live with him the next two years, knowing I would be desperate to see you. If I saw you, it meant seeing him, as well. He wants to rise in society."

"I would never live with that slithering eel," Leah proclaimed.

"Legally, he is your guardian," Catherine pointed out. "He would have every right to claim you. You would have no choice but to reside under his roof. There was more." She hesitated. "He wanted to marry Rachel when she made her come-out."

Leah's eyes widened in shock. "He's mad to think that would happen."

"He would keep you from me and demand Rachel's hand in exchange for maintaining silence about our births." Catherine clasped Leah's hands. "I couldn't let him have you. I certainly couldn't see myself convincing Rachel to marry him.

"And that means having the truth come out."

Catherine watched as her sister digested this information.

"The longer I waited, the more damaging the gossip would be. Especially for the St. Clairs."

Tears streamed down Leah's cheeks. "You love Jeremy enough to give him up."

"Yes. I want to protect him. The annulment does that. Naturally, there will be gossip when the scandal breaks, but he is a duke. A handsome, eligible man with a lofty title will be forgiven almost anything. I knew once our marriage was dissolved, Statham would tell what he knew to the *ton*. Not only would I be ruined, but you would never have a chance to wed. By leaving England, we give the St. Clairs some peace, knowing we'll never see them again, while you and I can forge a new life. Americans aren't interested in titles. We both have a chance to find husbands and lead a life not bowed by shame."

Leah wiped her cheeks. "What will we live on?" she asked, worry creasing her brow.

"I have the earnings from my children's books. Mr. Bellows promised to continue to buy my stories. He said there's a strong possibility of having them also published in America. If times grow hard, I will sell my sapphire necklace."

"No! Catherine, you can't. What would Papa say?"

"He would be proud that I had the fortitude and foresight to do so. It is worth a great deal. We could probably live off of what it fetched for several years."

The coach began to slow. She saw fear and uncertainty in her sister's eyes. They came to a stop and Strong jumped down and opened the door.

"I see you've told her," he said, sympathy in his eyes. "Don't you worry, Lady Leah. I'll make sure no harm comes to you or your sister."

"You're going with us, Strong?" Leah asked hopefully.

He winked at her. "I couldn't very well let you sail across an ocean on your own now, could I?"

Strong helped them from the coach and said, "It's a little after ten. We have tickets on the next mail coach which leaves at one. I know we're early but I needed to get you and your luggage here and go back across town to return the rented horse and carriage."

Catherine made a quick decision. She opened her reticule and withdrew a folded handkerchief. Pressing it into Strong's palm, she said, "I want you to sell my necklace. I believe I will get a better price for it in London than Boston. With the money, we will be able to buy a small home for the three of us. Would you have time to find a jeweler once you return the carriage?"

He nodded. "I have just the right buyer in mind." He slipped the handkerchief into his pocket. "Let me get your luggage."

Strong retrieved Leah's valise and Catherine's trunk that rested atop the carriage. She'd only packed simple things to wear during her week at Eversleigh, with no ball gowns or fancy items included. The wardrobe in the trunk would be much more suitable for her new life and she could buy Leah whatever she needed once they arrived in Boston.

"You'll need to stay with these," Strong advised. "I will be gone for a few hours."

"But you will make it back in time to board the mail coach?" Catherine asked.

"I'll be back, my lady. Hopefully, in time to bring you something to eat before we depart."

Leah took Catherine's hand and, together, they watched the loyal servant depart.

***

Jeremy entered the small office, his anger barely contained. A clerk looked up, blinking rapidly several times and leaped to his feet.

"The Duke of Everton. I'm expected."

"Yes, Your Grace," the clerk said nervously. "If you'll follow me."

He led Jeremy down a narrow hallway and paused to rap on the doorframe. A man looked up and, like the clerk, shot to his feet, looking flustered.

"Your Grace. Please. Come in. Have a seat."

Jeremy sat in the available chair placed in front of the desk and glared at the solicitor.

"You're Davidson? The one who sent me the message?"

"Yes, Your Grace. Her Grace has already come and gone this morning."

His heart sank. He hadn't thought Catherine would act so quickly in filing for an annulment, much less have already committed her signature to the document. He had to find her and tell her what a grave mistake he'd made, hoping to change her mind before he gave up on their marriage.

"Did Her Grace mention where she was going when she left your office?"

If anyone might be able to point him in the right direction, it was this man. He prayed the solicitor could reveal Catherine's whereabouts.

"Only that . . . she would be traveling," Davidson managed to get out. "She didn't say where." He pushed some papers toward Jeremy, his eyes pleading for the duke to sign the documents.

Jeremy smiled. Catherine would never go anywhere without Leah. *And Leah was at his London townhome.*

He stood quickly, knowing how urgently he needed to get home. No wonder Catherine had Davidson send the message for him to come sign at once. It was because she needed to spirit Leah away. He decided to take the annulment agreement with him—unsigned—and see if he might somehow get Catherine to tear it up.

When he reached for the papers, his eyes fell to a folded page on the desk. It bore his name.

"What's this?" he asked and picked it up.

Panic filled Davidson's face. He reached for it and quickly withdrew his hand when Jeremy glowered at him.

"Th-that's . . . not for you, Your Grace," the man sputtered.

"I beg to differ. My name appears on it."

"Yes, it does, but it's not for you. Not now. Her Grace was most specific about that."

"Oh, she was? Do tell, Davidson."

The poor man looked as if he might collapse. "She was adamant that you be summoned to sign the annulment papers this morning. She wanted the annulment to go on record today." He cleared his throat. "And the letter she left was to be sent to you in exactly one week. Not any earlier."

"Do you know what it states?"

The solicitor looked appalled. "Certainly not."

"I will take it with me now," he said firmly.

"Will you wait the week, Your Grace? I would hate to disappointment—"

"Are you married, Davidson?" Jeremy asked suddenly.

"Y-yes. Yes, I am."

"Do you love your wife?"

A smile emerged amidst the dismay. "I do."

"Well, I love my wife, too. I need to make sure she knows that before I sign your document." He scooped up the papers Davidson had previously offered. "I'll take these with me. If Catherine still wants an annulment after I've spoken with her, I will return tomorrow and sign them before you. And if she doesn't? I hope never to see you again, Davidson."

Jeremy folded the papers and slid them inside his jacket. He still clutched the letter Catherine had written him in his hand. "Good day."

With that, he strode from the office and back to his carriage. He instructed his driver to get him home as quickly as possible and then climbed inside. As the coach took off, he opened the single page.

He raced through the contents once and then read it again more slowly. The letter thoroughly confused him.

What rumors did Catherine refer to? She said she'd married him under false pretenses and made some veiled reference to her birth. She mentioned not wanting to embarrass him or his family and begged him to find a more suitable wife. Who would be more suitable than Catherine Crawford? She was the daughter of an earl. Beautiful. Well spoken. Intelligent. He was more confounded now than before he'd read it.

She did write that disclosing whatever she needed to might have caused him to withdraw his offer. In his heart, Jeremy believed nothing she could ever have revealed would be so awful as to make him set her aside. Apparently, she thought it would—so she had withdrawn from the marriage herself.

Once again, hope sprang within him. If she didn't love him, she wouldn't have sacrificed her own happiness to free him from their union.

He folded the page. No rumors had reached his ears but Catherine had believed they would in a week's time. Who would know something so awful about her and use the information to destroy her reputation?

Statham.

He was the only choice. The only family she had left. If anyone knew some vile secret that Catherine felt would embarrass him and his family, it would be her cousin.

Jeremy determined that once he found Catherine and learned the truth from her, he would confront Statham—and destroy him.

Chapter Twenty-Six

The coach hadn't come to a complete stop when Jeremy flung open the door and jumped to the ground. He raced to the front door and barreled through it.

"Catherine!" he shouted. "Catherine!"

Racing up the stairs, he headed for Rachel's room. When Leah Crawford moved in, she'd taken up residence with Rachel instead of moving to her own bedchamber.

Catherine had to be there. She had to.

Jeremy threw open the door, only to find Rachel sitting in the window seat, a book in her hand. He turned in circles, desperation filling him.

She looked at him. "Why are you here? You're supposed to be at Eversleigh."

"Leah. Where is she?"

"I haven't seen her this morning. I had a headache last night so she decided to sleep across the hall."

He ran from the room and found the bedchamber empty. He went back to Rachel's room, fearful Catherine had already come for her sister.

"Get up. Look around. See if Leah's clothes are gone."

Rachel looked at him as if he'd gone mad but did as he asked. She opened a trunk and combed through it and then went to the wardrobe.

"Her blue gown is missing. And a yellow one trimmed in green."

"Jeremy?" Cor stood in the doorway.

"Cor. Have you seen Leah? Or Catherine?"

"No."

"Damnation!"

He left the room and hurried downstairs. Matthew emerged from the study, concern on his face.

"What's wrong, Your Grace?"

"Have you seen Lady Leah this morning?"

"I did when I arrived. She was going outside as I came in. When I didn't see a maid accompanying her, I asked where she was going. She told me Rachel was unwell and she was going to pick a few flowers for her in order to cheer her up."

"Well, she didn't bring me any," Rachel grumbled, having come downstairs. "What's going on, Jeremy?"

Before he could answer, the doorbell rang. He ran to it blindly, hoping against hope that Leah or Catherine would be standing there when he opened it.

"Your Grace, I need to speak with you at once."

"Strong?"

The former valet pushed his way in. "You must listen to me. Time is of the essence."

If anyone might know where Catherine was, it would be this loyal servant.

"I ask for ten minutes of your time." He glanced around. "In private, Your Grace."

"Do you know where Catherine is?" Jeremy demanded.

"I do."

"Then take me to her!"

"No," Strong said. "Once I speak my piece, if you still wish me to bring you to her, I will gladly do so. If you choose not to accompany me, I will never tell her that we spoke."

Jeremy studied him. "You know what she referred to in the letter."

"I do."

"Come along. All of you."

When Strong hesitated to follow, Jeremy said, "This is Catherine's family now. They will hear what you have to say."

The servant nodded. Jeremy led the group to the library and indicated for Strong to sit.

"I ask for ten minutes, Your Grace. You'll understand by then. But please, no questions while I speak."

He thought the servant bordered on impudence but kept his mouth shut because he so desperately wanted to know where his wife was.

"I worked in the Crawford household for many years, most of them as valet to Lord Statham. There are only a handful of us who know the real story," Strong began. "It was no secret in society how much Lord and Lady Statham loved one another. Even to the night Lady Statham died, if you saw the two together, you would know they were deeply in love."

Jeremy hid his impatience, wondering what this man was working up to.

"After ten years, no child had come. Both the earl and countess were bitterly disappointed. That's when Lady Statham told the earl she needed a baby. His baby." Strong paused. "Even if it meant coming from a different woman."

His head reeled in surprise as Rachel gasped.

"The Stathams had always been fond of going to the theater. Lady Statham particularly liked the looks of an actress who played a few minor roles. She had me approach the woman and invite her to tea. That afternoon, the actress agreed to have the earl's child—if she were properly compensated."

Strong ran his hands through his hair. Jeremy went and poured out a drink. He handed the whiskey to the servant, who tipped it back.

"The Season was ending so Lady Statham returned to the country. Lord Statham stayed in London long enough to ensure the actress was with child and then he retreated from London, as well. I returned to the city and brought the woman back to Statham Manor. An unoccupied cottage had been prepared for her. Two days before she gave birth, I smuggled her into the household. Lady Statham had spent the past several months in her rooms. Word was put out that the pregnancy was a difficult one and that she was on bedrest.

"When the time came, the local doctor was summoned. He was in on it, of course. Lady Catherine was the result. The actress, knowing she didn't have the talent to remain on stage, took the settlement from Lord Statham. I drove her back to London, where she took a mail coach to her childhood home."

Strong stood and began pacing. "Lady Statham remained home that Season to care for the child while Lord Statham went to the session in Parliament. They returned the next Season to London with Lady Catherine in hand and were quite happy." He paused. "Until Lady Statham found herself with child. She lost the baby at six months and almost her life. That's when she begged the earl for another child, hoping this time for a boy. He'd still be of Statham's blood and inherit the title since all of society would think the child theirs."

The valet took a seat again. "We've no time for the details. Suffice it to say that another woman was found and Lady Leah was the result."

When Strong fell silent, Cor asked, "Why is this coming out now?" She looked to Jeremy. "Is this the source of the trouble between you?"

"This is the first I've heard of it," Jeremy replied. He looked to the servant. "This is why she left me? Does she think her being a bastard makes any difference to me?"

"It's the blackmail, Your Grace."

He stilled. "Is it Statham?"

Strong nodded in confirmation. "Lady Catherine never knew any of this while her parents were alive. Statham is the only one who could have told her. He was going to take Lady Leah away from her, asserting his rights as her guardian." The servant's eyes flicked to Rachel. "And the earl demanded that when she made her come-out, Lady Catherine must guarantee him that Lady Rachel would be his bride."

"What?" Rachel cried. "That's horrible."

"He is a horrible man, my lady," Strong agreed. "Lady Catherine couldn't live with herself if she forced Lady Rachel into marriage with Statham. That meant in two years, the ugly truth would come out. She didn't want to shame you, Your Grace, or your family. Thus, she pushed for the annulment." He paused. "They're leaving London today. Bound for Bristol. From there, they'll go to America. That way, you—and the *ton*—would never have to see her again and be reminded of the scandal. It was a way to make a new life for her and her sister. We're to leave on the one o'clock mail coach."

"We?" he asked.

Strong shrugged. "I couldn't let them go off on their own."

Jeremy couldn't believe the depth of sacrifice Catherine was willing to go to. All for him and his family. Yet he knew how much family had meant to her. How sad that her only living relative had betrayed her so cruelly.

"Take me to her. At once," he demanded, seeing Cor's nod of approval.

Strong retrieved a handkerchief from his pocket and handed it to Jeremy.

"She sent me to sell this so we'd have enough to purchase a small place in Boston. I think it only right that you return it to her, Your Grace."

He unfolded it and found Catherine's sapphire necklace. His throat grew thick with emotion.

Placing his hand on Strong's shoulder, he told the valet, "I owe you a debt I may never be able to repay."

"I just want to see her happy, Your Grace."

Jeremy said, "Horseback will be quicker. Follow me in the coach, Strong. We'll need a way to bring them home."

The servant beamed. "Certainly, Your Grace."

STRONG HADN'T RETURNED. Catherine tamped down her fears, trying to appear confident for Leah's sake. She watched as their coach arrived and passengers disembarked. Once the luggage was unloaded, the team of horses was traded out and a man called for those leaving to begin boarding.

"What are we to do, Catherine?" Leah asked anxiously.

"We'll go to Bristol. I'm sure Strong is trying to get the best price possible for my necklace. He knows where we're headed. We'll wait for him there."

She summoned one of the men who was gathering luggage and indicated her trunk and Leah's valise. When the last of the luggage was strapped down, she took her sister's arm and moved them toward the carriage. They were the last passengers to board. Leah went up the stairs and entered the coach. Catherine stepped onto the first rung.

A commotion caught her attention. Someone was shouting and riding a horse hell-bent in their direction. Catherine drew a sharp breath. Her worst nightmare had come to pass.

It was Jeremy.

He drew up the reins, his gaze locked upon hers.

"Don't get on that coach, Catherine," he ordered.

Summoning her courage, she raised her chin a notch. "You are no longer my husband, Everton. You cannot tell me what to do."

He withdrew a sheaf of papers from his pocket. "I didn't sign the annulment. You are still my wife."

Without taking his eyes from hers, he tore the pages again and again and then flung them into the air. The pieces fluttered on the breeze and drifted to the ground.

Jeremy dismounted and slowly walked toward her.

"I know the truth, Catherine. I read your letter."

She knew she hadn't confessed to her illegitimacy in it. "No, Jeremy. You don't know the whole truth. If you did, you wouldn't be here."

He smiled. "The letter only gave me a piece of the puzzle. Strong filled in the missing parts."

Catherine couldn't believe that Strong had betrayed her.

Jeremy continued steadily walking toward her. He reached her and his hands spanned her waist. Being a step from the ground made them stand at eye level.

"I know about the blackmail. I know why you demanded the annulment. You thought the St. Clairs would be humiliated."

"Yes," she hissed. "I couldn't have you and your family humiliated, Jeremy. It's true that some gentlemen in the *ton* produce bastards. But none of them have tried to pass those bastards off as their legitimate offspring to society. The truth will get out. Leah and I will be ruined. And you and your family would share in our disgrace. I can't allow that."

Tears filled her eyes. "I always prized family above all else, never knowing it was all a lie. I'm a mongrel. Not good enough for the St. Clairs and their rich heritage."

His hands tightened on her waist. "I think your parents are the greatest love story I've ever heard. Your father loved your mother so much he was willing to give her children the only way he could. And your mother loved the two of you girls deeply. You were hers. From the start. Most of the *ton* will see it the same way. Those that don't aren't worth our time. You and Leah are innocents in this, Catherine."

He lifted her to the ground and tenderly cupped her cheeks.

"Dukes are known for weathering scandals better than most, thanks to our lofty titles. And even if this became the scandal of all scandals, it wouldn't matter. Because I love you. I was a fool before. An utter fool." His thumbs stroked her cheeks. "I want to have children with you, Catherine St. Clair. As many as we can. I want to love you every day for the rest of our lives.

"I have to ask—are you brave enough to love me? Scandal or no scandal? For better or worse?"

She'd never said aloud the words that filled her heart.

Until now.

With tears blinding her, she could barely make him out, but Catherine told him, "I do love you, Jeremy. I always have."

He kissed her with a tenderness that let Catherine know how cherished she was. From a distance, she heard the rousing cheers of the coach passengers and bystanders who'd taken a keen interest in this entertaining conversation.

"Excuse me, Your Grace?"

Jeremy broke the kiss and smiled down at her. Then he looked to the driver who sat in the box. "Yes?"

"We've got a schedule to keep, Your Grace."

"Of course. Leah, come down."

Catherine saw her sister standing in the coach's doorway, grinning shamelessly. She started down the steps and Jeremy caught her waist, lowering her to the ground. Leah fell into Catherine's arms.

The coach started off and Catherine said, "Oh, no! Our luggage."

Jeremy laughed. "I am a duke, you know. I can buy you both new wardrobes."

Her wonderful husband took her in his arms again. "I love you, Catherine St. Clair. I plan to take you home now and make love to you the rest of the day."

He kissed her again, long and deep. She returned it openly, happily, love swelling in her heart.

When they finally parted, Leah stood nearby with an amused look on her face. Strong stood beside her.

"Your coach awaits," Strong said, not bothering to hide his smile.

Catherine rushed to the valet and threw her arms about him.

"You do realize you meddled in the life of a duchess," she teased and kissed his cheek.

He turned bright red. "I do, Your Grace. And it was worth it, I see."

She looked back at her husband. "Yes, it was, Strong."

Jeremy joined them, his arm possessively going around her waist. "Attach my horse to the back of the coach, Strong."

"Certainly, Your Grace."

Jeremy led her to the grand carriage with the St. Clair ducal seal on its doors. He hoisted her into it and turned to help Leah.

Her sister laughed. "I believe I will ride up in the box with Strong." She winked at Jeremy.

He encompassed Leah in a bear hug and then turned her loose. "You are a very smart woman, Lady Leah. You're going to make some man very happy one day."

She looked at him wistfully. "Even if I'm a bastard?"

He took her chin in hand.

"You're the daughter of an earl. A sister-in-law to a duke. And you're smart and beautiful and vivacious. Men will be clamoring at my doorstep the moment you attend your first ball. I'll have to make them take a number and wait their turn to enter the house."

Jeremy kissed her forehead and then climbed into the carriage. He sat and pulled Catherine into his lap.

"That was sweet what you said to Leah. Do you believe it?"

"I do. She will make an excellent match. Just as her sister did." Giving her a rakish grin, he asked, "Now, where were we, Duchess?"

Catherine kissed him soundly in response.

Chapter Twenty-Seven

Jeremy led Catherine into the house, Leah trailing behind them. Immediately, Cor and Rachel appeared, Matthew not far behind them. The women began peppering him with questions.

Glancing over his shoulder, he told Leah, "Tell them everything. And make sure the servants know to keep out."

Leah's eyes twinkled with mischief. She curtseyed and said, "Whatever you say, Everton." Turning to face the others, she said, "Come into the parlor and I'll tell you everything." She began sweeping the others in the opposite direction.

Jeremy swept Catherine off her feet.

She looped her arms around his neck as he carried her up the stairs. She couldn't stop smiling at him.

"I'm sorry I didn't trust you enough to tell you the truth," she apologized.

He reached the top of the stairs and proceeded down the hallway.

"Your letter said you thought I wouldn't marry you if I learned about your origins."

"I didn't think you would."

They arrived in front of the door to his rooms and he opened it.

"And yet you selfishly accepted my proposal and married me."

Catherine bit her lip. "I couldn't help myself."

"Because you loved me," he insisted.

"Because I loved you," she agreed happily.

"You're going to have to prove that," he said solemnly as he ventured into the room and kicked the door closed. "And I will do the same."

Jeremy set her down and took her in his arms. His kiss was thorough. Unhurried. Magical. When he finally broke it, Catherine found herself breathless, trembling with anticipation.

"I plan to kiss every inch of you," he shared.

She felt her face flame at the thought.

"To do that, I'll need to have access to every inch," he explained as he removed her bonnet and tossed it aside. Jeremy carefully slipped the pins from her hair until it spilled down her back.

He fingered a lock and then brushed his lips against it. "Your hair is one of my favorite things about you."

"You don't think it's too red?" she asked, knowing now it came from the actress who was her mother.

"Not at all. It warms under the light inside. Outside, it blazes like fire." He ran his fingers through it, satisfaction filling him.

Taking her hand, he led her to the bed and had her sit. He knelt and removed her pumps and then reached under her skirts, his fingers gliding up her calves and to her garter. He unfastened the silk stockings and rolled them down her legs before slipping them from her feet. Catherine's heart already raced so that she thought it might burst from her chest.

Still kneeling, he reached for her hand and removed her gloves. Reverently, he pressed a kiss into each bared palm.

"Your turn," he said, sitting on the bed.

She rose and lifted his hat from his head, placing it on the nearby chair. Catherine ran her fingers through his thick, dark hair, watching his emerald eyes glow at her. She backed away and he held out a leg, his polished Hessians gleaming. Grasping firmly, she pulled the boot from his foot. His other leg rose and she removed the second boot.

Frowning, she said, "Your buckskin breeches are too tight for me to get to your stockings."

"Then take them off." He leaned back on his hands, a smile playing about his lips.

"I will. Eventually."

Instead, she pulled him to his feet and took off his coat and then unbuttoned his waistcoat. Peeling it from him, she bit her lip, thinking what she should do next.

Jeremy locked his legs around the back of hers and she braced her hands on his shoulders to keep from falling. She moved them to his cravat and undid it sensuously, sliding it from his neck. The shirt buttons came next and once she'd unbuttoned them, he raised his arms so she could pull it from him.

Catherine couldn't help but gasp. He was bare to the waist now, his sleek, muscled torso a thing of beauty. A dark matting of hair covered his chest and ran in a line into his breeches. She gave in to temptation and placed her palms on it, moving them slowly. He sucked in a quick breath and she realized how moved he was by her touch. His eyes had closed. The corners of his mouth turned up. She pushed him back against the mattress and leaned over, kissing his throat, feeling his pulse jump. Her hands continued to roam, her fingertips finding his nipples and playing with them.

Jeremy's hands shot out and grabbed her wrists. "My turn," he said, pushing up until they both stood.

"I wasn't through," she protested.

"In time, Duchess," he promised.

He bent until he grasped the hem of her green overdress and pulled it over her head. The simple silk underdress followed. He kissed her again, pulling her close, his hands running through her hair and over her back. His bare skin felt on fire.

Jeremy nuzzled her throat, licking and nipping, causing her breasts to grow heavy and a pounding to start in her nether regions. He removed her petticoat. His eyes feel to the curve of her breasts, pushed upward by her corset. His thumbs rubbed along the curve, over and over.

"Your skin is like satin," he told her as he gently turned her and loosed the stays.

Catherine only wore her chemise now. His fingers went to her shoulders and slipped under the sleeveless garment, causing her breath to quicken. Slowly, he pulled the chemise from her. She stood naked in front of him. Surprisingly, she felt no embarrassment as his admiring gaze took her in.

"You are exquisite." He pressed a soft kiss to her mouth and another few along her collarbone.

"My turn, Duke," she proclaimed boldly.

She bent and unbuttoned the buttons at his waist and then the ones at his fall. Immediately, his manhood spilled out, standing at full attention. She swallowed, wondering how it was ever going to fit within her. Worried now, she pushed the breeches down his thighs and they fell to the floor. He sat again so she could pull them off. Now, it was easy to get to his thick, cotton stockings and she removed those, as well.

Jeremy stood again, looking like an Adonis who rose from the seas. One hand moved to cradle her neck as his arm went around her waist. His hungry mouth descended upon hers, taking his fill. His body burned against hers, the skin heated. Passion sparked between them. Kissing was no longer enough. They collapsed onto the bed, both their hands roaming. Her tongue glided along his neck, tasting the salt of his skin, as she breathed in his musk. He pinned her wrists above her head and held them with one hand as he feasted upon her breasts. Catherine writhed beneath him, the blood pounding in her ears.

Then his fingers danced along her belly and down to her womanhood. Her body knew what was coming when they entered her as before. She gasped his name, over and over, as he brought her to a height she'd never known. The orgasm spilled from her, her body jerking, trembling, as she rode the crest of passion.

Jeremy moved over her, twining his fingers through hers. She felt his manhood brushing against her.

"Don't be afraid," he said.

"I'm not," she told him. "I'll never be afraid when I am with you."

He entered her with a single thrust and stopped. A sharp pain erupted. As she cried out, his mouth covered hers, kissing her, encouraging her. The pain quickly subsided and Catherine was aware he was now inside her.

They were one.

Jeremy kissed her again deeply and began to slowly move. The friction of their bodies caused a beautiful sensation. His fingers tightened on hers as he began thrusting. Gradually, he increased his pace and she found herself meeting each thrust. Living for it. The same feeling from before began building within her. She held tightly to him. Suddenly, it erupted in a halo of colors and sensations, more powerful than anything she'd experienced.

He called out her name and buried his face against her throat as he collapsed. She welcomed his weight, which pushed her into the mattress. She felt treasured. Protected.

Loved . . .

Jeremy rolled off her but brought her along, pinning her to his side as he lay on his back. Her cheek rested against his chest and she heard the furious beating of his heart. Her legs tangled with his. Her hand stroked his side.

"I love you, Duke," she said softly.

He ran his hand along her back, up and down, the motion soothing.

"I love you, Duchess," he answered.

Catherine had never felt such peace.

Jeremy awoke, feeling the warmth of Catherine's back pressed against his chest. His arm held her to him, even in sleep. He didn't know how he'd lived so long without her. They were perfectly matched.

She stirred, a little sigh escaping. He kissed her bare shoulder.

"Good morning, my love."

Her hand stroked his forearm. "Good morning."

He pressed his lips to the side of her throat.

"Mmm."

He idly wondered if they could stay in bed all day. They had for much of yesterday. After several bouts of making love, he'd rung for Manfry and had his valet bring them something to eat. After eating and sleeping and making love again, Catherine declared herself famished. He'd given her one of his dressing gowns and they'd sneaked down to the kitchen to retrieve a midnight snack.

Now that she was awake, he thought they could start the process over again.

"Jeremy?"

"Yes?" His thumb stroked her bare belly.

"I'm disappointed in you."

He froze.

"I had no idea in marrying a slightly older man, you would prove to be senile at your age."

She turned to face him, her fingers playing with the hair on his chest.

"You don't remember?" she asked, a frown marring her lovely face.

"Apparently not," he said guardedly.

She sighed heavily. "I seem to remember marrying a man who told me I would tire of hearing him tell me how much he loved me." She paused. "I believe he said he would tell me in the morning when we awakened. As we dressed and ate. When we made love. When we fell asleep each night." She sniffed. "I've been awake a good minute now and haven't heard the words once."

He grinned. "I love you."

"I suppose that's a start."

Jeremy kissed her. "I love you."

"That's better."

He kissed her again. "I'll tell you a hundred times today," he promised.

"No, that's not good enough. You were remiss as we started the day. Two hundred," Catherine declared, mischief shining in her bright, blue eyes.

"Two hundred it is," he agreed. "I love you, Catherine St. Clair." He kissed her brow. "I love you." Her cheek. "I love you." The tip of her nose. "I love you." Her chin.

Jeremy worked his way all over her body, from her ears to her toes.

"Satisfied?" he asked.

"Not until you make love to me."

He needed no further invitation.

When they finished, he told her to stay in bed. She smiled lazily as she watched him dress.

"You know, the way you're watching me, it's as if you're undressing me, Duchess," he teased.

Catherine shrugged. "And what if I am, Duke?"

"I love you."

She smiled. "I know. I love you, too."

"Come on." He threw back the covers and scooped her up, already wanting to return to their bed. "Time for you to get dressed. If you don't, we may never make it downstairs to breakfast and I know just how hungry you can get."

"Hungry for you," she murmured into his ear, her teeth tugging on his earlobe.

"I love you."

"I'm counting, you know."

He grinned. "I'm sure you are."

Carrying her through his dressing room to hers, he set her down and then played lady's maid, getting her ready for the day. Every time he put on a new piece of clothing, he told her he loved her. With every stroke as he brushed her hair, Jeremy did the same. He left it to his wife to pin up her hair, knowing he'd only pull them out again so he could run his hands through her waves.

"Can we go see Jenny before breakfasting?" she asked.

"Of course." A warm feeling spread through him, knowing that Catherine would care for his daughter as if Jenny were her own.

They climbed the stairs to the top floor, where the nursery lay, and Jeremy told her he loved her on each step. When they reached the door, he kissed her once more.

She laughed. "You made me lose count," she complained good-naturedly.

He sighed. "Then I suppose I'll have to start all over again."

"Better make it three hundred this time. You want to stay in my good graces, Your Grace."

They spent half an hour in the nursery, helping feed Jenny and playing with her. As they stepped back into the corridor, Jeremy pulled Catherine into his arms.

"I love you, Duchess," he said. "That's one."

"Only two hundred and ninety-nine more to go, Duke."

"Do you think you'll like being a duchess?" he asked.

"As long as you're my duke, I don't see why not. Do you like being a duke?"

"I suppose so."

"Well, if you ever change your mind, I can most certainly write you a reference."

"As what?"

Catherine laughed. "A lady's maid."

He kissed her. "I love you. Two. I could also write you a recommendation."

Her eyes sparkled with mischief. "As your mistress?"

"You saucy wench." Jeremy kissed her hard, desire for her rippling through him. He broke the kiss. "I was thinking of a nursery maid."

Catherine glanced over his shoulder toward the schoolroom. "I suppose I could also recommend you as a tutor. In the art of love."

His lips grazed her jaw. "If you don't watch that smart mouth of yours, I'll take you to the schoolroom right now and teach you a new lesson in love."

Her stomach growled and they both laughed.

"Perhaps that lesson can wait," she suggested.

As he led her downstairs, Jeremy thought of several lessons they could share.

Chapter Twenty-Eight

CATHERINE DIDN'T LIKE what Jeremy had planned. Not one bit.

The carriage hit a bump and she bounced off the seat. He quickly caught her and pulled her back—into his lap.

Looping her arms about his neck, she said, "I can't always go riding in your lap."

"I love you," he said sweetly.

"I'm beginning to wish I hadn't reminded you this morning."

He brushed his lips softly against hers in reply.

She pulled away. "Do we really have to go see Statham?" she pleaded.

Her husband's green eyes grew hard. "Yes."

"Must you challenge him to a duel?"

"It may not come to that," Jeremy said.

Catherine hoped it wouldn't.

They arrived at what once had been her home in London. She'd spent spring and summer in the city each year while her father conducted business in Parliament. The structure before her looked so familiar and yet seemed oddly cold.

Jeremy handed her down and she saw Morefield waiting for them. The only reason he would be present would be as Jeremy's second. Dread filled her.

Morefield greeted them and her husband handed his friend a letter. She saw Statham's name on it.

"Wait outside," Jeremy cautioned. "I hope it won't come to issuing Statham a challenge but if it does, then I will indicate you are to deliver it to him."

"Can I ask what this is about, Everton? What slight Statham might have caused?"

"You may not," Jeremy said curtly.

Morefield's eyes met hers. Catherine shrugged helplessly. He had to know somehow that the possible duel involved her.

"We'll return shortly," Jeremy said, taking her arm and escorting her to the door.

He rang the bell. Jervis answered it, his eyes widening in surprise.

"We wish to see Lord Statham," Jeremy said.

"Please, come in, Your Graces," Jervis said.

They entered the foyer and Jeremy produced his card, which he gave to the butler.

"My wife would like you to give up your position here and come to work for my family. If you're still interested, you should give Statham your resignation. I don't know which of my houses you'll be placed in. That's up to Her Grace and my secretary."

"I am eager to join your service, Your Grace," Jervis said. "Things are . . . not as they used to be here and at Statham Manor."

"You might want to wait until after my business with Statham is concluded," Jeremy advised. "And if you don't mind, we'll come along with you. Announce us but I want access to Statham immediately afterward."

Catherine knew he wanted to keep her cousin off-balance.

"Very good, Your Grace. If you'll follow me."

The butler led them to a drawing room. They waited as he knocked and opened the door. She knew he handed Statham Jeremy's card as she heard, "The Duke and Duchess of Everton, my lord."

Before Statham could give Jervis an excuse, Jeremy stepped into the room with her on his arm. Catherine tried to look unflustered but her heart sped up when she caught sight of her cousin.

He didn't look good. Martin had always been prone to being red in the face, she guessed from excessive drinking. It was barely eleven in the morning and she saw a crystal tumbler of brandy at his elbow.

"Statham," Jeremy said with a brisk nod.

Her cousin rose to his feet. "Your Grace." His eyes flicked to her in unease. Catherine stared, not bothering to greet him.

After a moment, he said, "Sit, please," as if he only remembered his hosting duties. "Would you care for any refreshment?"

"No. We won't be here long."

Jeremy led them to a settee and they sat. "We're here to discuss your blackmailing my wife," he said as pleasantly as if he were remarking on the weather.

Statham's face reddened further. "Blackmail?" he sputtered. "I haven't the faintest—"

"Let's dispense with the lies, Statham. You've threatened my duchess." After a long pause, he added, "That means you've threatened me."

Catherine watched the various emotions flit across Statham's face. He'd been confronted and was trying to think of a way to weasel out of it.

"Listen to me, Everton. I don't know what your wife has been telling you, but it's all lies. Blackmail? Why would I wish to blackmail my dearest cousin? What information might I even possess that would lead to my acting in such a despicable, dishonorable manner? Catherine's the one lying, Everton. Not me."

"Lying?" Jeremy asked calmly, idly flicking a piece of lint from his trousers. "You think my duchess is lying to me?"

Statham's face grew redder. "That's exactly what I'm saying, Everton. Catherine was a lying bitch when we were children and she hasn't changed in the least. She made up nonsense all the time about me bullying her, telling my father and her parents outrageous falsehoods, trying to see me punished."

Catherine choked and then sputtered, "You were awful to me when we were children. How dare you pretend you never intimidated me. Hurt me. You were mean. Cruel. Spiteful. And you bragged to me how your father never punished you for what you did to me."

Jeremy took her hand, lacing his fingers through hers. It brought her comfort and gave her strength. She leaned back, trying to control her surging anger.

"See?" Statham said, leaning forward. "She's still lying. She was incredibly spoiled as a child and lied when she didn't get her way. Though she's a woman now, she still thinks she can fabricate nonsense and be believed."

He paused, looking earnest, and Catherine wanted to claw out his eyes. "Look at me, Everton. We are two reasonable, rational gentlemen. Our word is our bond. I give you mine and swear that I have never threatened Catherine—either as a child or an adult. There's been no blackmail on my part. I promise to forgive her for making such false accusations against me. I only hope that you can get her under control. Madness runs in the family, you know. Her mother was as batty as they come."

This time, Catherine leaped to her feet. It was bad enough her cousin belittled her but to drag her beloved mother into the situation and utter such blatant lies was unthinkable. Before she could deny his accusations, Jeremy clasped her wrist and pulled her back beside him. His thumb massaged her wrist, calming her. Without looking at her, she knew he was telling her to trust him. That he would take care of her—and her horrid cousin—for good.

"You've told Her Grace that if she doesn't do as you say, you will ruin her and her sister," her husband said coolly, disregarding everything Statham had said.

Catherine saw Statham's confidence fade as he realized her husband was taking his wife's word over a fellow, titled gentleman. His face turned bright red now and his eyes narrowed.

"I can. And will," he blustered. "You can't do anything to stop me, Everton. Catherine and Leah are bastards that my uncle pawned off on the *ton* as purebloods. He presented them as his true daughters, not the by-blows of an actress and some shopkeeper's daughter. They are barely Crawfords, certainly not ones I'd acknowledge. It's time society found out who they were."

She sensed the tension running through him now and knew Jeremy struggled to control his anger.

He did, though, as he coldly said, "You threatened to hold my sister-in-law hostage. You wanted to coerce my wife into forcing my sister to marry you. And if she didn't, you planned to destroy your cousins' reputations—and sully my family's name. Have I got everything correct?"

Statham blanched as Jeremy spoke.

"I wouldn't quite put it that way, Your Grace."

"Oh? How would you explain it?"

Statham shook his head helplessly.

"Traditionally, when a gentleman has been grossly offended, he demands satisfaction from the offender, especially when it deals with honor. Waiting outside is my good friend, Morefield, who holds a letter issuing a challenge to you. It details my grievances and insists I receive justice. If Morefield delivers this letter, you may choose to accept or refuse my challenge. If you accept it, my terms will be harsh. I won't see our duel end with first blood. I won't find it acceptable if you are physically unable to proceed.

"I'll only agree to death, Statham. Yours." Jeremy paused. "And believe me when I tell you that I'm an excellent shot."

Her cousin grabbed the tumbler and downed the rest of his brandy in a single swallow.

"If you reject the challenge, you would gravely insult me—and prove what a coward you are." He stopped and waited until Statham met his gaze. "That's *if* I have Morefield give you the letter."

"What... what would it take for that not to occur?" Statham asked hoarsely.

"Only for you to keep what you know to yourself, as any gentleman worthy of that title would," Jeremy said. "Your silence—for your life. It's your choice, Statham."

Her cousin licked his lips nervously.

Jeremy stood. "Very well. I'll—"

"No! Wait!"

"You have something to say?"

Statham swallowed nervously. "Yes, Your Grace. I'm sorry—"

"No," her husband said, his irritation plain. "Apologize to my duchess."

Statham came and stood before her and then bent upon one knee. "I ask for forgiveness, Your Grace. I beg you to show me mercy. I promise never to reveal the origins of your birth. Or Cousin Leah's. If you choose, I will never speak to you—or of you—again in society."

She stared into his eyes, thinking how this worthless man had taken the title her father had held with honor.

"You will cede guardianship of Leah to Everton."

"Of course," he quickly agreed.

"You will greet us cordially at any *ton* event but keep your distance. We will never invite you into our homes nor will we expect to visit you in yours."

"I understand."

"If you even think of betrayal, my husband will know. He is a very clever man, Statham. I would not have him duel with you. Instead, I would have him ruin you financially. And then see that you're judged to be incompetent and placed in an asylum. You would have many years of suffering ahead of you. So many that you might truly go mad."

He shuddered. "I vow never to speak ill of you, Your Grace."

"Good." Catherine glanced at her husband, who looked upon her in awe. He offered his hand and helped her rise.

Jeremy escorted her halfway across the room and halted. He kissed her cheek and said, "I'll be back."

Confused, she watched him cross the room and return to where Statham stood. With such speed that it seemed a blur, her husband threw a punch that landed on the earl's jaw, knocking him to the ground.

Hovering over Statham, he said, "I want the papers regarding Leah's guardianship delivered to me by the end of the day. And then I want you gone from England for at least five years. Longer would be better. You've insulted my duchess and made a mockery of calling yourself a gentleman. It will take a long time for my temper to cool, Statham. See that you never cross me again else I will issue that challenge and see you dead."

Jeremy returned to Catherine's side and tucked her hand through the crook of his arm before leading her from the room.

Jervis stood just outside the door. It was obvious from the look on his face that he had heard everything. He nodded deferentially.

As he saw them out, the butler said, "I will submit my resignation, effective immediately. I won't require a reference from Lord Statham."

"We'll be expecting you," Jeremy told the older man. "Please inform Lady Leah to pack her things. I'll send the carriage for you both in two hours."

"Very good, Your Grace."

Morefield paced along the sidewalk. He hurried toward them as they emerged from the townhouse.

"Should I be concerned? I opened the letter, you know. You didn't bother to seal it, Everton."

Jeremy grinned. "I figured you would."

"By the look on your face, I'm assuming that I will not have to act as your second and give Statham your challenge."

"No, you won't."

"Thank goodness."

"Morefield, you and Charlotte should come to dinner tonight. We have much to catch up on."

The viscount sighed in relief. "Charlotte will be delighted. We have tickets for the theatre tonight if you'd care to join us after dinner."

Jeremy looked to her and Catherine nodded. "That would be lovely, Morefield. We'll see you then."

They returned to where Strong waited with their carriage. As they settled against the seat back, her husband's arm went around her shoulders.

"Remind me never to cross you, Duchess," he teased. "Financial ruin? The madhouse?"

Catherine shrugged. "I'm sure there's nothing you can't do, Duke."

"Have I told you today that I love you?"

She smiled radiantly. "I believe you have. But I'd much rather you show me instead."

Her husband framed her face with his hands. "Then we'll start with a kiss."

EPILOGUE

One year—and many "I love you" proclamations—later . . .

CATHERINE TRIED BREATHING slowly and evenly. The pains came and went more quickly in the last few minutes. The midwife had checked moments ago and told her the birth was minutes away.

She allowed Jeremy to bathe her face again with the wet washcloth. Her attentive husband hadn't left her side since this morning when her water broke. That had been almost twelve hours ago. Twelve long hours. But it would be worth it. Soon, they would be adding to their family. Their Jenny would have a brother or sister.

He set aside the washcloth and took her hand again, his other palm caressing her cheek.

"You have been extraordinary, my love." He kissed her fingers.

She sighed. "I haven't done anything yet but lie here and complain. Wait until I produce our child. Then you can tell me how wonderful I am."

Another contraction hit and she gripped his hand tightly as her face screwed up in agony.

The midwife came over and checked under the sheet. "The head's crowning. It's time to push, Your Grace." She frowned at Jeremy. "And time for you to say your goodbyes, Your Grace."

"I'm not leaving my wife," he said stubbornly. "I'm a duke. You can't make me."

They had talked several times over the past few months about his fears. Catherine had been in good health throughout the pregnancy, though a month ago she had been spotting some and both the doctor and midwife suggested bedrest, especially since she'd grown quite large. Jeremy had spent almost every waking moment with her—reading to her, brushing her hair, talking about their future. He'd told her then that he would stay with her throughout the birth.

Jeremy released her hand. "I have an idea, sweetheart."

He helped her to sit up and removed the pillows behind her, tossing them aside. He slid behind her, her legs between his, her back leaning against his chest.

"Take my hands, Duchess."

She did just as another pain struck and squeezed so tightly he groaned.

"I hope if it's a son, he'll be as strong as his mother. No, if it's a girl, I hope she, too, will have her mother's strength."

"Push, Your Grace," the midwife instructed.

Catherine bore down, gritting her teeth and crushing her husband's hands. He encouraged her with soft words of praise.

"I love you," he said. "You're doing magnificently."

"I . . . love . . . *you!*" she ground out, bearing down as much as she could.

"That's it, Your Grace. Do it again. The shoulders are through."

"I . . . love . . . oh!" she said, as she felt the baby slip from her.

Her head fell back against his shoulder. She was so weary she might sleep until Christmas.

"It's a boy," the midwife told them, cleaning the infant and wrapping him in soft linen.

"We have a boy."

She heard the pride in her husband's voice. And then another, terrible pain struck her. Catherine groaned loudly.

The midwife handed the baby to a servant and peered under the sheet again. "Your Grace, prepare yourself. Push again, with all your might."

"Again?"

She leaned against Jeremy, holding his hands tightly as she pushed again.

"Once more. Now!"

"I love you, Catherine," Jeremy said softly. "You can do this, love."

"Aagghh!"

Again, she felt a release of pressure and saw the midwife lift another baby.

Two?

"This one is a girl," the midwife shared.

"We have a girl!" Jeremy proclaimed.

Catherine felt tears of joy sliding down her cheeks. Her husband mopped them away, pressing kisses against her temple.

The midwife brought one bundled baby and the servant brought the other. Jeremy eased from under her and took their daughter while she held their son.

"They both have the St. Clair hair," she noted, "though their eyes are as blue as mine."

"That may change," the midwife said. "Many babes are born with blue eyes and then they darken. It can take a year for eye color to be determined."

She smiled at her husband, the man who made every day worth living. "Then I guess we'll have to wait and see if either of them turns green-eyed." She paused. "We weren't expecting twins. Goodness, we hadn't even settled on one name—and now we must come up with two."

He gazed down at their daughter and then looked to their son. "Do you have any ideas?"

"Actually, I do," Catherine said. "What about Timothy for our boy?"

Jeremy's smile spread as he looked at their son. "Timothy, it is.

And our girl?"

"I'm rather partial to Cordelia. Of course, we already have one Cor in the family. What if this Cordelia becomes Delia?"

"I like it." He kissed his daughter's forehead. "What do you think, Delia?"

Her response was to howl loudly. Her brother chimed in.

"They're hungry, Your Grace," the midwife said.

"Then I'd best feed them."

The woman shook her head in disapproval. Though they had a wet nurse standing by, Catherine had made the unusual choice to nurse if she could. With two mouths to feed, it was probably best that someone was there to help her out.

The wet nurse came in and, between them, both babies were fed and then taken to the nursery by Sara. Jeremy helped Catherine from the bed as a pair of maids changed the sheets. He took her to the warm bath awaiting her and bathed her himself, even toweling her off and slipping the night rail over her head.

He led her back to the bed, pulling his boots off before he got in with her. His arms went around her and Catherine laid her head on his chest. They had Jenny. And now these precious twins. Along with Leah, Rachel, Luke, and Cor, this was a house full of love.

"I need you now more than ever," he said softly. "You complete me, Catherine. You and our children."

She gazed up at him. "Have I told you today that I love you, Duke?"

His lips curved into a smile. "I love you, too, Duchess."

THE END

About the Author

Native Texan and former history teacher Alexa Aston lives with her husband in a Dallas suburb, where she eats her fair share of dark chocolate and plots out stories while she walks every morning. She enjoys reading, Netflix binge-watching, and attending sporting events when she's not watching *Survivor* or *The Crown*.

Alexa's Medieval and Regency historical romances bring to life dashing knights and loveable rogues and include the series *The Knights of Honor, The King's Cousins,* and *The St. Clairs.*

Made in the USA
Middletown, DE
06 May 2019